The

Monster

The story of a Great Sperm Whale,

and a rotting tub full of Greek Seamen

by

DIMITRI KISSOFF

Published by Kissoff De'Ath Publications
GITS Ltd, Liverpool Road, Manchester, England
Copyright ©1988 & 2013

First Edition in Paperback Printed and Bound
by Dolman Scott Ltd, www.dolmanscott.com
Set in Baskerville Old Face

A catalogue record of this paperback is available from
the British Library.
ISBN 978-0-9927966-2-4

Illustrations by

Steve Currie

www.dimitrikissoff.com

Dimitri was born in 1951 in Birmingham, England. He has been awarded no prizes for this, and none for literature. Raised in a far-off colony in darkest Africa, then sent to school near Liverpool, where notably he received a cup for boxing and had his appendix removed. Eventually, he was allowed through a hallowed portal somewhere in deepest Shropshire. There he discovered Tradition. University in the North of England followed. Here he learned of the joys of Sex, Drugs and Rock 'n' Roll, as did all his friends. Leaving without a degree or ambition, he wallowed in a world of rock music for many years, discovered truck driving, travel, wine, food, acting and small human creation – a hobby that produced four or five approximate facsimiles. At the time of writing, the old man is still alive, though aches somewhat …

'Praise' for
The Totnes Monster

* * * * * * * *

'Pretentious!'
Tom Sharpe

'Very Funny!'
Tony Booth

'Who is that guy?'
Don Van Vliet

'Are you serious?'
Christopher Hibbert

'You need help, Dimitri ...'
Barry Humphries

* * * * * * * *

Contents

In memory of my brother in life

Denis Edet Essien

laid to rest on publication day

28th February 2014

The River Dart
flows through Totnes
near where it joins the sea.
Some of the actions described in this book
could not possibly have occurred there.
The characters, too, are all
totally imaginary.
As, of course,
is SLIM.

GENESIS

In The Beginning Big Anna was at one with the world.

And the world was good. She stretched out her six-foot frame on the grass under the shade of the huge elm and breathed in the colours of the apple she had been given three hours before, the core of which she still clutched in her hand. She smelt the sky. She saw the noise of the London traffic encircling Hyde Park as a ripple of pulsating joy. She heard all the colours surrounding her as audible rainbows and the people speaking in rising modulations. She thankfully took some wine, felt it slip down her throat into her stomach, felt her body absorb it. She pulled hard on the proffered neat joint. She danced ecstatically, rolled on the freshly mown grass, then threw off her clothes and dived into the mercuric Serpentine, wave upon wave of water retreating from her vast bulk and crashing into the shore. And the spirit of Guru moved upon the face of the waters.

As she emerged from the lake, her new friends wrapped her in a long white robe – friends who also wore white, whose heads were shaved, and around whose necks were hung medallions containing the picture of a man's face – a dark, doleful face. It was the face of a man to be reckoned with – stock exchanges would crash in its close proximity; above all, a man not to be challenged.

Her glowing, shining new friends, all whiter than white, who now seemed to have been her close friends for many years gone by, took her by the hand, led her to their land, and laid her in a room on huge floaty cushions. And then the men laid her.

And laid her. And laid her again.

1

Anna then slept ten long eventfully dreamy hours after her first bite.

She had been given an Eve's apple, heavily laced with lysergic acid diethylamide. Once again LSD had done its trick. Another young dissatisfied soul had been extracted from the melee of humanity, to be re-educated and taught the true meaning of life, a soul who would see The Light, who would find happiness and satisfaction in the teachings of a man who had overnight become her God Almighty, who had in fact done nothing more than escape his own poverty trap and created enormous wealth for himself just by scrambling youthful minds.

For Guru had said 'Let there be Light' – and there was Light.

Eight out of ten similar mind-snapped cases would awake the next day a hard and fast part of his cause, as she undeniably did. And Guru saw that this was good.

And so for nigh on twenty years Anna was totally loyal to her new friends, and above all to her Guru – the man in the medallions' pictures all those years before. Not only was she loyal, but she became his companion, lover, his copesmate. She nursed him when ill, soothed his furrowed brow, bent over backwards, forwards, every which way for him, and always did his bidding.

And then, as it happens, one day she turned away ...

* * * * * * * * * * *

2

London's royal parks in the halcyon days of the summer of 1968 were a minefield of drugged-up and generally lazy youth waiting to be swept away. Though some were swept into psychiatric hospitals, just under the carpet or even back into straight society, some found their way into the clutches of the many religious and pseudo-religious groups set up by various Gurus, dubious Reverends and the like. The beneficiaries of these organizations by and large, of course, were the same dubious Gurus and Reverends.

So this, dear reader, is the story of one of these poor souls, her subcontinental Guru, a nasty Virus, a Vicar, a Duke, and many too numerous to mention here.

It is also, truly, the story of a Great Sperm Whale and a rotting tub full of Greek seamen.

* * * * * * * * * * * *

1. The Councillor

It was just one of those lovely days. The sun contentedly beamed down, a light breeze rustled the leaves on the trees and the town basked in the hot sunshine. It was high summer in Totnes.

Of the towns on what is known kindly as the English Riviera, though surprisingly not on the sea, Totnes is the most ancient. For over a thousand years it has been the central market town for this area, neatly split in two by the River Dart, tidal right up to the town. Great quayside timber yards accessible to mighty vessels from exotic foreign parts once lined its banks, and for hundreds of years these timber ships were the only substantial objects to be seen on, and occasionally in, the river; until, that is, a whale, a submarine, and finally a navy edged their way very slowly but surely into this story that, my friends, will steadily unfold. And on that bright, sunny, and apparently friendly day, Totnes Parish Council was meeting, and about to adjourn for lunch.

"Councillor Lukes. PLEASE!"

Fred jumped at the sound of his name. Now where was he?

To place him with a touch more precision, Councillor Frederick Lukes, OBE, DFC, was standing framed in the mullioned windows of the Town Hall Council Chamber, thoughtfully looking out over his town, hands clasped firmly behind his back, legs spread solidly on the shiny wooden floor.

To his left, on Crumbleigh Hill, he could see the ancient parish church dominating Totnes, to his right the River Dart, and on its bank a mile or two upstream the newly whitewashed 'religious' facility known as

4

Carnal House.

Fred Lukes was Chairman of the Council. He loved Totnes. He had devoted all his working life to it. He had been born there, brought up there, and wanted to die there, or at least be buried there – but not just yet.

Things though were changing too fast, and Fred put most of the changes down to the people in white, with whom some of his councillors now appeared to be siding. They were a new and, in his opinion, totally unwelcome element.

He'd heard about the goings-on at *the Big White House by the River* – the Carnal House place – and he didn't like what he heard one bit. It looked as though he would have his work cut out. Usually calm and affable, he was now a very worried man. He'd have to do something.

His eyes went back to the river, to the shimmering sunshine on its surface and to the green hills on the other river bank. It was a word he'd heard a lot recently – 'Green'; and not in its usual context. It seemed to Fred that everyone in Totnes now had an intense desire to be as 'Green' as possible.

And then ... the Church. He'd heard that in parts of the parish, late at night, there were small gatherings talking to the dead, taking part in ancient pagan ceremonies, performing rites unrelated to the teachings of Christ, all to increase the Vicar's flock, and all, he now had heard, to no avail. Fred Lukes was sure it was the Guru and his 'Carnal House' that was emptying the churches of Totnes.

Finally, he thought of the River Dart. So they were drilling for oil just three miles off Totnes, were they? What might happen to his beloved town?

"Councillor   Lukes   ...   COUNCILLOR LUKES!" His reverie was finally broken. Just that one item still remained on the pre-lunch agenda; an item which Fred knew had to be handled with kid gloves.

"My apologies," he said, as he turned back from the window, nervously tugging at his ear lobe. He looked at his notes on the table, made a sucking noise with the wet ends of his moustache and spoke in his slow Devonian drawl.

"Ladies and gentlemen, I wish to make you aware of a possible problem concerning our town. Let me explain, as the reasons for the recent tidal waves, which some people have attributed to our legendary Totnes Monster, have now surfaced, so to speak. I shall be as brief as possible; it is a fine day and I'm sure we would all like to break for luncheon. It will only take five minutes and then we can adjourn – shall we try to keep to that? So, without further ado, and of this I beg you not to breathe a word outside of this chamber – Oil!"

Eyebrows were lifted in surprise. Two councillors wearing only white appeared to awaken. They leaned forward. This worried Fred. There had been rumours. Strange men were known to have been staying in the town. Muffled explosions had been heard on the Dart, followed shortly afterwards by mini tidal waves. And now he thought he knew why. Anxiously, Fred cleared his throat and spoke.

"Council, we have received confidential reports of a possible oil strike – yes, oil ... three miles from the centre of town. The problem is that we are coming up to the holidays very soon; the area is very popular with leisure sailors and, as you know, there are literally thousands of pleasure craft on the river." His big red hands gripped the back of his chair. "The substantial funds that could come into the town from the oil, etc., have to be weighed against the possible loss to the environment, and more importantly for the town, its tourist industry."

Unusually, the whole Council was awake and listening. "The find," he proudly but nervously announced, "is approximately mid-channel, beneath the bed of the Dart – the recent tidal waves were presumably caused by seismic tests on the rock strata. So there we have it. We could all be sitting on a gold mine – er ... oil – well – you know what I mean."

Fred paused to sip a glass of water, blew his nose vehemently, slowly lifted his head of thick grey hair and looked about the council chamber.

"Ladies and gentlemen," he said, "this is something about which I felt you needed immediately to be made aware. The report only came through today. There is little point in discussing it now – maybe we should do so after lunch – but in the meantime, please think on all the information I have given you, which, as I have said, is of course highly confidential. If this news got out, it would play hell with land prices." His bushy eyebrows twitched nervously. "Is it the feeling of the meeting that we adjourn? Very well, thank you all for your time; meeting adjourned." Picking up his notes whilst mumbling something about the minutes to his secretary, he turned back to the meeting. "Meeting reconvenes at two-thirty, and remember, please keep all this in total confidence." Something was just not quite right. He felt it in his bones.

A tired Councillor Fred Lukes was almost apoplectic with rage that night as, sat in his favourite armchair waiting for the late TV news, he picked up the Totnes *Bugle*. Inside was a four-page pull-out feature on the Guru, plus a free colour poster. Bad enough. But much worse to Fred was that in banner headlines it screamed ...

COUNCILLOR SPRINGS OIL LEAK!

2. The Swami

Two miles down from the Council Offices in *the Big White House by the River*, the appositely named Carnal House, there was a knock at a door. Swami Tikka Masala, on the point of clinching an important deal, was somewhat stressed, and sweating. Having just heard that the Guru was coming to England, presumably to poke his nose into what he considered was *his* business, and notwithstanding the good news about the oil – which he had just received from his man on the Parish Council – he had jumped at the sudden sound. Now standing by his grand mock-leather desk, framed by a huge bay window overlooking the sloping lawns and gardens of the Totnes Randicentre, he was dreaming of girls, beaches, palm trees and numbered bank accounts, meditating, one might say, in order to calm himself. In any case, sweating or not, Swami Tikka Masala certainly looked impressively powerful – and he was.

Tikka was in an enviable position.

His head totally shaven save for a small band of hair down the centre of his skull, dressed in a large cotton sheet, and with what looked like a bird dropping in the centre of his forehead, he was nevertheless the respected man to whom all of his Guru's European devotees listened. He gave a mean Satsang, and if you received The Knowledge from Tikka, you were fairly special. Reckoned to be the best pituitary gland stimulator in the world, he could turn on The Light at will, though virtually any gland was his metier. As a result of this proven ability, girl devotees were happy to be around him – especially happy when in his great king-size bed. He had a job in which he could fully extend himself, and the way they sometimes bent over backwards for him was very touching indeed. But all that sort of thing would have to be put on hold for a while; for when his boss the Guru was around, the older man took precedence, and a lot more besides. At least he would be bringing Nurse with him. Swami would have to behave for a while.

He looked out towards the gardens of Carnal House, to the laburnum arches, the herbaceous borders, to the shrubs, the trees, the rose garden, the fountain, the vast lawn gently sloping to the river, all maintained lovingly by an army of white-clad volunteers. It was magnificent, entirely the result of kind, charitable donations. He strolled up to the windows, took a few deep breaths and stretched his arms upwards and out, away from his body.

Swami Tikka Masala – a moniker personally chosen by his Guru, as were most Devo names (invariably from A. Verri Delibelli's great masterpiece *India Through The Stomach* – Motley Head 1978) – was the one who now made all key decisions concerning the European operations of Randco (Grand Cayman) Ltd: he who spent tens of thousands from generous donations to further the cause, he who was one of the Guru's long-time confidants. Yet it was he who salted away further tens of thousands to a numbered bank account in a Swiss canton in order one day to set up his very own Ashram. If the Guru only knew – good job he didn't. They say power corrupts, and in the sad case of Swami Tikka Masala, this was certainly true.

Indubitably he had started out a devoted servant of the Guru, a true Devo, but over the years he had felt the need to improve his personal situation in life, for who knows what might be around the next corner? He had made millions in share deals, mainly for his own benefit, but had made sure that, to avoid any questions that might be asked by his usually suspicious Guru, at least some of the profit receipts did find their way into Randco's coffers, and for that Guru had congratulated him. He himself had set up the Randi Rubber Company as in-house manufacturer and supplier of all things rubber, when Guru had insisted on prophylactics always being available and mandatory for all Devos everywhere, and Guru had been so happy to see his name stamped on every piece. More praise.

Top seller was the reliable Randicond, an item made in many different shapes, colours and sizes, a product so well made that the worldwide rubber industry in its wisdom had bestowed many safety and other awards on the Randi Rubber Company; for these condoms surprisingly never, ever burst. And each time a new award was given, Tikka sold a few more of his shares at a profit, and banked the money.

Whilst it is true the Guru would have been hopping mad, literally, if he had known about the money going Tikka's way, he would have been even more incensed had he found out the reason behind the amazing reliability of the Randicond. For in order to make them so reliable, Tikka had surreptitiously arranged for a tiny hole to be made in the tip of each one to dissipate any pressure build-up within at the moment of release. As the Guru's name was being stamped on the item, the pin hole was made. A slight modification of the stamp template was all that was needed. Of course, these items were well-nigh useless now for the purpose for which they were intended, but did that bother Tikka? You bet it didn't: he was laughing all the way to his favourite offshore bank.

At the knock on the door, Tikka quickly sat down in his huge executive chair, swivelled round until he was facing the desk, leant forward over it, picked up his pen and was apparently working hard as his secretary had walked in.

"Yes," he said lazily in his pillow-talk voice, "what is it?"

"A Mr. Hopeworthy is on the line, Swami," she said, handing him some papers to sign. "Shall I put him through?"

"I was meditating," he suggested. "Yes, of course, it's about time I finalised the deal. Put him through." The Swami was about to greatly upset one Inigo Hopeworthy, Property Director to the Church Commissioners – up till that moment the proud owners of most of the River Dart.

"So you see, Inigo," he said after a few minutes' conversation, trying to appear relaxed and in total control, "you don't mind me calling you by your first name? I thought not. Well, as I said, we wish to exercise our option to purchase the River Dart." Noises were heard coming down the telephone line – gurgling, choking noises, which Tikka ignored. "Yes," Tikka said, "I know I said it was unlikely we ever would. But circumstances have chang ..."

"You mean the oil has changed things – that's what it is," the aggravated Property Director spluttered, for he too had heard rumours about the oil. He was sure the newly installed Bishop, a man of formidable character to whom he was answerable, would not take kindly to the loss of millions from the Church coffers. "That's it, isn't it?" he wailed, two rows of neat bridgework gnashing nicely together. "You've heard about the oil, haven't you?"

"Oil – what oil?" Tikka asked innocently, but with some difficulty, his tongue being firmly in his cheek.

"You know very well. What oil indeed! I shall

12

probably lose my job over this – let alone my head. Why did I ever ...?"

"So you will draw up the contracts and send me my copy. Tonight? Good. Thank you so much, Inigo." Tikka put down the handset with a flourish of pride, and started happily to sing a slightly altered old Stephen Foster song ... 'Way down upon the Swami's ...'

Later that evening, in the newly white-washed Carnal House, he was still somewhat full of bliss, humming away to himself, still tickled absolutely pink. But, sad to relate, in a nearby Bishop's Palace, one Inigo Hopeworthy was not. Property Director for twenty years to the Church of England Commissioners, he was tendering his resignation. It was back to the family estate agency in Hampstead – if they would have him after so long.

As he collected his personal belongings, and his thoughts, he realized he had been expecting too much for a Bishop of the Church of England to look kindly with love and charity on someone who had let the Church down so badly. The new Bishop had never liked him, thinking him too old-fashioned for the modern Church, and had, on hearing the news of the lost oil revenue, stormed out of their afternoon crisis meeting shouting something that was anathema to Inigo. For the Bishop had summed up the situation with one sentence ...

... "The Church isn't a bloody charity!"

Inigo Hopeworthy was sure that, once upon a time, it had been.

3. The Guru

Meanwhile, on another part of the planet, thousands of miles to the west of Totnes, Guru Shami Randi, God, The Enlightener, and self-proclaimed Master of the Vagina, was lying back in the Olympic pool-sized bath in the private rooms of his gold-plated palace in Randiville, U.S.A., preparing, to the great relief of most of his inner circle, for a trip to Europe.

Born of peasant stock high in the Nepalese hills at a rumoured early age, Randi was a diminutive man who would have been insignificant and totally unknown to the rest of the world had it not been for his once acute business sense (sadly now dormant due to his ingestion of too many mind-expanding substances), his powerful public relations organization and his somewhat startling appearance. With shoulder-length frizzy grey hair on the sides of his head and none on top (this lack of hair always being concealed by a rainbow turban, even when in his bath), and with a misplaced right foot (lost to a sea monster when still a child), he had, with just a leg to stand on, single-mindedly transformed various eastern mystic ideas into a brilliant multi-million dollar business.

From the successful marketing of breakfast muesli with a mantra on the back of the packet and a free medallion of himself inside, to a chain of centres where, in the hope of stemming the flow of the highly infectious disease SLIM, free rubber appliances were mandatory in all guest rooms, he had certainly cornered a market.

His notorious Randicentres were places where the displaced, dispirited and sometimes disturbed could drop in for a chat, stay a night, and then wake up

15

surprised, yet happy, to find that they had handed over all they possessed to Randco. They themselves had become that very thing – possessed – and many said by the devil himself.

As a rule of thumb, Eastern religions talked about Light, Inner Order, Tranquillity, whilst Randi talked about Knowledge always through Love – Love that had no restrictions. There were naked tea parties in the grounds of his many Randicentres; tea parties that started fairly demurely and ended in games such as 'find the cream bun' and 'watch the éclair'. And games such as these, in the context of self-fulfilment and finding oneself, were easy for all to comprehend.

Randi, however, was now taking as few personal risks as possible, and with the worldwide onset of the dreaded SLIM he was insisting on the use of rubber gloves and condoms at all tea parties he attended. These rubber items were delivered on silver salvers, and their wearing was becoming ritualized; first, a short mantra was said, then they were donned in unison. He had created a new kind of sterilized foreplay.

Essentially, what he had long ago discovered was that people much enjoyed orgies, and were willing to pay, and pay plenty, for the privilege of indulging in them. Knowing biblically as many different people as possible had been one of the foremost beliefs he had originally expounded. His own philosophy had been simple – take as much as possible and give back as little as possible; keep the wealth created for Randco – the Great Guru Himself – but let the kids who gave him his wealth have enough of a good time to keep them hanging on.

The catalyst had been his own favourite hobby – sex ... carnal knowledge, fornication – call it what you will – and each day, to make sure he received substantial

16

daily doses of this favourite pastime, three different young Devo girls were accorded the privilege of attending the Great Man. This day was no exception.

Having had their assistance in his ablutions, Randi presently hopped gingerly from his bath. The girls dried him down and helped him gently onto a couch. He then instructed two of them to massage him from top to toe, and the third to prepare a long white line of cocaine and a joint of neat Thai marijuana.

Randi enjoyed his drugs, often imbibing cocktails that could kill horses. When stoned thus and with his brain absent, he liked being taken up in the Randair Learjet125, for this made him feel even more God-like than usual. Once, flying high over the desert in more senses than one, he had spied a long white line five miles below. He had insisted on snorting it, but was only stopped from depressurizing the aircraft and leaning out to do so by minders from his very own Royal Guard – the Peace Force – who managed to explain to the tongue-biting Guru that, 'yes, it was his own personal white line, but that it was a line of white cars, his cars, his Rolls Royces, and that it would not be a good idea, Sire, to try to snort them up his nose – from such a height'.

His bad habits had led to the destruction of the membrane between his nostrils and the subsequent collapse of his nose and so, to avoid looking completely pig-like, he had arranged for a new nose to be created by one of America's top plastic surgeons. The surgeon had rearranged it (after pleasurably breaking it in a surgical vice) so that the end result would look retroussé. Unfortunately, The Guru's face did not suit his new nose: he now had great difficulty snorting anything up it, and, due to an erroneous injection whilst on the table, all the melanin in it had been destroyed. He now looked somewhat like a brown one-legged pig with a white nose.

But, my friend, we digress ...

The line of cocaine was now ready and Randi tilted his head back. While one girl was already massaging his lower regions orally, something that sent shock waves reverberating around his body, the second lit a reefer, reversed it in her mouth and hovered above his trembling lips, whilst the third loaded a special double-snap syringe with the cocaine destined for the depths of his nasal passages. The little Guru waited, anxiously coiled up, ready to spring into his daily drug-induced euphoria.

The girls knew their job well. All three had been carefully checked that very morning in the Randiville medical centre for signs of the deadly SLIM virus, had been given a clean bill of health, and had been kept in secure isolation till his bath-time, the whole time watched over by two thugs from the Peace Force. They bent down and, all experts in their various fields, gave the little man from Nepal the most wonderful private service he had ever had. Three in one, and one in three; he came, took a draw, and was zonkered.

Presently, after some top-ups from the girls, Randi was seated, one would say only by a whisker, in one of his fifty-five Rolls Royces, ten of which were being used that day for the trip to the airport. His efficient, neatly starched Nurse with the upside down timepiece was as usual in attendance, supporting him in more ways than one.

After being figuratively scraped off his massage table and dressed by the three little maids, his Nurse had attempted to remind him in what direction he was headed that day, and had at the last moment thankfully remembered to strap on his shiny prosthetic leg. Even so, it had been found necessary for two strong men from the Peace Force to carry him to the appointed car.

Petals were then confettied on him, a wreath was hung around him and his hands were taped together from his neck with clear tape – he being incapable of now holding them up in his traditional eastern sign of humility.

Garlanded thus and dressed in white robes, with his rainbow turban at a jaunty angle, he looked at the same time serene, ready for burial, yet frankly comical. The grass had worked well: certain parts of him ached terribly as though he had been pumped dry (he had been), and the cocaine had turned him into more of a babbling idiot than usual. Nurse knew she'd have her work cut out keeping him away from his Devos, for they must not see him in this state, especially with his hands taped up.

"Wagons ... ROLL!" the Devo in the first Rolls barked into his handset – and slowly the motorcade of ten white Rolls Royces, flanked by gun-toting motorcycle outriders on white Harley Davidson Electraglides and a multitude of white-clad singing and chanting Devos, gathered momentum. The eight-mile drive to the local airport would be a suitably grand affair, for Guru Shami Randi deserved grand entrances and exits; at least, in his own humble opinion he did – this was how he travelled everywhere, it was nothing unusual for a God.

At the airport, crowded with thousands more specially bused in Devos, all dancing, singing and chanting, the local dignitaries were out in force to send off the Guru they so disliked and despised. They were obliged to be there, for the original small town had grown very rich with Randiville next door. The singing and chanting that had preceded his arrival at the airport intensified as the motorcade pulled in.

The Mayor's official greeting was drowned out and largely ignored as men and girls flung themselves at

19

his feet; they flung their clothes at his car, they flung flowers, they flung anything they could fling, including themselves, as they followed him and his party, still chanting and hand clapping, onto the tarmac right up to the Randair Learjet. None, though, were allowed sufficiently near the babbling wreck of a Guru to notice his calcified state, Nurse had made sure of that. Then slowly the chant unified and, to the tune of a well-known National Anthem, a thousand voices sang

Guru Shami Randi,
You mean so much to me,
Oh yes you do!
Godhead, Enlightenah,
Saviour and Brightenah,
Master o'er't Vagina,
We love you, our Lord, etc., etc.
(Ad Nauseam)

By this time some of the Devos were already naked, and Randi, having been bundled into his white jet, was smiling malignantly as the dignitaries, police and Mayor looked on aghast. The aircraft handlers first had to remove the flowers and clothes which were draping the aeroplane before they could find the wheel chocks, and, having removed these, it was able to taxi to the runway's end. As the Great Guru slumped into his throne-like seat, his Nurse removed the tape holding up his hands and without thinking massaged his neck to calm his hypertension.

20

As she clicked out the knots and looked down at his well-hidden bald pate, she inwardly thought how nice it would be if it was a fractured, not just a fractious neck. But she removed her hands quickly and sat in her own less grandiose seat behind as the plane gathered speed.

The aeroplane took to the air and hundreds of the most devoted, and most naked, ran after it, waving their hands and everything else madly about; then, unable to do anything else to halt their beloved's departure, they buried themselves on top of one another on the grass. As the Randair Learjet took to the sky, it flew past over them, dipped its wings in salute, and out dropped thousands of rubber Randiconds, all of which were quickly donned.

The end of runway 21 East was never the same again.

4. Big Dirk

High in the sky, a vapour trail showed the track of the Learjet, racing towards Totnes at 39,000 feet, and far below it, in the ocean, a school of Great Sperm Whales surfaced, sounded, and dived. And one whale in particular looked up, eyed the writing in the sky and strangely recalled something from his distant past.

Thus, dear reader, and with deep respect, may I introduce to you our Cetacean protagonist in this house of cards ...

Call me ... Dirk. Big Dirk. Tis I, and I want to tell you a story ...

Some time past – I know not when – having nothing much to interest me at sea, I thought I would move around a bit and see the drier part of the world. It's one way I have of letting off steam. The other is blowing it out my nasal passage. Whenever I find myself growing bored with life, frustrated at my loneliness; whenever I find myself involuntarily pausing before passing a whaler, then turning and moving fast (twenty knots max.) the other way; and especially whenever my paranoia gets the upper hand, it takes dedication to stop me from deliberately ramming a factory ship, or knocking the harpooner off with one flick of a fluke. Then, it's then high time to get to land as soon as I can. There is nothing surprising in this. If they but knew it, almost all men in their degree, some time or other, cherish very nearly the same feelings towards the ocean as me.

Now there is an island in the cooler climes, an island sometimes breezed by warming winds, an island set in a once-clean and pleasant sea, that I know. I like

22

the isle, but not the sea round thereabouts, for so much noise, sonorous, deep, comes from ships that pass around, and so much flotsam, jetsam, and so much ... well, ambergris (may be too fine a word) floats therein, it has become a mire. But the hypo gets me, and gets me bad, and I have to go.

So, in a manner of speaking, I don my cap, tighten my scarf, pull up my collar, and go. And will I meet a friend on the way? Shall I come across another like soul searching for the secret of life? Will I (and why, oh Lord, why not yet?) find a lover to hold, albeit in a brief embrace, a brief encounter to continue the chain of genes aching to be continued, a mate to cherish for those few precious seconds it takes to move the ocean? Will I? Well, shall I? I must be patient! The Lord will provide ...

So I adjust my cap, loosen my scarf for so hot 'neath collar, and go.

I look up. Far above me, far, far above, I see writing in the sky, a long thin line slowly increasing its length, and guilt floods my mind. But why? I think back, back through my life, and I am hit in the face, struck by a feeling so intense I shudder.

Once, in warmer climes, I had played with a furry little brown boy near a shoreline. I had let him ride me, I had gambolled with him in the surf. And then I had tried to toss him high in the air – playful, mind. I recall it so clear now. A gentle snap, a tearing noise of foot from leg, a boy disappearing upwards, spurting blood, screams, family from the palm-fringed beach running into the water to rescue almost drowning now footless boy; lump, oh Lord, foot-long lump in throat.

I swallow hard, as I had that time so long ago.

I dive to escape the dream, the nightmare, so vivid, surreal. So then to sleep.

23

And now ... I dream my dream again, of a little brown boy flying up, up and away, who leaves his leg behind. I'll just have to chew on that ...

And far above the ocean, Guru Shami Randi bent down to rub the stump where his foot should have been, and instantly had felt someone's evil eye on him. He looked around. All were asleep, meditating, or probably both. But someone **was** watching.

Vhat a very odd feeling ...

As they flew onwards to Totnes, Nurse thought on the chaos they had left behind as they'd taken to the air. The Devos on the runway would not be in any trouble – there should be no arrests considering the amount Randco paid in donations to the local police benevolent fund, now one of the richest in the U.S.A. However, she did notice that Guru appeared to be having an uncomfortable ride. He was sweating and shivering, unbeknownst to her being unable to think of anything save the giant millstone around his life – his dreaded Sperm Whale, Big Dirk. He shuddered uncontrollably, cold clammy sweat breaking out of every pore of his body. Best leave him be, she thought.

"Excuse me, Holiness," a rather timid Randair stewardess said after a while, from a seemingly very uncomfortable point somewhere near the carpet at Randi's foot. His high-flying paranoid reverie interrupted, the frightened man twitched, but with the drugs he had imbibed having less effect due to the normal passage of time, he managed to look down at her, happy in the knowledge that his instructions concerning humility in his magnificent presence were being adhered to.

"Yes, child?" came the patronising reply. "Vhat is it?"

"Captain Swami Pre Sambodi's compliments, Holiness. He has received a message from Randi One and wishes to share the communication with you." She held out a note from the pilot which the Nurse took, she not being sure that Randi would be able to read at that very moment.

"Vhat does it say, Nurse?" squeaked the Guru. She scanned the message quickly. It originated from Swami Tikka Masala in Totnes, someone to whom the Nurse had become very close on their last English trip.

"Guru," said the Nurse, "it is from England – it concerns the river my beautiful Swami bought." She couldn't wait to see him again!

Guru frowned. "He has bought a rivah?! ... Vhy? Did I, Guru Shami Randi, order this? No, I did not! Does no varn listen? That Swami ..."

"Guru," she interrupted calmly, "he says it is good news – Gospel. Beneath the river there is oil; now you own the river above. That's why he bought it, and now he wants to send for your submarine to assist the exploration for your own liquid gold ... the *Obtuse* will be on its way ..."

" - That Swami ... did well to follow my instructions and purchase the river."

"Yes, Guru ..." Nurse took a deep breath, and held it. Randi blithely continued, turning to the Devo girl still crouching painfully at his feet.

"Tell Sambodi to send this message to Randi One for onward transmission to the Swami in Totnes ...

'BRATAVISHNU, SWAMI. YOU HAVE DONE VELL. YOU CAN KEEP THE ROLLS I LENT YOU ...' Signed by me. Oh, and add, 'YES, SEND FOR THE *OBTUSE*. FIND CAPTAIN KAMAKIS WHEREVER HE AND THE SUBMARINE ARE IN THE WORLD, AND UNDER MY ORDERS TELL HIM TO MAKE FULL SPEED FOR TOTNES IMMEDIATELY. I VILL MEET HIM THERE. THE *OBTUSE* CAN HELP WITH

THE EXPLORATION.' Is that clear?"

"Yes, Holiness, but who shall I tell?" questioned the girl.

"Vhat do you mean – who?"

"Who shall I get to radio this message?"

"Good Lord above and below ... and here," cried Randi. "Sambodi!"

"Will anybody do, Holiness?"

The Nurse interrupted to save the situation – and the girl's bacon. "Tell the pilot, girl, he is S-a-m-bodi." An embarrassed look of comprehension crossed the crouching girl's face and she backed down the aircraft's aisle on all fours, her eyes averted from Randi's.

"Who is that girl, Nurse?" asked the lecherous Guru, forgetting his annoyance yet peeved at not obtaining a good look at the girl's rear. "She is both foolish and ... er ... good looking. A perfect combination for a vooman. Can she make tea? Does she type?"

Nurse took another deep breath to calm herself. "She is Ma Prem Dansak, Holiness," she said in measured tones, "recently arrived in Randiville from Randi Six Stockholm, yet to receive Knowledge. A new loyal Devo, Guru. Beautiful, don't you think?"

"I do indeed," the great one said. "Have her accompany you from now. She vill come in handy. I maybe can give it to her ... The ... er ... Knowledge ..."

"Yes, of course, Holiness," replied the patient Nurse, straightening up, and flattening her starched white uniform.

26

She smiled inwardly, knowing just how 'lucky'
the girl was.

5. An Officer's Mess

Captain Halitosis Kamakis, formerly of the Royal Hellenic Navy and whose only decorations weren't even the sort one hangs on the Christmas tree, was randomly snapping out instructions to his crew. The Randco submarine, the *Obtuse*, was at last thankfully leaving the NATO arms dump, and dump it was, on the Greek island of Corfu – that jewel, as the holiday brochures say, set in the Ionian Sea. Captain Kamakis was wondering now just what to do next.

Some days before, he and his crew had sailed into the base at Paleocastritsa on the island's west coast under the influence of an awful lot of Ouzo, the well-known life-giving Greek elixir, drunkenly hoping to defraud the base commander out of some stores they sorely needed, and the next morning had totally regretted the move. But by then the harbour boom was down, and there was no turning back. Now, four days later, they were happily sailing out of the base in an unusually pristine submarine, with a substantial supply of arms, a top secret torpedo or two, a new deck gun, and full tanks of diesel.

Halitosis Kamakis, in charge of the Guru's one and only submarine, lived by his wits, wits which were rumoured to be in the seat of his pants, and up till that week he had commanded nought but a rotting tub crewed by some fairly unwashed Greek seamen.

Now all was changed.

The crew were dressed in smart new uniforms, the sub was full of diesel, new batteries had been installed, one engine had been overhauled and it had been given a coat of paint. The *Obtuse* was almost as good as new. But it had been a nervous four days for him, and he had wondered just what had made him risk all. He blamed the Ouzo. The base commander might end up at the wrong end of a Greek firing squad, but that would be his problem. Kamakis' was to get himself and his men away from the base.

Randco had acquired the *Obtuse* when the British government had sold off its fleet of Oberon class submarines. In order to liquidate the fleet as fast as possible, they had been offering two subs for the price of one, and Kamakis, hired as Captain on Swami Tikka Masala's suggestion, had cleverly gone out and bought the opposite two ends of the same sub, thus halving the cost, negating any tax liability, and saving Randco tens of thousands. The British, as usual, were confused by this good example of eastern Mediterranean business acumen, but too late – the sub, technically in kit form, so tax free, was gone.

Following the sub's purchase, he had then worked for Randco for nigh on six years, though they hadn't exactly been the best years of his life. He had become so bored! Maybe it was his very own mid-life crisis, for he often wondered just what he was doing meandering around the seas of the world in an ancient tub, which might spring a leak at any point, with no ultimate purpose in mind. Halitosis Kamakis often thought – just what was the point? Well, friend, let me attempt to elucidate.

The *Obtuse* had originally been intended for use as an underwater Randicentre – the Devotees' own Atlantis. The Guru had thought of all the young Devo girls breast-stroking on the sea bed, clad in nothing save for a gas bottle strapped to their taut, firm backsides – his personal mermaids – and he had immediately ordered its purchase. Since then, though, it had done little or nothing, and the crew, on his only visit to them, had put the Guru off the submariner's life for ever. He hated bad smells at the best of times – as it is well known no-one smelling remotely evil was allowed anywhere near him, and in the sub the smell of a strong male human presence could be pungent in the extreme. From that time the Guru had always referred to the crew as revolting, and tried always to keep a fathom, if not a league, away.

The Greek navy too was now equipped with Oberon class subs, and Kamakis had in his drunken state somehow assumed correctly that it would not be a problem for his sub to enter the base, one of the most secret in Europe. His crew were Greek, the *Obtuse* looked like one of their navy subs, no-one would think anything of it. Then he could get the badly needed stores. Maybe someone would check if they wanted something unusual, but the drunken Kamakis was sure he could talk his way around that one. So he and his crew had arrived in Paleocastritsa unannounced and unexpected, a motley crew much more disparate than usual, steering an ancient submarine fairly haphazardly into the normally secure naval base.

After docking, and, to his surprise, being welcomed by the base commander, Kamakis attempted his first small purchase from the stores – the latest model captain's chair he had recently seen advertised in a marine catalogue. This went without a hitch, or even a half-hitch, and it was only when, after much miscellaneous purchasing, he asked for a complete paint job for his submarine, two very classified torpedoes, a few thousand gallons of fuel and a new deck gun that dark eyebrows were raised.

There was, however, only a short delay before authorization came all the way from NATO HQ, and both he and the commander, a tall thin and now

30

nervous specimen of humanity, were singularly surprised and pleased when it did. Little did they know of the involvement of The Lord Above in the matter of this authorization, for The Lord had looked down on the *Obtuse* and her crew in their moment of need and had moved things, mysteriously as usual, so that normal naval security procedures were not followed. The Lord knew that very soon Kamakis would receive his unexpected sailing orders for Totnes; it was in His Plan, and with little or no fuel the *Obtuse* would be going nowhere fast. He so liked to be of service, did The Lord.

The base shipyard hands were let loose on the *Obtuse* and swarmed over it like ants – painting, scrubbing, polishing, installing, renovating, until at the end of its short sojourn in Paleocastritsa the small submarine was extremely ship shape, and if a submersible could smile, was smiling all the way from its sharp to its blunt end. As there seemed little point in his men staying around the *Obtuse* while this was going on, Kamakis had given most of them a couple of days off during the refit. Some he ordered to stay on duty in shifts, but even these had, in their typically undisciplined way, drifted away and joined their mates in bars, tavernas and doorways in various states of inebriation. They then went off to look for somewhere to stay.

That same day, Flight JL 203 had arrived in from Tokyo. The Japan Airlines 757, *the Spirit of Hirohito*, limped into Corfu International Airport on one engine. Captain Watanabe had once or twice seriously doubted that his flight would make it, but he hadn't told the passengers of his fears, for he knew that none of the women he was carrying had ever flown before; well, not in an aeroplane. As he saw the aptly named terminal building, he breathed a great Japanese

31

sigh of relief.

He knew then they could not take off again – certainly not until the flight of birds now neatly shredded in the port engine were removed, and the engine checked. That could take days. He had never landed at Corfu before; the runway had reminded him of old Hong Kong, stuck out into the sea like that, and so short he had to pull up hard. And where was the nearest Boeing agent? Knowing his luck, probably in Rome, where he had been heading when the birds had struck. Thank God the little island had been en route. Now he'd have to arrange accommodation for his passengers and crew.

Opening his flight manual, he turned to CFU for Corfu. So who was their local agent?

George Barbas stubbed out another Papastratos. He'd been waiting at his desk in the airport for four hours now, had seen ten flights arrive, and was full of ennui. Corfu airport in the height of summer was not his idea of fun. He was hot – no, he was HOT! And right next to the very smelly toilets. The delayed flight from Bermincham could have maybe ten more minutes, then it was home for George. He'd been up since first light, could stand the awful smell of drains no more and was about to ring his office to tell them what they could do with their job, when an unusual thing happened – a smart, uniformed, oriental gentleman, trailing a long line of equally polished oriental women, walked up to his desk. George looked up indolently and lit another cigarette. "Can I kelp you, sair?" he asked, unctuousness oozing from every pore.

"Ahhh. Capitain Ahhhh Watanabe," announced the man, bowing stiffly. "Ahhh. Japan Airlines. Oowagh." Thank God, thought Barbas, his desk was so conveniently positioned next to the lavatories, for the

32

man sounded as though he was about to explode. He pushed the tip saucer forward.

"The gentleman's is here," said George, pointing the oriental towards the barely hidden urinals; then deferentially, "and the ladies ... thair." He smiled. The Captain grunted once more, then explained that it was George's agency that represented JAL in Corfu and that they needed accommodation and not the toilets. George swiftly stubbed out his cigarette, lit another, and picked up the telephone. He was soon talking fast and furiously with his cousin Jannis on the other side of the island – a cousin who just happened to own a hotel. The hotel building work was almost finished, and he had spare room. He always had room space – no problem!

And so sixty-six Japanese Geisha girls, on a tour of Europe, unexpectedly arrived in Paleocastritsa that evening. George's cousin now had a full hotel; in fact, it was overfull – he had, in the international jargon of hoteliers, an overbooking situation. As George arrived with the Japanese contingent, he saw cousin Jannis in a heated discussion with a bunch of sailors who appeared to be from the local NATO base. They too had been promised the rooms ...

Soon everyone repaired to the hotel bar to discuss the 'room space' problem further and slowly but surely the heat was taken out of the sailors' sails, not though by cousin Jannis. It was the Geisha girls who were trained to soothe man's aching brow, and soothe it they did.

Much, much later that night, whilst Captain Watanabe and his crew were still picking bits of perfectly shredded dead duck from a formerly pristine engine and wondering where on Corfu they could obtain some pancakes, the girls were soothing more than just these men's aching brows. Everyone had become very friendly. Things were so friendly, in fact, that the 'overbooking' had been resolved as, hand in hand, couples tip-toed off to bedrooms intended for one. But, my friend, these girls did not only want Greek seamen: any male matelot would do, and this proclivity of theirs had been vividly borne out back home in Japan just two months before. Stay with me, I will explain ...

For when the 90,000-ton aircraft carrier the USS *Richard Milhous* had then been on a courtesy call to Yokohama, this very same bunch of Geishas had entertained its US crew just as they were now entertaining what was, of course, to the trained eye, the crew of the *Obtuse.* Little did they know, though, just what calling cards the US sailors would leave, for the USS *Richard Milhous* was not just a carrier of aircraft.

And so for three days in Corfu, whilst Captain Halitosis Kamakis watched his submarine gleam a little more each day, his men were enjoying all the pleasures of the Orient; and whilst Captain Watanabe watched a new engine being slowly installed on the *Spirit of Hirohito*, his girls were, so to speak, up to their necks with Greek seamen.

Not wishing to overstay his unanticipated welcome, on the fourth day of the sojourn on the Greek island Hal Kamakis recalled his men, now happy and revived. However, whilst being thus revived and relieved, often, they had between them contracted, courtesy of the globe-trotting Geishas, and inadvertently the US Navy, virtually every sexually contagious disease known to man, including the awful, the dreaded, and the always fatal ... SLIM. And so we continue ...

The *Obtuse* left Corfu and was about to dive when the Guru's order arrived from Swami Tikka Masala, instructing Kamakis to make for Totnes at full speed, and for almost the first time since the sub had been purchased, Kamakis, who now had found a purpose in life, was able to oblige. The sub's tanks were full of diesel, it had new batteries, everything was ship-shape, and the crew, especially, were happily satisfied. Kamakis replied and confirmed their course. They were now under way, though they should have been under a doctor, for his crew was now the nearest thing to a biological time-bomb that was humanly possible. He ordered them to trace a generally westerly course for Gibraltar, sat back in his newly acquired Captain's chair, and contemplated his navel.

Things appeared to be going well. At last they might see some long-awaited action; but what did the Guru want now? Something to do with oil. ... What would they be doing?

He placed his chin on the tips of his arched fingers, looked deep into the region of his belly button and thought on the mysteries of life. Why had it been so easy? If he could extract top-secret lethal stores without hesitation or deviation, then couldn't anyone? The thought quite worried him, but only for a moment.

He swung forward, attempting to extract himself from his new chair, only to find its tilt mechanism had jammed. He was still flat on his back with his legs in the air. No amount of swinging forward helped. And obviously he couldn't take the damn thing back to the store. He was stuck in the tiny officers' mess in an extremely ignominious position. Either he would have to wait for a passing hand or attempt a crash landing on deck.

As he waited for the aid that seemed as though it would never arrive, he recalled the extremely hot day in Athens when the straps on his sandals had snapped, and he had badly burnt the soles of his feet on the scorching city pavement running to the nearest shoe shop. Little thongs sometimes cause big problems. Still no-one was coming to help him.

He decided to wait, not wishing to be found in a heap on the floor by a subordinate. His cries for help were drowned out by the general noise inside a busy submarine just getting under way, and he couldn't quite reach the intercom. But maybe he could, just. He stretched out until his arm felt as though it would leave his socket, but to no avail. One last try was attempted at reaching over to the wall-mounted hand piece, just another inch, just half an inch, and then ... disaster!

It was all too much for the laws of physics, which laws suddenly came into play as Kamakis, with chair in tow, over-balanced and, just as his number two annoyingly entered the room, he landed in a heap on the floor with the chair firmly in place on his back. As they hit the deck, the small gas cylinder, which provided the hydraulics for the chair, ruptured and exploded with a bang. Kamakis was, in more senses than one, truly in an officer's mess. Maybe it was only prestige that seemed to be visibly draining from his face, but probably not. Groaning noises appeared audible, noises emanating from below the overturned chair, and after surveying the scene for a moment, his number two, one Spiro Sporades, bent down to help. As he did so, Kamakis croaked out a warning.

"Please be careful with the chair, Spiro, it has entered my bottom."

"It has entered where, Captain?" replied the confused Spiro.

"My bottom, there is something in my bottom," creaked Kamakis.

By the whiskers of St. Spiridon, thought the Corfiot Spiro (all men on Corfu being named Spiro), the Captain has received a bump on the head and is confused.

"Captain," he said, "the chair is simply lying on you, nothing else - look"; and he reached forward to pull it off.

"Please, Spiro, be careful - something hard has pushed itself into my rear, I fear." From under the chair Kamakis pointed to his bottom. "I know the feeling - I mean, I know what I am feeling."

Spiro once again lent forward and took great pains, something Kamakis appeared to be experiencing, to pull the chair off his back slowly and gently. Two ratings were summoned to give assistance and finally, with a little 'plop', the chair and the Captain were disconnected. Kamakis was helped to his unsteady feet, took one step and collapsed with pain in Spiro's arms.

"Lay me down on the couch, Spiro. I'm buggered," said Kamakis. Though Spiro still did not believe it, Kamakis really was, or at least just had been. In the crash and explosion, the nine-inch shaft on which the whole chair was supported had broken through the seat's upholstery, broken through the seat of his pants, and ended up embedded deep within him. He had been verily and explosively shafted.

For the next week Halitosis Kamakis had a great deal of difficulty walking without pain, his stride being somewhat wide, almost in the style of John Marion Wayne, and though the record books omit to mention the fact, he, to this day, is the only man alive to have had anal relations with his own chair, underwater.

6. A Spurned Whale

This is Dirk once more. Greetings from the ocean! My journey log continues ...

Moons pass; winds pick up, die down; the sun comes up, drops, rises again, thank the Lord, forty, fifty, I lose track times and I know I am still far from my island. I look about. What is about looks back. Nothing. No thing. Not a jot, nor a tittle. Nix. Rien. Nada. Τιπότα.

I send out a pulse or two, a click or five, for this feels like gaol, with no inmates nor warder, an ocean of nothing, a sea of aquatic boredom ...

My passage must soon be over for I hunger for company; my school has gone. Where is the love I cherish, the friend I wish to treasure, to share my life, to share my great unseen torpedo, my humungous whalehood? How long must I keep it like a sword in its scabbard? So long hidden from view! Oh, where are you my love, where?

And then – a reply!

I swim towards the source, clicking with joy. I get no joyclicks back. Not one. Nonetheless, I be glad to see her. She is shiny, steely, cold, longer than I! And she does have a great aft.

I move alongside, close, touching. She does not respond.

Such a cold, cold fish.

I move behind her to feel her aft. Why? For there is a stirring below in me, a twitching, a trembling, what is occurring? But yet she does not answer.

Something still grows beneath me, something expanding, a feeling so intense I know not what to do.

Now I slide up onto her back. My sense is going,

what am I doing? It is my torpedo that is enlarging and searching for a way in to enter her!! I cannot stop it!

My whale of a seacock stands to attention, erect and proud, like a sergeant-at-arms would salute on parade. A mind of its own!

I try to grasp her with my flippers, lest I should slide off to the deep. My whalehood commences throbbing, pushing, thrusting forwards. I cannot, it will not ... STOP! She and I are locked in an embrace the like of which I do not comprehend. I thrust once more, harder and harder. Bang, Bang, BANG! And I am in! But I am in pain. I have penetrated her for why I know not. I have broken her rear doors, her stern caps are gone, but I too am broken, for if this is love I WANT IT NOT!!

In haste I withdraw, my privates in agony, slashed by I know not what. She too pulls away fast, propelled by spinning discs that nearly slice me more. A stinging liquid, that clouds and turns milky white, escapes from her stern tube, a liquid that touches my lips and I recoil at the taste, something much worse than the ink of a startled squid. What can it be?

What a creature, so strange!

I lick my wounds to recover.

My whalebone retreats back from whence it came.

Methinks it should stay there.

Back in the real world, Hal Kamakis had selfishly commandeered the Officers' Mess, and undoubtedly in one he truly was. As the days went by, and the old tub steered its merry way towards Totnes, the health of his rear end improved somewhat, but at the same time some indications of what his men may have picked up from the Geishas of Corfu were becoming apparent. Small hints that all was not, for them, well, were manifesting themselves in various ways that would have been obvious to a trained eye; or, more to the point, a nose. But no heed was taken – the motion in the ocean was blamed.

The *Obtuse* left the warm waters of the Mediterranean and turned to starboard, due north towards England. At Cape Saint Vincent the changes became noticeable, with a swell rocking the boat sufficiently to make yet more of the crew unwell, who reacted accordingly in unison with a yawning of many hues. But, as we know, the sea was not the only swell that would be rocking the *Obtuse* ... So, friends, let us now see Dirk's previous intercourse from the submariners' point of view.

One day Hal had been as usual trying to take his afternoon nap, only to be awoken much too soon by a strange thudding from the stern. For no reason he could fathom, the sub was tossing all over the place and his agitated crew were being thrown from side to side; so he reluctantly rose on unsteady feet to investigate.

"Spiro," he shouted to his number two, "what is occurring? What is the thumping? Is it a big end?"

"I don't know, Captain," countered Spiro, "there's something up in the stern tubes ..." Little did they know, in a manner of speaking, just how right they both were.

The two men charged aft towards the trouble,

vomiting crew pushed aside as they hurried through the boat. The rocking became more intense and the sub shuddered violently, the volume of the banging increasing as they reached the last bulkhead. Stepping through the door, they rushed up to the rear tube doors, under pressure from the other side – as if the stern caps had gone and the sea was rushing in. But what was the repetitive pounding? They scratched their heads. Then they tried to fathom the problem. Hal excitedly spoke first ... "My Ouzo!" he screamed, realizing "someone is trying to steal my Ouzo!"

"What?" yelled Spiro. "Your Ouzo?? What Ouzo?"

"My Ouzo!" shouted Hal, trying to make himself heard above the constant hammering. "My Ouzo!" he said again. For a few moments all that could be heard in the stern torpedo room was a constant pounding noise and the word 'Ouzo!' repeated over and over. Suddenly, Hal grabbed the port torpedo door handle, yanking it up forcefully.

"Captain!" screamed Spiro. "If the stern caps have gone ...!" But he was too late. As the door opened, a torrent of milky water exploded into the room, smashing both men against the bulkhead. "Ouzo!!" they both cried in unison, licking their lips. Now Hal knew what had happened, though Spiro was yet to comprehend.

"My Ouzo!" shouted Hal, yet again. "Someone has tried to steal my Ouzo! The thieves have broken in from the other side; that's why the stern caps have gone. My Ouzo was stored in the port tube! Oh, Theo Moo!" But calling out to The Lord Above was by now pointless, as a multitude of cases of broken bottles of the best liquor Greece could offer were ejected forcibly from the port torpedo tube into the room, which was now fast filling with a milky cocktail of ouzo and sea water.

"Captain! Secure the bulkhead door!" shrieked Spiro, who could see a bit of a problem emerging. "We must get out, or the *Obtuse* will sink!!!"

"But my Ouzo," repeated Hal for the umpteenth time, "what can we do?"

"Escape," screamed Spiro, jumping through the bulkhead door, "and quick! Now, get out! Leave the bottles, they are all broken, we will sink!!" But Hal Kamakis stood his ground, by now up to his ankles in diluted Greek spirit. "Captain! I shall count to three and then secure this bulkhead! Now GET OUT! One ... Two ... Thr..." A wretched Hal knew when he had to jump, and in the nick of time he did, as Spiro slammed the bulkhead door shut, ramming the handle upwards into the locked position.

Halitosis was now crying. "My Ouzo collection ... all gone, broken, smashed! What has caused this catastrophe??" he wailed.

Both men leant back against the bulkhead door, panting, drenched, and stinking of aniseed. Their crew came forward, necks craned to see what had transpired, all confused by the sight of their exhausted officers, questioning the pounding, which had now thankfully ceased, and wanting an explanation for the unusually strong Greek bar-room smell.

"Show is over," announced Spiro. "I will discuss this with the Captain, and a notice will be posted. Now go back to your posts, men!" He turned to Hal, who had slid to the floor, and was crying into his hands.

"No point crying over spilt milk, Captain. Now, what is this all about?"

7. Kelp!

Some days later, when they were in deep water in more senses than one (for by now NATO badly wanted back its purloined equipment), and when Hal had finally admitted to Spiro that he had for some time been using the port stern torpedo tube as a repository for his life's collection of Greek liquor, the decision was made to surface soon to inspect, and mend if possible, the presumed external damage to the stern caps, and then pump out the torpedo room. The weight of the unwelcome sea water in the sub so far aft was giving the helm problems keeping it trim. Spiro had pointed out to Hal that there was no way whoever it was who had broken the stern caps could have had any knowledge of his prized collection of Ouzo, Mastika, Metaxa, etc., etc. No-one knew. There must have been another reason for the incursion. Furthermore, they had noticed that the air in the sub was not as sweet as it should be. The mixed smell of Ouzo and vomit was just not clearing.

They had very quietly passed Vigo on Galicia's Atlantic coast, having been at periscope depth most of the way there. Sufficient fresh air should have been circulating in the ship from the breather mounted on the conning tower, and considering that all the air filters had just been renewed, the presence of stale and smelly air was most problematic. Kamakis instructed that there should also be an inspection of the external filter when they surfaced – this they agreed to do the following day, the air having become noticeably worse. Happily, the Bay of Biscay that day was not too stormy, though a fairly strong swell had developed on the surface. Kamakis searched the expanse of sea through his periscope and, satisfied that they were visually alone, gave the order to surface.

The *Obtuse* started feeling the surface waves, the boat gently rocking. As they hit the surface, Spiro clambered up the ladder, opened the hatch and climbed through onto the deck with his technical crew, who set to mending the port stern cap. They found it had been split in two by some considerable force from outside the sub, but the crew had no immediate explanation. They replaced the cap, tested the pressure seal, and went back on board to pump out the torpedo room.

Not wanting to see the remains of his collection being washed away, and though still in pain, Hal Kamakis had bravely followed Spiro up the conning tower to attend to the bad air problem. And there, right on top of the breather pipe, blocking the intake of fresh air, he had seen a mass of seaweed. It was out of reach – just. He shouted down to the crew below for a broom and handle, positioned himself on the edge of the conning tower, and waved the broom madly in the air in the very general direction of the seaweed. He had his back to the sea, his bottom still very painful. Preoccupied as he was with it (nothing was new), he failed to see a large dark object, similar in size and shape to the *Obtuse*, come up alongside. Spiro, though, facing the other way, was rooted to the spot, with mouth hanging wide open.

"Spiro, what is it – for God's sake, give me a hand." Kamakis held out his hand for help, but Spiro was still immobile. "Spiro, Spiro – aaahr!" There was the sound of splashing stage right. Hal had once more overbalanced and now had fallen in the water with the broom. He still did not know what was behind, though his own was beginning to hurt like hell. "Kelp!" shouted Hal from the briny, "Kelp!"

"Yes, Captain, I know. Seaweed: it was blocking

44

the breather ..."

"No ... Kelp! It is, how you say, my accent ... please kelp me now!!"

Spiro was still in shock, then realized what sort of pickle Kamakis was in. "Captain, look out," he screamed, pointing. "It's behind you!"

"This is not a pantomime, Spiro," roared Kamakis, waving the broom in the air. "I order you to get me out of here NOW!"

"No, really, Captain, it's behind you!" Spiro bellowed, pointing. "I think I know what broke into the torpedo room!"

"What are you talking about, Spiro? Oh, for God's sake, get hold of the broom so I can get back on board. We must dive immediately or we might be observed. What is it?" The sea swell slowly swivelled Kamakis around ...

Dirk had heard the noises of the technical crew's administrations from some way away, for sound travels far in his watery part of the world, and he had, after plucking some last pieces of broken glass from his very sore undercarriage, mooched over to take a gander. Seeing the humans hard at work, he now understood that the object of his previous affections was nought but some kind of underwater human transporter. He now sincerely understood, and with deep humility regretted the mistaken error of his ways, and was grateful that the men were able to put right the mess he, and his whalehood, had excessively made to the thing's rear end, which had at the time, inexplicably to Dirk, seemed rather attractive. Feeling so profoundly apologetic, he was about to confirm this for you in his log, but the following events, which happened suddenly and without warning, have precluded this.

Hal now saw the whale and froze; as is well

45

known, in water this is only recommended for icebergs. For humans it is like treading water too carefully. It invariably leads to drowning, and for the first time since his accident, he felt like using his bottom for more than just sitting on. He had that distinct sinking feeling.

And he *was* sinking. He had become unable to move, in the cold, dark waters of the Bay of Biscay, when he turned and laid eyes on Dirk. Only very few humans can passively float in sea water, and the great majority of these are already knocking on St. Peter's Gate when they do. Hal had seen great whales before, but only in books, or from a distance, and, as the waters closed over his jet black curly hair, he quickly realized he had no intention of meeting St. Peter just yet.

Defrosting unusually quickly, he struggled upwards, bravely fighting against the still-rising tide of pain from his rear, when inexplicably someone put out the lights. Everything had gone dark. He was still floating, now apparently on the surface, but without any effort and yet able to breathe. He looked around, but could see nothing. What on earth had happened? A chink of light appeared and went, then another. He turned towards the light, waiting for the next ray to appear. He bumped into something, something wet and warm. Where was he?

A ray of sunshine appeared; he turned towards it, shielding his eyes from the brightness, wiping the water from them, and focused. Was he going mad? Something smelt very fishy. And then what looked to Hal like a ferry's bow doors slowly opened. Light and water flooded in. For God's sake, Halitosis Kamakis, wake up! He pinched himself; then he saw the teeth. Row upon row was neatly placed around the bottom bow door, all glinting merrily in the sunshine. He was on the inside looking out; the inside of ...

Big Dirk had seen the man fall in the water. Humans seemed to do the craziest things. The other man on the boat had been pointing, waving, shouting, jumping up and down and, as more men appeared out of the top of the strange tower stuck in the middle, the man in the water disappeared.

Dirk had lugubriously swung into action. He knew many humans were unable to swim, even with all their appendages intact, and assumed this must be one of the many. He knew he should help save the man to make amends to humanity and there was only one way. He dived just under the surface, being careful not to make too many waves and knock any of the other crazy humans into the sea – one was enough. He started searching. After about a minute, he bumped into a fast-descending object which now appeared to be struggling. It must be the man: no other creature would make so much fuss over nothing. The sonar in his enormous forehead confirmed it was.

He caught the man in his mouth and surfaced, but, unfortunately for Hal, Dirk had been distracted for a moment by the sight of the men on deck of the *Obtuse* furiously jumping up and down. They reminded him a bit too much of whalers. In a panic, he had forgotten all about Hal Kamakis, had snapped his mouth shut and dived.

Hal felt his arm break. He knew it was broken, he'd heard the snap, recognized the searing pain coming from a now-limp arm. When he had seen Spiro and the other men, he'd thought it was about time to get out, so he'd struggled forward.

He had got one arm out of the damn whale's mouth and was about to make a swift exit when unexpectedly the mouth had banged shut and he was hurled to the back of the wet, smelly cavern. He had

47

been lucky to get his arm out still attached. Things had gone from the benign to the ridiculous.

Now he seemed to be on a free Nantucket-type sleigh ride. Water was rushing into the mouth, forcing him back further and further. The pressure was building up in his head; his ears popped, then popped again. He swallowed, trying to lessen the pressure, but he sincerely hoped the whale wouldn't do the same. And for the first time in years, Kamakis prayed.

On board the *Obtuse*, First Mate Spiro Sporades had seen Hal's arm being broken in the whale's jaw, he'd seen the monster sound and was sure he would see Hal no more. All they could do would be to get under way and head on to their original destination. There they could pick up supplies and carry on with their job, whatever it was. Halitosis Kamakis would have wanted that.

With a heavy heart, Spiro ordered the men back into the sub. The whale was nowhere to be seen. He stayed on deck a few moments longer, but nothing appeared, not even a scrap of evidence suggesting the demise, or not, of his boss. Rain started falling gently, the swell was increasing, and dark clouds were forming to the west. He slowly climbed the ladder up to the hatch, took one last look around, and then lowered himself into the submarine.

"Periscope depth, forward dead slow," he ordered to a forlorn crew, all obviously heartbroken. No-one spoke, the silence pierced only by the sound of the old diesels lurching into life. "Up 'scope," said Sporades after a few minutes. The *Obtuse* was hardly moving, none of the crew wanting to leave the area just in case, in case their boss was still alive. Sporades slowly grabbed the periscope handles and brought them down. His heart was not in the job. He looked into the

48

eyepiece.

"Surface, you sons of Artemis, SURFACE! NOW, NOW, NOW!" he screamed as soon as he had focussed. There, hanging onto the breather pipe with one arm, his face being continuously slapped by a rather large piece of seaweed, white as a sheet, was Captain Hal.

The sub almost exploded out of the water, twin bowhead fountains of water ballast shooting skywards. Spiro leapt out of the hatch.

"Spiro, Spiro," cried Kamakis, "thank God! My arm - look, it is broke." Spiro grabbed it to check, shook it, and agreed it was broken. Hal screamed with pain.

"You can let go of my arm now, Spiro," he said, wincing once more, "and get this submarine under the waves. We have been up far too long." Worriedly, he looked up at a vapour trail high in the sky.

Kamakis slowly climbed down the ladder, followed by Spiro, who helped him to lie down. An anaesthetic injection was then administered to his arm. Two short planks and some bandage later a sling was hung around his neck and his arm shoved unceremoniously in. Only then did anyone think of drying out their poor sodden Captain. Off painfully came the sling and all his clothes, he was wrapped in a multitude of blankets, and the sling replaced.

And thus was one Halitosis Kamakis, Captain of the *Obtuse*, conveyed to Totnes, naked save for some old itchy blankets, with his arm sandwiched between two short planks and his bottom still feeling the effects of a tubular steel invasion. As they might say of him in the valleys, he was the luckiest man to come out of whales since Jonah.

Big Dirk knew nothing of Jonah, nor the Welsh

valleys, but had felt a sense of responsibility towards Hal. He knew he shouldn't have taken him on the dive; after all, he had saved his life, then nearly killed him. That was stupid. He started following the *Obtuse* at a discreet distance, diving in and out of its wake, not quite sure why he was in tow. Was it guilt? Loneliness? Or had he discovered a new emotion?

Now, a whale with a guilt complex was one thing, but an unsatisfied one such as Dirk's – well, that was something else. Big Dirk felt very beholden towards the man he had nearly swallowed; now, though, the steel hull of the *Obtuse*, onto which he had finally deposited him, was coming between him and the object of his, well ... new affections. He moved alongside it, gently rubbing his soft underbelly down its length, but making sure this time he didn't become too excited.

He followed the *Obtuse* all the way from Biscay, easily keeping up with the relic of a great British past, but had been a touch worried as the submarine had entered the Dart, never liking one-way streets that much. Nevertheless, he had continued to follow close behind, sensing that he had at last reached the island of his dreams. His journey was nearly over ...

The submarine had stopped in mid-channel after travelling three or four miles up the river, and Dirk had seen it up its periscope, deploying its low-frequency radio aerial at the same time. He had known that this moment was the only chance he would have to communicate with his friend, somewhere deep within the vessel. He had swum over to the *Obtuse* and had once more rubbed his long belly on its side. He now liked that feeling – cold steel between his flippers – but it was no way to get through to the men inside.

As the periscope had slowly turned, he knew someone inside the sub was surveying the scene and had an idea. He had to do something to catch their attention and they weren't noticing the gentle rocking that he had created when he'd come alongside. As the 'scope swivelled slowly towards him, he got ready, lowering his head in the water and taking aim. And then, at the last second, he let go a torrent of water from his blow hole which hit the middle of the periscope's lens with considerable force. Positioning his huge left eye inches from the lens, he waited for the water to clear, and winked sweetly.

Inside the *Obtuse*, Spiro Sporades blinked, took another look, froze, swore, crossed himself twice, then screamed, "Dive, Dive, Dive! Down periscope!" The crew looked at him with pain in their hearts, for they were all sincerely looking forward to escaping from the hell hole that the renewed *Obtuse* had quickly become. For the last few days there had been little food, nowhere to rest – the entire mess was still their Captain's personal sanatorium, and with the breather still partially blocked, the air had become fouler and fouler. And when Spiro shouted, 'It's the whale again!' they had all audibly groaned. Suddenly, the excited radio operator shouted, "Spiro, I got through, I got through!"

"You get through – what they say?" Spiro's heart was in his mouth, a somewhat rash relocation of human organs once more making it a touch tricky for their owner to speak grammatically.

"They say there's a berth in the boathouse." The radio operator hastily did some figures. "Four hundred metres north on the west bank. There is a channel – here." He pointed at a line of deep water on the chart.

"Birth ... canal ...?" Kamakis poked his head around the mess door. "Where are we ...?" Sporades ignored him, and swiftly ordered the changes.

"Ahead, Dead Slow," he said. "Extreme caution,

51

we don't want it to hit the bottom." He glanced at Kamakis, who was rubbing his.

Though originally used for pleasure craft, the facilities in Carnal House's innocent-looking boathouse had recently, on Guru's orders, been extended back underground to accommodate the *Obtuse*. This had created a huge cavern of a dock, the entrance of which looked like nought but a sleepy summerhouse by a river. The sub very slowly but surely edged up the channel towards its secret berth. A motorboat came out to greet them, to lead them to the Guru's grotto – their hidden home for the weeks to come.

On seeing the boat, Dirk had sounded and quietly moved away, being wary of its intentions.

The boat was too small for a whaler, but it was better to be safe than perfume.

8. The Vicar

Lunch, for some, was over. For a lonely Councillor Fred Lukes, it had simply not happened. He had looked at the contents of his sandwich box, so lovingly packed by his wife that morning. He had poked at the pork pie and lifted, then replaced, the edge of the salad sandwich. He just was not hungry. He had too much on his plate, figuratively speaking.

As he waited for the meeting to convene, he surveyed the street scene below the Council Chamber, and his mind wandered to the next item on the agenda. As he looked down, he saw many white-clad people dotted about the streets. The place was definitely taking on an unreal feel. No more was it just tourists and bored sailors. There was another pestilence about. And look – his colleague and friend Councillor Frank Lee, making his way back, leaving *that* whitewashed Cafe, with another two councillors both head to foot in white ... peculiar. He and Frank normally had lunch together, had done for years. Why was he there? Councillors drifted in and the meeting reconvened, somewhat leisurely, thought Fred, if not lazily, for he wanted to get on.

"Good afternoon, ladies and gentlemen," he said after the formalities, and then, straightway fixing his gaze on the two councillors dressed head to foot in white, "There may be an 'Elephant' in the room!"

Councillors looked around, confused and startled. This was not like Fred. He held up his arms to calm the meeting, for there was a distinct low murmuring sound to be heard.

"I spoke this morning in confidence," he continued, "and I do so now, for something new and

53

evil has entered our town, something we must fight. Carnal House!" He spat out the hated words. "I believe this establishment, this 'White Elephant', just outside town on the banks of our beautiful river is – detrimental ... to the area, and that is putting my personal feelings politely."

He looked up, the two white-clad councillors doing a fair imitation of rats in a cage. He continued. "In my opinion, it is a very bad influence, mainly on the young, especially as I understand its main teachings seem to refer to ... er ... sexual love. Our hard-working Vicar tells me that after a short resurgence of interest in things ... er ... Christian, his church is once again emptying. He blames this place – and I have here a letter from him in which he expresses his feelings most succinctly."

He was about to start reading.

"Point of order, Mr. Chairman: is this relevant?" interrupted one of the white-clad councillors.

"This is the 'Parish' Council, my friend," said Lukes, for once somewhat patronisingly. "May I continue? Thank you. So ... the Vicar's letter ... ah ... and I quote ...

'After a resurgence in numbers attending Matins, Evensong, Communion and my highly successful', and remember," said Fred, "this is a letter from our town's traditional spiritual leader, so to speak ... 'my highly successful Astral Travel seminars, there has been a marked dropping-off in church attendance. It cannot have passed your notice, Councillor Lukes, that there are many white-gowned people roaming our streets. I believe their leader – a so-called "Guru" – is the Devil Incarnate, for the evils of the flesh so freely available at his Carnal House, er ... are drawing my flock away. Something has to be done' ..." Fred put down the letter.

"Those are the feelings," he announced to the faces looking up at him, "of our Vicar; feelings we must respect. And I believe that we as a council must – er – find out exactly what ... benefit the town gains from this building's presence and the goings on there. I notice its Victorian red brick is now white! Are planning and environmental regulations being adhered to, and so on? Do we know enough? Can we do more? Maybe someone here can help?"

He lifted his head of thick grey hair and looked about the council chamber at his allies. He sucked on his moustache. His eyes met his friend Frank Lee's, then Lorraine Simpsons – the landed farmer's wife – then Colonel North's – the retired major – and finally the gnarled pupils of Captain Ayeup – the seafarer. Surely, none of them would turn against him. None of them would turn up all in white. He tugged at his ear lobe nervously. No, of course not, of course they wouldn't.

So the meeting, like the Dart, meandered on ...

Now, dear friends, it is time to meet this Cleric. Priestley by name and, yes, at times even priestly by nature, struggling to sell his wares in the market place of life, to promote and maintain a foothold for his beliefs in this green and pleasant land, beliefs about which, to be sure, he himself was often somewhat confused. I give you ... The Vicar!

John Priestley was fifty-five. Once.

Just how long he had been fifty-five no-one could remember. It had been a long time. His friends and acquaintances did realize though that, with the normal passage of time, he was probably not still, and was way past, fifty-five. Estimations varied. Some said sixty-five, some seventy-five, some even eighty-five, for this Long John seemed ageless. It was, however, common knowledge that he was not as old as his ancient church, a structure in even worse state of repair than his own decrepit and creaking frame.

He knew now that he had reached the pinnacle, if one could call it that, of his career when he had been appointed Vicar of Crumbleigh in Totnes all those years before. The timing had been unfortunate, though prophetic, for few came to his ordination service as this had precisely coincided with the funeral service of his ultimate Lord and Master – here, of course, discounting the Deity – for as they were burying Archbishop William Temple in his coffin, Reverend John Priestley was being installed in his parish. Alas, a religious-sounding name was all these two men of cloth would ever have in common.

As a youthful clerical aspirant, he had moderate success at his seminary, though more through good luck than hard work, and passed his theology exams with distinction. This was something about which his father, General Alastair 'The Dog' Priestley, late of the Boer War in southern Africa (and late for it – as he arrived in Cape Town the last shot had just been fired), had been unusually surprised, nothing normally affecting his equally gaunt exterior; for John had, so to speak, been the runt of the litter – the older sons being put through Sandhurst and Dartmouth with their intended final destination the Army or the Navy. The girls were swiftly married off to similar young men, one even producing heirs, though without much grace – so John had been sent to a minor public school in Shropshire which was known to turn out a good proportion of 'clerical workers', as old Dog Priestley was wont to call priests.

He was expelled twice from the school, if such a

thing is possible, for indulging in unusually intimate relationships with young men from the town. Indubitably, young John Priestley had not been a success at school. However, in the equally intimate atmosphere of the seminary towards which he was subsequently propelled on the suggestion of the headmaster (and by a profoundly angry father who never lost the habit of referring to it as a seminal college), he was more fortunate.

He learnt much at his seminary: what was good in the eyes of the Lord, and oft times what was not so good; but always at the back of his mind was the deep-rooted belief that the Lord moved in mysterious ways his wonders to perform, a belief borne out and witnessed every day as he observed so many young men struggling (or maybe not) with their own sexual inclination. All religiously appeared to maintain that same-sex attraction was intrinsically a disordered condition, one to which the priesthood was not in any way subject.

It seemed that his seminary attracted more than its fair share of the less able, at the same time providing a smokescreen for those who would otherwise face questions about girlfriends, fiancées and married life. And, at the end of a hard day's study of the scriptures, hard liquor would often be used by teachers and students alike to round off the day's work, to 'get to know each other better' and, of course, to praise and give thanks to the Lord. And if these sessions should sometimes lead to occasional lewd, indecent acts, drunken fumbling and inappropriate touching ... so be it. For the Lord moves ...

At twenty-one years of age, John's world was his oyster, or words to that effect. Besides collecting a minor degree in theology, he had also received a minor dose of something much worse from one of the underground workers in the town. Soon he was posted as curate to the small country village of Pringle Priory and taken under the wing of its bachelor vicar, under whose wing he was to learn the full and unexpurgated meaning of brotherly love.

His stay at Pee Pee, which name he and the Vicar gave to their parish, lasted unusually long for a curate so wet under the collar, this being partly due to the ministrations of his Vicar, who always complained to his Bishop that he needed yet more time with Priestley 'to bring out what was still so deep-seated within the lad'. Eventually, Curate Priestley was able to leave Pringle Priory, his departure coming shortly after his Vicar's own forced retirement, for one day the kind Vicar had been discovered by the Verger in the vestry ardently pursuing investigations into just how deep-seated 'the lad' really was.

Recovering from his ordeal at the hands of his Vicar, John Priestley was sent, after a period of recuperation in hospital, where he had undergone surgery for the removal of some very painful consequential piles (that is, if piles can indeed be consequential), to assist once again as curate, this time in a parish deep in the heart of the West Country. He found himself near the sea, overlooking a river, high on a hill, in the ancient parish of Crumbleigh, once the most salubrious part of the town of Totnes, now marred visually by the prominent hilltop sight of the dilapidated church. He remembered the day he arrived, striding up the hill with his bag over his shoulder, humming 'There is a green hill far away' to anyone that cared to listen.

And, dear friends, someone was listening, for as Priestley had reached the massive doors of the church, his new Vicar, the Very Reverend (and very old) James

Ethelrick, had stepped forward with both arms outstretched. "My boy, my boy, how wonderful to meet you," he had said. "I have heard so much about you. Come, let me take your bag, let me show you your new church, let me – would you like a cup of tea? And a biscuit or two? You must be tired after your journey. We'll go to the vicarage – in a bit of a state, though – since my wife died it's not been the same. I don't keep the old place as Beryl would have, though Mrs Jenkins is a great solace. But no matter, this way ..."

Years passed and the old Vicar died. A new Vicar, one John Priestley, former Curate, earlier black marks with his previous Vicar if not this time removed surgically, simply and conveniently forgotten, shuffled down the corridor in the vicarage to the larger bedroom, and took up his bedpost.

Now much more gaunt, set in his ways, his feet invariably in slippers and odd socks, he looked out from his bedroom window over his new domain and mused thoughtfully. It was the only way to muse, he thought ruefully as he looked towards the river. He rued his loneliness, never having known any woman biblically, only ever having been in the company of young men, save for the one painful occasion with his first old Vicar. He just did not understand women, and they probably reciprocated the feeling. There was a knock at the bedroom door.

"Yes!" he said, slightly startled. "Who, er ... what is it?" But, of course, it could only be the housekeeper Mrs Jenkins, faithful Mrs Jenkins. He was not sure if there ever had actually been a Mister Jenkins, but that didn't really matter in The Lord's great scheme of things.

"Ah, Mrs Jenkins!" he said, as if surprised, for

there was no-one else in the house. "What can I do for you?"

"Oh, Vicar," she said, "such a sad time, so sad, the old Vicar passing on so sudden. I thought you might need some company."

"Why, Mrs Jenkins, how thoughtful of you, er ..." Priestley noticed the room was void of chairs and so waved towards the huge feather bed. "Please sit yourself down. My apologies for the poor seating arrangements. Yes, it is sad, but life must go on ..."

Mrs Jenkins sat down right on the edge of the bed, her ample frame sinking solidly in; her skirt rode up until the tops of her stockings, and the plump pinky white flesh overlapping above, could be clearly seen.

Priestley licked his lips, for his mouth was suddenly dry. Now there were just the two of them. Alas, there would be no Curate – the Bishop had told him the church could now not even afford the miniscule stipend. If God's will, then so be it. Perchance they would be seeing out their lives together. Mrs Jenkins stretched one of her hands behind her back and grimaced slightly.

"What is it, Mrs Jenkins? You do not look very comfortable. Can I do anything to help?" Priestley moved towards her, his tongue working overtime.

"Well," said Mrs Jenkins, "it's sort of, fibrositis, here in the middle of my back. The old Vicar, bless his soul, used to, well, rub it with unguent when it got like this. I wonder ...?"

Oh dear, thought Priestley, she does look in pain. And so, comrades, it came to pass that the Vicar and his Housekeeper became very close on that feather bed, the soft down giving gently under the combined weight of the two remaining occupants of the vicarage. It was the day that John Priestley became a man, if a man knowing a woman biblically for the first time can be defined thus, and though it must be said that every now (and again) the Vicar did stray back to his old roots and the pleasant company of his friends from the seminary, what came to pass on that feather bed came to pass often, and right up to the end of his life, when alas he went to meet the Lord his maker, he and Mrs Jenkins were often the best of friends. But to the matter in hand we must, for once again we digress ...

One day a Guru came to the town. And stayed. To begin with, the Vicar took the upstart in his stride, but then he noticed, slowly but surely, his own congregation diminishing. Each Sunday fewer and fewer people made it up the green hill; not that they had fallen by the wayside due to fatigue: they had not even started up the hill, and most of his congregation were now to be found in *The Big White House by the River.*

John Priestley fought back. He started Astral Travel seminars, and for a short while his flock once more turned back to him; he had truly become the good shepherd. He installed Mrs Jenkins in the cellar, with broom in hand ready and waiting to thump with it on the ceiling – the vicarage dining room floor, for when the Astral Travellers arrived back on Earth, John Priestley would press the footswitch concealed under the carpet, a bell would ring in the cellar, she would thump hard and the travellers would feel their landing bump. But soon the travellers tired of their astral projections, and when one accidentally pressed the Vicar's footswitch when they were all apparently still out Betelgeuse way, their landing was somewhat sudden and premature. No-one came for the next take-off. Slowly but surely John Priestley's worshippers finally drifted away.

One Sunday morn, soon after he realized what a big flocking problem he had, he was dressing for Matins, his faithful housekeeper as usual in attendance. "I think, Mrs Jenkins," he said, "that as today is so special, for as you know the new Lord Bishop is giving the sermon, I shall wear the cream surplice, and the ... navy cassock. Yes, that will be nice. Do you know, Mrs J., there is so little variety now in clerical clothes, it is most annoying. A pink or a purple maybe, no ... purple wouldn't do – that would upset the Bishop – it is so boring all this black and white. Even some frills wouldn't go amiss. That reminds me – I have not seen anyone in an alb and amice for ages – I refer, of course, to the shoulder linen and not the fur hood, though that in itself would be rather unusual. What would the Lord Bishop say?" And, for a moment forgetting his problem, Priestley chuckled merrily into his cassock.

As he finished dressing, he could be heard humming to himself, practising the Agnus Dei, a thing of which his Lord Bishop would also most definitely not approve, for the two clerics' traditions were diametrically opposed. Some would say that Priestley should have joined the Church of Rome, and further that his Bishop was naught but a Wesleyan in disguise. It was obvious that the two were, or soon would be, very much at loggerheads.

Having perfected his rendition of the Agnus Dei (for he had decided ecumenically to perform this masterpiece just prior to Matins), Priestley finished dressing and made his way from the vicarage to the church. Positioning himself at the church door to greet his patron, he sincerely hoped that on this special day at least there would be a somewhat larger congregation than usual.

The new Bishop's old Bentley drove up to the door at the appointed hour. The Bishop stepped out, the Vicar stepped up, and they shook hands; the Bishop was then seen to vigorously wipe his own on his flowing cassock. Priestley's hands had been nervously damp for, though a star attraction in the shape of the Bishop was on offer, the well-nigh impossible seemed to be happening.

Even fewer parishioners than usual were turning up to worship, and in the church porch there had been much priestly ringing of hands which, besides dampening the Vicar's palms, only seemed to serve one other purpose – to compensate for the rather lacklustre ringing of bells coming from the church tower. With a worried and heavy heart, Priestley entered his near-empty church.

He did not like what he found. As a result of the choir being greatly depleted due to a local Boy Scout jamboree, tone-deaf Priestley was forced to sing his Agnus Dei solo. The Misses Henderson had unfortunately been knocked down in the High Street earlier that week by a rubbish cart (which, besides covering the two old ladies with a mountain of rotting vegetation, had reduced the total congregation by half) and were now recovering in hospital. Out of the corner of his eye the Vicar could see the puffing bell ringers slinking off to the pub next door – also aptly named the Church – just as he and the Bishop entered. And what transpired next was also, putting it mildly, not at all helpful to this now suffering Vicar's career.

The Agnus Dei he sang as best he could. The lesson(s) he read (in a manner of speaking). He prayed on bended knee, though the Lord was not listening. He swung the incense boat beautifully, he genuflected perfectly, he broke the bread magnificently, and he served the wine with much more panache than even the wine waiter at Chez Paul's – but it was all to no avail, and almost to no congregation, something certainly noticed by the fuming Bishop, who rose to give his sermon to the assembled single numbers, condemned and blasted Popery, Rome, and graven images in general, then sat down well before his allotted time. It had been a short (with the emphasis on the word short) sermon.

As the day was so special, Priestley had arranged for a joyful peal of bells to be rung at the end of the service. However, the service was now, he noted astutely, at that very point, and all the campanologists were still in the other Church next door. He had to think fast. Knowing well that he badly needed to impress the recently installed Bishop, he purposefully strode out into the aisle, inadvertently angered his new patron by bowing and scraping before the high altar, then hurried to the bell tower – for without the ringers present he knew that he himself would have to ring the chimes.

He knew about bell ringing – he vaguely recalled the optional campanology course at the seminary – and he'd stood in a few times when one of the ringers had been ill. Now, which rope did he pull first? He grabbed one of the sallies. A most unexpected thing then transpired. The bell rang all right, but continued on its travel after the first chime, and as John Priestley was hanging on for dear life, so did he – upwards. For in their hurry to get to the pub, the ringers had left the bells in the 'up' position, ready for the end-of-service chimes, and, as is well known in campanology circles, this is not recommended.

From the Church next door the bell ringers rushed over, for they knew when something was up: in this case the Vicar. The Bishop too proceeded post-haste to the bell tower to investigate the source of the cacophony. As the bells erratically continued to chime, six pairs of eyes and six shocked faces stared up at the harassed Vicar, who gingerly lowered himself to the floor, sallies flying all around him and slapping him in the face. By then he was doing a fair imitation of a bat, his dark cassock flapping wildly about his person as he touched the stone floor.

"Oh, dear Lord," he said, and looked up towards the heaven ...

But the Lord, not for the first time, was not listening.

9. Exorcism

The day after the unfortunate Vicar had been caught hanging around the belfry, the General Synod of the Church of England commenced its annual session.

Ears were bent, laymen lobbied by clerics, clerics by laymen, bewigged lawyers by frocked bishops, and an unusual number of the gentlemen of the press were also present.

It was to be a contentious week's debate.

For two days the talk was mainly about sex – women priests, gay priests, the new dreaded disease SLIM – so it had been sincerely hoped that John Priestley's own Bishop's speech, due on the third day, would stop the press continuing to refer to that year's gathering as 'The Synod of Sex', and thus save further embarrassment. Partly leaked to the press the day before, the speech promised to contain little Christian charity, or hope, and almost no love, for its theme was the simple cut-throat rationalization of church resources. An expectant hush fell over the gathering as the Bishop rose. His speech was long, involved, controversial. All three houses of Synod listened hard, and in the mood in which they were (when anything would have been somehow better than sex), they generally received it well, though by the end the reporter from the *Church Times* had, as usual, nodded off.

"And so," the Bishop continued, turning slowly to look at the assembled mass for some reaction, "to sum up. In the interests of Christians everywhere – our shareholders, if you like – we must do what Dr. Beeching did so well to the railways of this land. We must rationalize. We must cut out the branch lines, we must close some stations, we must re-route our resources and we must concentrate on the areas of greatest need. Our inner cities are crying out for help, our poor are becoming poorer, whilst the rich become richer. How can we do the will of God if scarce money is being spent supporting loss-making premises in well-to-do areas? To this end I suggest we set up a working party under the auspices of the Church Commissioners to undertake a viability study on, at first, just one parish. I have one in mind in my diocese which is in need of a great deal of work, renovation and so on, and one that sadly only supports a regular congregation of single figures." He looked up at the multitude. "My Lord Bishops, Clergy, Laity – we must ... Cut the Crap!"

The Bishop sat down to a gentle murmuring from the assembled throng, some mildly questioning such colloquial language; but for once the Bishops, the Clergy and the Laity, probably due to a sense of relief that Synod had at least one thing to discuss other than just sex, all spake with one voice, and voted in favour of his motion to set up the working party with a view to 'Cutting the Crap'.

In a private letter from his Bishop, a man later referred to in *Crockford's* preface as the 'Butcher', due to all the excess fat he trimmed from his diocese (and who was never one to even mince words), Vicar John Priestley received the bad news. A viability study-team would be arriving in his parish – soon. He had to 'pull out his finger', 'put his nose to the grindstone', 'his shoulder to the wall' and 'work his fingers to the bone', having, of course, first extracted them. What shape exactly his body would be in after such application he was not sure, but now he had not the time to worry.

Only two days later, under the Bishop's very own orders, a group of young ecclesiastical high-flyers attached to the Church Commissioners' office in

London arrived in Totnes. Surveyors, estate specialists, accountants and statisticians, they came armed with tape measures, surveying equipment, notebooks, calculators, personal organizers, mobile telephones each, and shiny, shiny suits. All had similar efficient haircuts and not one would have been out of place canvassing for the Church of the Latter Day Saints, or selling Life Assurance, though a difference would have been hard to glean. They set to work with a vengeance, ignoring the Vicar's kind offer of help and (unheard of before in Totnes) Mrs Jenkins' tea and cakes. These men, and boy were they men, but only just, meant Business.

The surveyors surveyed, as they are wont. Calculators calculated. Graded poles and tripods were positioned in every part of the church; tape measures were deployed from the retrochoir, down the chancel, across the nave, and up to the portico. Notes were taken and filed. The estate specialists estimated, picked up first this piece of silver, that bit of gold, noted and filed the estimates. And the accountants and statisticians all crammed into John Priestley's small office to study the parish records, its returns and accounts. Notes were once again duly filed.

A tradition was inadvertently being observed. Bishop Eadnoth of Crediton, who had a millennium before offered the good folk of Totnes a piece of nearby land in return for a not insubstantial monetary loan, would have been proud of them. Priestley, though, was sure that Jesus would personally have slung these men out of the temple by their ears, stamped on their ubiquitous telephones and torn up their personal organizers.

On the evening of the first day, the men left for the Imperial Hotel in nearby Torquay, where they had generously been allowed by the Church Commissioners' finance department, which they indeed controlled, to take over a whole floor. They were due for dinner with the Bishop at nine – and they would still be having Cognac and Havanas at midnight.

The oppressed Vicar, with Mrs Jenkins' help, was now attempting to put a semblance of order back into his tiny study. The accountants had left a mountain of papers and ledgers strewn all about, interspersed with half-empty bottles of water, cups of cold coffee with floating cigarette ends, and full stinking ashtrays.

Mrs Jenkins was piling the papers high, but handing to the Vicar anything that looked remotely contentious. She had just given him a file headed 'Strictly Private and Confidential', when suddenly he visibly blanched.

"By the Lord Jesus Christ, I knew it!" he cried, looking to the heavens. "Forgive me, Father ... Mrs J. – look at this. I knew it. I knew the Bishop had something up the sleeve of his cassock. See ... here – 'Optional Contract to purchase the' ..."

"Yes ...?"

"... 'freehold of the parish church and grounds of Crumbleigh'. No wonder they're doing this audit. I had assumed it was just my empty church on Sunday. My God! Forgive me ... further – er ... Father ... Why me?! How could they have found a buyer? The place needs tens of thousands spending on it."

He rifled a bit further, paper carelessly falling to the floor, and then, ashen-faced, slumped into his armchair.

"What is it, Vicar?" cried Mrs Jenkins. "What's occurring?"

"It – it's ... the Guru!" he moaned, pointing at the proposed purchaser's name. "It's him – whatever he's called ... Him! He's put in the offer. He's the one that's been emptying our church these months past. Now he wants to take it away."

"What can you do?" said Mrs Jenkins. "There must be something!" The Vicar thought for a few minutes.

"There is, I believe, maybe just one thing," he said, now calmer and more thoughtful, gazing out into the middle distance with bright, wide-open eyes. "I believe there is an evil spirit about, an evil spirit that needs to be annihilated, that needs destroying, that needs ... exorcising. But I must wait for a sign, a sign from God. If he wishes me to do this thing, then he will send one, but in what form I know not now. Though I believe He will send it soon, maybe as a portent or omen, something out of the ordinary course of nature – perchance a manifestation. And when it comes it will be shown to me, and me alone. I will know then that the time will have come to save my parish from destruction by the forces of evil embodied in this vile person. And I shall be strong!"

As he stopped speaking, a shaft of eerie moonlight fell on his upturned face. Mrs Jenkins sharply caught her breath.

It grew very, very cold.

Two days later, Priestley became ever more perturbed. Now the surveyors had found dry rot in the roof. Soon he would be giving outdoor services from inside his church. Something had to be done about the Guru. Priestley knew he was the reason attendances had been steadily falling off, though he couldn't really blame him for the same thing now happening to his roof tiles. The collections had been terrible of late, and, as in most leisure industries, he needed his gratuities to survive. The bottom was definitely falling out of this market.

70

That evening, the Vicar went out for a walk by the River Dart to mull over his problems and maybe clear his muddled head somewhat, and as he walked along a headland late in the twilight he thought gently to himself of ways of improving his lot, if it could now be called that. In his opinion, it was fast becoming a little. Maybe he could extend the next medieval day into a pageant, with all the receipts going to his purse. Or he could make a giant jelly and people could pay to eat some of it, or perhaps he could roast a hog or two: no, not inclusive, maybe it would have to be beef. There had to be something he could do.

But what?

The sun was fast descending and a gentle breeze lifting from the wide expanse of river. He hummed himself a tune, though many would not call it such – for, as we have heard, this Vicar was well-nigh tone deaf. He looked out across the water to the heavily wooded east bank a mile or so away, where the trees came right down to the water's edge. One or two cotton wool clouds drifted seaward. What a beautiful part of the world! Things were, presumably thanks to the Lord, peaceful and relaxed. He sat down on the grass in thought, pulled out his penknife and commenced some thoughtful whittling – an action that always made him feel at ease.

He would have to fight the Guru's people, but how? Perhaps he should use the Guru's own techniques. But he couldn't; it would be immoral. After all, his astral travellers had enjoyed their trips, and they had been brought back to the Church – The Lord's own Church; that had been the intention.

He picked up a stone and threw it down the cliff into the river, watching the ripples fan out. The surface now was still as a mill pond, the breeze dropped, there was peace on earth. He stood up and walked down towards the beach, still whittling away. He could hear the birds singing their twilight song as the last rays of the sun disappeared in the west. Oh how he loved this land. He threw another stone, this one to skim the surface. He whittled on. The stone splashed once, twice, thrice, and then John Priestley, unassuming Vicar of Crumbleigh in Totnes, stumbled backwards in fright and pain. His knife had slipped and had stabbed him in the leg. Happily, this was not due to any mishandling on his part, nor any normal mishap, but in truth because he had just had a monster vision.

Suddenly it seemed to Priestley that the birds had stopped singing, a cold wind had sprung up from nowhere, the sky had blackened and out of the depths of the river, half a mile away, a large dark hump had risen. Great ripples spread out from it, and then, as suddenly as it had appeared, it was gone.

The Vicar swung around: had anyone else seen it? There was no-one. He turned back. Again the hump rose: there was a great splashing, he distinctly saw a fin. And then he ran, he gathered his cassock around him and tried to run as fast as his injured, ancient legs would carry him, back to the sanctuary of his parish church, rotting roof and all. He bolted the door behind him, ignored the blood still dripping down his leg, rushed to the nearest pew, knelt down, and prayed.

Not being totally sure just what he had seen in the twilight, he prayed and prayed until his knees gave out.

But *was* it for what he had been waiting? Was it *his* sign, *his* omen? So it must be! He knew his duty. He must exorcise its spirit, then his problems would be over. He hobbled back to the Vicarage, his body a minor disaster area. What was the Bishop's telephone number? Hurriedly he looked it up in the convenient

Yellow Pages, the pages flying about, torn out as he ferociously searched for the correct category. Finally, neatly sandwiched between chariot-makers and charm schools, he found it under the heading 'Charities – Church of England'. He grabbed the telephone and dialled.

"Oh, hullo," he said breathlessly when connected, rubbing his chest, "is His Grace there?" There was an audible gap before the answer came from a voice even more decrepit than the vicar's own.

"No ... His Grace is not in at the moment," croaked the reply. "He's ... out." Logic was obviously one of the respondent's strong points.

"Well, when will he be back? This is important," shouted Priestley.

"When will he be – what did you say?"

Priestley groaned. "Back, Back, the opposite of Front!" he howled like a dog in exasperation.

"No – he's not back at the font," said the voice. "Let me look at the schedule – he doesn't usually do christenings these days ... no ... I was right, today he's – ah, yes, day off! It's a Church holiday – did you not know? Er ... who's speaking?"

"You are," snapped Priestley angrily. "What holiday?"

"It's a Saint's day today: Saint Elmo's." Priestley was sure Saint Elmo was just something nautical, on fire like his chest, or both.

"Could I leave a message for the Bishop?" he said, running out of patience.

"You may of course do so. I should be pleased to ..."

"Very well." Priestley knew he should not do this. "Please tell His Grace when he returns from the golf course, or wherever, that the Vicar of Crumbleigh called, that I am about to perform the exorcism of a monster, and that I am informing him of the exorcism as required by Church Law."

"Oh, how nice ... you're walking a dog. Is it a Saint Bernard? I do like large dogs ..." creaked the voice.

"No, it's Saint Elmo's ..." (sarcasm was not his forte). "I am exorcising a spirit – do you understand – not exercising! EXORCISING. And on with it I must get! Have you got that?"

There was no reply whilst Priestley kept the line open, as the Lord Bishop's verger was painfully writing down the rather long, difficult to spell and very unused word. As he was about to reply, Priestley cut the line, fearing that time was fast running out. He had to free the town from the influence of the monster's unclean spirits, and do it urgently. There was little enough time for the ceremonies, let alone all the adjurations and prayers. A trail of blood followed him into the church ...

Now the Lord Above, who sits on high and as you know moves in mysterious ways, had once more been watching, as was his wont (and presumably his right as Master of the Universe) and had moved the hand of the editor of the local daily paper so that the headlines in the next day's Totnes *Bugle*, that erudite organ of the Riviera said it all ...

TOTNES MONSTER FOUND!

Hey! Hang on a minute here! I am but Dirk ... Big Dirk. No monster me! This be outrageous!

See here, I was yet consuming some squid in this one-way street of a river. Not too many here, mind, all too small, truly no giants of the deep. I was ravening. So I dived a piece, sounded, that typo thing, splashed about here and there. Trapped some in my plank mouth, was munching them. Biding my time, waiting on my friend hiding in his strange black tube, minding my business. Floating up and down this tedious river, dealing with life ... Some journey I have had, but why for?

Then this man in black appeared onshore, long flowing clothes – a tall, thin, lanky man. He spied me. So I made my presence felt for him, did flaunt myself a tad. Dove here and there, clapped my fins, flashed my whalebone, showed him my hump, flapped my flukes. Times there's nought to do but shake the tail feather!

Now I sounded, then I blew.

And he spied me once more. This time he jumped up, arms awaving, screaming, some sort of terror. What is this?

I'm only Dirk ... Big Dirk.

Presently he runs away, stumbling, but fast, mind. So what is this Monster tale??

Tis I ... Dirk ... is all ...

10. Ma Anna Poona

Totnes was buzzing. News of the town's very own monster was on everyone's lips. The Vicar had been interviewed on the *Bugle*'s front page and had announced that the evidence of the monster was some sort of prognostication. This had taken no-one by surprise, though many had no idea what it meant. The Vicar's pronouncements were many, varied and usually there were few who took them seriously, but this time some did give heed to his words. There had been inexplicable tidal waves over the previous few weeks, and yet, not knowing of the secret search for black gold, the good folk of Totnes now had an explanation. In any case, there was the legend of The Totnes Monster to keep alive. At last someone, the Vicar to boot, had actually seen the monster. It could only be good for the town and its tourist business.

The day was market day, when as a rule the town would in any case be bursting at its seams; but that day, though this may possibly be an oxymoronic concept, there was only almost as much breathing space as in a middle eastern jail, for an inordinate number of monster watchers were also present, binoculars and long-lensed cameras dangling proudly from their necks. Into this hectic scene squeezed one Phillipa Throssell, her son Nathan, and friend Jemmima.

"I'm hungry, Pippa, I'm hungry!" squealed Nathan.

"Better get a sandwich," said Jemma; "does Nathan eat meat?"

"Never, Jemma, never," lied Pippa, as they attempted to squeeze up the High Street, she tightly holding the little boy's hand. "Shall we go in Ma's

Cafe?"

"Will we get in? It's so full," said Jemma, eyeing the great white-arched M above the entrance with trepidation. However, Pippa had already opened the door to one of the most popular cafes in Totnes: a family was just leaving and they were able to sit down without further ado.

"That was lucky, Pippa," said Nathan, who had been brought up to call his mother by her nickname. "Here's a menu, Jemma," he said, for once polite.

Jemmima Waine snatched the menu from the boy. A tall woman with striking red hair, she had been at school, private of course, with Pippa. Now she lived close to her in the village of Stoke Gabriel. Pippa lived just across the river in Dittisham, though it wasn't only the river that now separated them.

Jemma looked hard at her old school chum sitting across the table, dressed head to foot in white, with her strong face, her flowing blonde hair and yet her blue-black eyebrows. Pippa had, in her opinion, recently been taking a very unhealthy interest in some Eastern Guru whose name escaped her; she had warned her, and now she was sitting with her in one of his very own establishments.

For years she had thought Pippa's lifestyle far too trendy, and recently it had become most odd. She, her husband Tom and son Nathan were nowadays always, but always, dressed in white or cream clothes, as were many others in the town. How she kept the child looking clean, heaven only knew. Even their Range Rover was a whiter shade of pale; and yes, there it was, the picture of the doleful-looking man, hanging around Pippa's neck on a string of beads.

Well, dear friends, not only was it market day – it was Elizabethan market day, when normally sane men and women would dress up in, amongst other things, frilly neck braces and codpieces, and Jemma even spied a man through the window of the cafe being locked in the town stocks, about to be pelted for charity. She could see much Mead being supped, market carts steered erratically, even spinning and weaving in the road, for once not from drunken drivers. But amongst all this mayhem, which was normal for Totnes, she noticed many white-clad persons, adding a totally surreal feel to the ancient market. To the casual onlooker, these people might have been a colony of plague victims; to the locals, and Jemma, they certainly were. The town was being taken over.

"Would you like to order now?" said a voice a foot or two above her shoulder, seemingly emanating from a large white circus tent. They all looked up together, and Jemma jumped in her seat – something probably prompted by the size and general demeanour of the woman taking the order.

"Mum," squeaked Nathan, "it's the Totnes Monster!"

"Nathan!" said his mother Pippa, sharply, for she knew the apparition. "Hello, Anna, er ... Brata... vishnu," she continued, at the same time gingerly giving a four-fingered V-sign with the palm of her hand. Jemma looked on aghast.

"Bratavishnu to you," replied the said Anna, pointing with pen poised and ignoring Nathan's slight, not bothering with the greeting sign; "you're – Pippa – aren't you? We must have an Eastern name sorted for you soon. And this is your child? And your friend? How nice ... You must come in more often. Now, what can I get you?"

As Pippa ordered various pulses and salads, Jemma looked around. The place was half full of customers wearing white, and half in normal greyish brown colours. All the staff were pristinely white, and working very hard. All had medallions with the same doleful face staring out; some were wearing wraparound saris, whilst some looked as though they were out for a game of croquet or real tennis. Towering above all these people and definitely making her presence felt was the woman taking their order.

Ma Anna Poona, to call her by her given name, was simply huge. Six foot three inches in her natural cotton socks and with a girth and name to match, she was certainly a mountain of a woman. Somehow, without the aid of a safety net or visible means of support, twin mountainous peaks stayed attached to her chest, the top of her head was piled high with her shocking white hair, and in her voluminous canvas tent she looked very much like a mobile range in the Himalayas. Not surprisingly, she was often called 'MAP', partly because she was on such a large scale, but this was not usually said to her face, a craggy thing not totally dissimilar from the north face of the Eiger. And she always made a large impression – if she had landed on the moon she would have left behind a substantial crater; she had certainly made an impression on Jemma, at one point nearly suffocating her as people squeezed past on their way out. Furthermore, she was a qualified sex therapist, a position she took very seriously – but always varied, and twice a week she would lay on hands in her consulting room in her Guru's mansion by the river. And, dear reader, we have met her before, at the Genesis of our tale ...

For four years, besides being the town's only female sex therapist, she had been serving wholesome food and drink at her cafe in nearby Dirtington College, Jemma and Pippa's old school, and now, with the help of money from her extremely speculative Guru (in repayment for personal services she regularly rendered to him – for, as we know, he needed therapy, often), she had opened Ma's Cafe in Totnes town, the first of a chain of similarly named wholefood restaurants which soon were to spread across Western Europe.

She had a huge captive market which she had helped create with the work already done at Dirtington. Students who left the college often stayed on in Totnes, much against their parents' wishes, to work in one of the many trendy co-operatives, and many had also become Devotees, or Devos, of that same strange man with the doleful face. It was an old ploy that women were supposed to reach men's higher levels by shoving fibrous food down their gullets, and MAP certainly enjoyed doing that. And now she was using the same ploy in the town. Totnes was full of Jemmas who had Pippas for friends, and they were her new target.

"I'm so sorry, dear," she bellowed, as the squashed Jemma tried to extricate herself from somewhere within the tent surrounding her ample form. "People should be more polite," she added by way of apology, whilst glaring at the departing party. "So that's one cracked wheat and garlic, one lentil burger, one plate of mixed pakoras, a salad for you all and some nice wholesome rasmalai for the little one – anything to drink?"

"Just a jug of lassie, please, Anna," replied Pippa, feeling most at home and showing off just a little in front of her friend.

"Sweet or sour?" asked MAP.

"Bloody hell, I don't want any dog food, sweet or anything," squeaked the fast becoming awful Nathan. "Yuk, yuk, yuk!"

"Nathan, quiet! It's a nice milky drink which you

80

will love," snapped his mother.

"Will not, not, not!!" came the expected response.

"Shut it, kid," bellowed MAP. And Nathan shut. But he'd get his revenge.

The food arrived fairly quickly, and as promised was good and wholesome. The child took one look at it, refused to eat a mouthful and asked for fish fingers, chips, or both. As usual, with Nathan in tow, the meal was not exactly easy or relaxing for his mother.

After finishing her meal, Pippa did try to clear the plates herself, as leaving food was a very bad thing to do, she had been told, and was shovelling all and sundry down her throat when she remembered MAP must have been thinner once, and stopped. Nathan then started to create and it was obvious the two young wives needed to leave as swiftly as possible. MAP saw the commotion, and came over to say goodbye.

"You must come to Satsang tomorrow, Pippa. Guru will be back!" she said. "He'll be here this evening – and please bring your friend – we won't eat you – we're veggies, ha, ha, ha. Please come, it'll be a special occasion," she said, turning to Jemma, trying to make her feel more comfortable and accidentally spitting cracked wheat and garlic in her face. "We'll look after you and make you feel at home, I promise. Will you come?"

"Well, maybe," said Jemma, wiping her face. She'd been told about the sex parties and thought she might, life in Stoke Gabriel not being totally fulfilling.

"Oh do, Jem," pleaded Pippa. "Tom won't be there, and you can keep me company. Please? So Guru's returning! My Go... Ger... Guru!"

"Oh, all right," agreed the badgered Jemma. "Tomorrow then."

"Tomorrow it is," said MAP, "see you then. Do you want a doggy bag for the food you've left?"

Pippa cringed, and when the wondrous Nathan, who was at that moment skilfully operating with his index finger deep within the upper regions of his nasal passages, piped up, "First you give us lassie, then a doggy bag – we'll turn into blooming dogs – woof woof," and then started straining at his mother's arm to leave the shop, she knew it was time to make a quick exit.

"No thanks, Anna," said Pippa, "must go. Bye!"; and out they went into the bright sunshine, Nathan being propelled with difficulty at a rate of knots by his mother up the High Street and onto the steps of the Town Hall, where, after a certain amount of child scolding, the two girlfriends said their goodbyes.

"See you tomorrow, Jem, OK?" said Pippa. "You'll enjoy it, you know – don't look so unhappy about it. We'll have a lovely Satsang, you'll see, especially with Guru here." But Jemma wasn't so sure ...

Later that evening, a motorcade of white Rolls Royces approached Totnes. Nurse and a Peace Corps driver sat in the front of the first car and, deep in the comfortable back seat, Guru leaned back and talked.

"Swami," he said to Tikka, sat next to him, "I hope you are enjoying your new car ... is this the very Rolls? Hmmm?"

"Thank you, Guru; yes, this is the car. It is beautiful. I am so grateful. And how are you, oh illustrious one?"

"This body I inhabit continues its functions vell," lied the Guru, "but you do look a bit ... tired. Hmmm?" he said, indulging himself in yet another brief moment of interest in the rest of the world.

"I am good, Guru, very well. The Totnes facility

82

goes from strength to strength," said the Swami, changing the subject. "We have many new recruits every year, and the town itself is a source of much wonderment. We have five stalls in the market and gross a five-figure sum weekly."

"Vhat's the nett?" snapped the Guru quickly.

"Oh, about eighty per cent. There is much money in the environs," the Swami said, noting the Guru's apparent astuteness. He wondered if the rumours he had heard about his increasing inability to function normally were just malicious. He continued, "We will soon make more, but I feel the figure is good for now."

"I guess so," agreed the Guru. "And vhat of Dirtington College? Hmmm? You say Ma Anna Poona is still bringing them in – in droves?"

"Yes, sire, droves it is. The catchment area here is rich, especially the students and children at Dirtington – they all come from wealthy families. In cash terms, each Dirtington Premi is worth three from the town. Though the ones from town do work harder – we have a good mix of capital and labour."

The Guru was pleased with the news about the Premis, for these newly converted disciples were the life-blood of his organization due to the funds they all deposited when joining, and rich Premis were, of course, worth, literally, their weight in gold. Even if seventy per cent left soon after due to dissatisfaction and a feeling of having been tricked and conned, their money had by then somehow legally become the Guru's property, and that, to put it bluntly, was goodbye forever to many substantial inheritances for these poor unfortunates.

"And vhat of Ma Anna Poona? Is she still – big?" continued the Guru. "Does she still – lay on hands? Hmm?"

"Yes, sire," said the Swami, disrespectfully thinking to himself that the big woman would lay on anything, even the Guru. He had heard about the long 'arrangement' they had had before the Guru's departure for Minnesota. "As you know, one of her main functions in our community is therapy for the unfortunate ones not obtaining the full benefit from their love relations."

"I see," said the Guru, "and vhat of you?"

"I, indeed, now help her with the girls," replied the Swami, "and find it most rewarding. I have opened many doors for many repressed young women. It is most stimulating." So that's why he looks a touch wan, thought the Guru, who felt a surge of jealousy well up inside him, as did Nurse in the front seat, at the thought of the Swami sorting out teenagers' sexual problems in the most practical way possible – though Guru knew he himself was no longer the 'chaud lapin' of his youth. In fact, my dear bookworm, it was a long time since he had been in his youth ...

Now then, whilst the motorcade was moving at a steady pace towards Totnes, Ma Anna Poona could have been seen leaving her Cafe there and moving extremely fast – for a woman of her size. The only strenuous movement she abnormally ever made was in her capacity as a sex therapist, and today's relatively unusual physical activity – upright with both feet on the ground – could mean but one thing. The moment, for which she had been waiting the last few months during the Guru's absence had, or was about to, come. She could not wait to get her big mitts on the little man.

MAP was running, and everything was flowing – her hair, her long head band like a ship's flag in the breeze, her voluminous robes. Rush-hour commuters stared, people stopped in the street and looked twice, motorists narrowly missed bollards, each other, anything. She carried on totally blinkered. The Guru's motorcade was, of course, heading for the same destination, fortuitously taking a different route. As it entered Totnes town, the Guru quickly looked at himself in the aptly named vanity mirror, adjusted a hair or two (for that's all there was), replaced his turban, and prepared himself for his reception. As Totnes was his European HQ, he expected a reception on a grand scale; but, even to the Guru, what transpired was most unexpected.

"So, we are here," said the Swami, as they rounded a corner, stating the obvious. "The Totnes Randientre – Carnal House!"

The Guru recognized the large Victorian house looming on the right and, as if on cue, hundreds of white-draped people ran out from its gates into the roadway. They started cascading flowers over the Rolls, they ran beside it, they sang and chanted. In through the gates the opulent automobiles drove, up the grand gravel driveway, past huge rhododendron bushes and right up to the imposing front doors. Hundreds of young men and women ran out of the mansion and the Guru was swiftly surrounded by more flower-bearing Devos and Premis. The doors of the Rolls were opened and the great little Guru stepped out.

Above all the commotion, gravel crunching, singing and dancing, could be heard a loud voice, out of breath, screaming, "Let me at him! Gangway! We have business to attend to! Make way!" The Guru was slightly worried in case the voice might emanate from a policeman, a bailiff, writ server or just someone trying to make way while the sun shined, until to his relief he saw the sea of whiteness part and there, ten feet from him, was the aforementioned Ma Anna Poona.

They looked at each other for a moment. All the Devos hushed and then, like a Viking goddess, MAP charged forward, bodily lifted up the little man and, still towering above him, carried him headlong into the facility. She was showering him with flowers and kisses, screaming all the time, "We have business to attend to – make way!"; and almost before they had reached the front door she had managed to remove most of his outer garments.

Now, our illustrious Guru had had a long journey, he was tired, even his clothes were a bit off-white, he needed sustenance, and for once in his life he did not immediately want to be ravished. It was good, though, that someone wished to. Of course, the captive audience looking on all adhered to his strict views on open sexuality, that's mainly why they were there, and so the peer pressure made it hard to turn down MAP's kind offer. After all, he had to set an example to his Devos. And now, considering her fumblings and much possibly inappropriate touching beneath his linen loin cloth, it was getting harder and harder, even at his advancing years, not to give in. And to cut a short story shorter – he succumbed.

The huge woman and the little man fell onto one of the many mattresses in the Great Hall of Carnal House laid out ready for the following day's Satsang. Most of the other Devos and Premis looking on threw the flowers they were carrying into the air, stripped off, and joined in *en masse*, as did the Swami and his good friend the Nurse. Every mattress and spare bit of floor was being used, and a very relaxing time was had by all the many attending this important impromptu social event in the Devo calendar.

Sadly, though, it was not so relaxing for the poor uncomfortable souls who had bared all and had been unfortunate enough to roll onto some of the many rose stems now strewn liberally around the room; nor indeed, to **MAP**'s chagrin, did the occasion quite come up to the standard she had expected.

For most, though, it certainly did and the distinction between cries of passion and cries of pain disappeared as the hall was enveloped in a panting sea of sweat and lust – the whole edifice finally exploding in a simultaneous crescendo of satisfaction.

For, at last ... the Devos' come had timed.

11. Sex On The Beach

Early the next morning, Ma Anna Poona could be found immersing herself in the warm waters of the Dart. She had seen pictures of holy people in India doing this in the continent's various rivers, some with very long names, and it seemed only fair to give it a try. She needed to get out, it might purify her, for sex therapist that she was, she knew when something was up, or in the case of her Guru, when it wasn't.

The night before had been one big let-down for her. Or, had she let Guru down? Maybe, after a few months without him, her expectations had been too high. She wasn't sure. But, though it appeared everyone else had finally left the hall totally satisfied, she had not. Guru had not come, well, up to her expectations really, and, like her good self, these were pretty extensive. Could he be past it? Or was it she who was?

Pulling her saturated sari tightly around her ample form, she waded out deeper, totally immersing her body. When she had tried to do this in the swimming pool at Dirtington, most of the other swimmers, and the water too, had left in sympathy, for with proportions like hers the expression 'displacement activity' took on a new meaning. There would be no problems like that in the Dart. Slowly she started swimming, the slightly salty water easily supporting her weight; she realized how uncomplicated life in the water would have been for her and thought back over the years to her initiation in the Serpentine Lake. Maybe in the next life she should come back as a fish.

When she was fifty or so yards from the bank, she stopped for a rest and, as she hung there vertically in the water, something big brushed past her leg. Then again. She swallowed hard, trying not to move or panic. Not - Oh no, it couldn't be. Oh, Guru!! Was it the monster ..!?!

Suddenly, there was a great commotion around her, she felt herself rising up out of the water fast as it steamed around her, her legs straddled something big and most unexpectedly she received the most enormous douche she ever had. Poor Anna - and salty water too.

She adjusted her sari, which was of no use to her at all now, and thought quickly. After the initial shock, the jet of water became quite pleasant, and when it stopped, she wanted more. But she was scared, very scared. She'd never met a monster before. She was tingling all over from the initial shock, but guessed that the safest place for her was on its back, whatever it was – as long as it was on the surface. She stayed put.

Big Dirk could feel the substantial weight on the top of his head and wondered what to do. He started swimming, slowly, on the surface. MAP, not surprisingly, still wondered what was occurring. She looked around. And what she saw made her sigh a huge sigh of relief, for then she knew. This was no monster! She was sat slap bang on top of a whale! She couldn't believe it. So that's what the monster was. Just a huge Great Sperm Whale.

Dirk started to swim slightly faster, rising out of the water, then lowering himself to let the water lap her legs. Faster and faster he went, until her hair and sari were flying back in the breeze. She threw her head back with pleasure, tightened her legs around his head. He could feel that and knew she was enjoying the ride. Anna, on her part, thought it much nicer than anything on a horse; anyway, riding stables would not accept her any more for even Shire horses buckled under her weight. Now this was fun, exciting, breath-taking. She was no longer frightened, enjoying her ride on this big, silly whale.

Big Dirk continued his playing, for he could sense how happy this human was becoming. He became adventurous, diving so that only her head was above the water, swimming as fast as he could, bobbing in and out of the water until she had to clutch at her white sari to keep it with her. She clutched him tighter too, feeling the warm water run all over her body. Her long white hair was flowing back now, tangling with her clothes. Her knees clenched, then relaxed and clenched again. Dirk could feel the change in tempo. It was as though something was gently rubbing up and down on his head. In fact, dear friends, it was. Increasingly, it became more forceful until he could stand it no more. He quickly looked for the nearest land, and aimed for it.

Ma Anna Poona threw her head back once more as she saw the land approaching. Oh that this could go on forever. She grasped Dirk's head even tighter with her knees, forced her legs apart, together, apart, together, until she could do it no more. She let go of her sari as they neared the beach; she had not a care in the world – and neither now had Dirk, for when the water became too shallow, he gently rolled her over, looked down at the now naked, panting, super-sized human female form and did what instinct knew he must – he laid her down on the beach as she passed out into ecstatic unconsciousness. After this short intromission, he swam back to her sari, grabbed it in his mouth and brought it back to the beach for her. He then retreated a few yards and, new man that he felt he now was, waited.

A few minutes later, MAP opened her eyes, and somewhat bashfully looked about. She knew someone was watching her, but could not see a soul. What had happened? There was her sari. She picked it out of the water and modestly wrapped it around herself.

She must have been asleep and dreaming of a whale. She couldn't remember the last time she'd had an erotic dream – probably when she was an adolescent – and this one was out of all proportions. Now she knew all the ins and outs of whalebone. There was sand in her hair and she could hear waves as if she was on a beach. She sat up. No wonder she could hear waves, she *was* on a beach. She heard a splash, turned, looked out across the river with a start, and for a second or two froze, recalling what had just transpired.

There HE was, smiling back at her with the biggest, sweetest smile she'd ever seen in her life. Almost in slow motion, with the rays of the sun breaking out from behind the usual small cotton-wool cloud, she ran down the beach. She ran right up to the water's edge, then into the water, which splashed her all over, and up to Big Dirk.

She grabbed what she could of his head, then bent down and kissed his huge lips. This sent a shiver down Dirk, who vibrated briefly like a great tuning fork, so wired up was he. For a minute or two they looked at each other longingly, lovingly, and then, yes, lustfully.

Dirk could once more feel a tingling in his loins, loins of huge proportions, loins that no butcher's hook could ever have supported. MAP too felt the yearning, felt the same urge in her loins – that is, if the female of the species does have such things – felt the pace of her heart quicken. She looked at Dirk, mentally cradling his head in her arms, mothering him. This will never work, she thought. They had different backgrounds, different likes, and, not to beat about the bush, their genes were pretty different too.

Dirk gently grabbed her sari between his teeth and pulled. Slowly the wet one-piece garment slithered about her body until it was once again floating in the water and she was standing in front of Dirk in naught but her briefs, if a garment so vast can be called this.

Now Dirk knew that something was definitely up. It was a good feeling, though he still didn't understand it all that well. Last time this sort of thing had happened, the events that had followed had caused him much pain and suffering, both mental and physical. But he really had no wish to understand it, just to do it, and consequently what transpired next could in no way be blamed on the great mammal, so suddenly thrown into a somewhat unusual trans-species love affair.

Even with all the exercise, meditation and general posturing that MAP had taken in the last few years, it would still be problematic, physically, to do what she and Dirk certainly wanted. However, with the passion of the moment overriding all normal aspirations and inhibitions, she found herself slowly sliding down Dirk's great belly towards the focus of his affections. Dirk too found himself well stranded as he attempted time and again to consummate their union, forcing his bulk further and further out of the water.

Map too was becoming frustrated, feeling that, try as she might, she would be unable to fully extend her body's welcome to Dirk. She attempted every position that she knew the *Kama Sutra* would have suggested to conclude the affair to their joint satisfaction, to no avail. Dirk certainly had stamina, but was it getting him where he desired to be? No, dear friend, it wasn't.

Finally, she remembered to do for Dirk what she had done for the Guru many times ... she bent over backwards for him ... and so then, yes, slowly, delicately and with great tenderness, the two genera-challenged lovers were able, finally, with great satisfaction and yet some eye-watering difficulty, to consummate their affair.

As MAP threw her head back in a shudder of excitement, she once more passed out into the land of nod, for the events, and not only the events, had been all too much for her body to take in, in one go. After a few minutes, she stirred, then remembered and turned to the wide expanse of river. There he was, watching her, motionlessly, her huge silent lover. Once more he brought her sari back to her, no words spoken.

Dirk turned, flashed his tail, and was gone. Her hand lifted and she waved a loving adieu, and started walking with a great deal of difficulty back up through the fields to the grounds of Carnal House.

In her room, she peeled off her soaking sari, and started drawing water for a hot bath. She had a Satsang to run! She must prepare herself, and quickly, but she would allow herself a few moments' contemplation while the bath filled. She lay on her bed to try to recover. There was a groaning noise as the bed settled.

Well, now she was satisfied! The whale had done something that no man could have done for her. Even Guru had now failed her, and, try as she might, she couldn't focus on mankind – she wanted to, but couldn't.

Her very own Whale just kept swimming into view ...

Ma Anna Poona felt a tear roll down her cheek onto the pillow. She looked up through her window at the high thin clouds drifting slowly by the blue, blue sky. She felt a light breeze touch her face.

Her hand moved down between her legs. That was it.

MAP wanted her big friend Dirk there.
Just there.
Again ...
And again ...

Well, Wadayaknow!!! What was that?? Be I in love!! With Woman?!

Woah! there be a first time for everyone. And this was my first time. I promise on my mother's life what happened between me and the stern tubes of that submarine was just a mistake. Nothing, you know what I mean, came of it. The ocean certainly did not move for me, my whalebone was slashed and they sprayed a stingy milky fluid all over my sore, bleeding organ. Thank the Lord it recovered in time. Yipeeeeeee!!! I would punch the air, slap my thigh, dance the hornpipe (if I but could).

She is thinking of me, I knows it, can sense her vibrations through my humungous head melon. And she wants me too!!

No-one, said NO-ONE, has ever sat on my face like that before! Concern me it did to begin with, but, Dear Lord, soon gets used to it. And then! How did she do it???

So want more, much more. Not just her mind ...

WANT HER BODY!!!! Yeah!! Praise the Lord!!

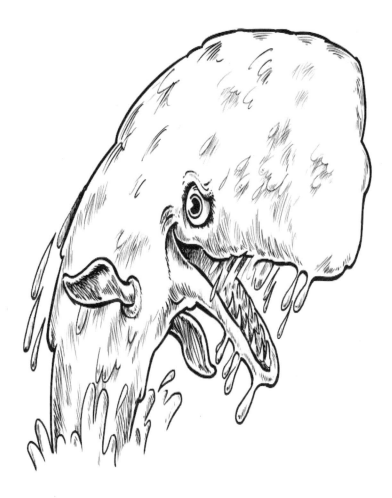

It was much later that Ma Anna Poona realized that Dirk's was the kindest, most unquestioning and, yes, largest face she had ever had the pleasure to sit upon, ever.

12. Satsang

Nathan Throssell sat at the kitchen table eating his beans on toast. He was in a mood – a bad one. Again. His mum Pippa was wisely keeping a good distance from him and was herself preparing to go into Totnes for the promised Satsang – the weekly mass meditation. She was nervous, as her friend Jemma was coming along – and she had to take Nathan. Jemma was also somewhat trepidatious, for she had heard a rumour about an orgy, as Mrs Hughes the newsagent's wife had described it, held in Carnal House the very night before and Nathan had made it clear that he did not want to go.

Now, dear friends, in case you had missed something so glaringly obvious, let me tell you that the Guru had some very peculiar ways. For instance, he could not stand certain smells (nasally he was highly sensitive), and he had instigated a sniff test which everyone had to pass before they could enter the great hall where Satsang was about to take place. It was unthinkable not to pass the test, and Pippa was worried that Jemma, not in white, might precipitate this terrible *faux pas*; for, in the Guru's case, a good smell was very much in the eye, not just the nostril, of the beholder.

"Couldn't you put this on, Jemma?" she asked nervously, holding up a spare white sari. "You'll blend so much better." But Jemma would have none of it.

"Look, Pips, I'm not a ... member. I don't believe in it, and I'm coming along, reluctant, mind, to see what it is all about – OK? I'll be alright; what are you worried about?" Pippa couldn't, or didn't want to, explain the niceties of being a Devo, or the test. After all, she was new to the whole thing herself – she'd noticed the first monthly bank payment to the Guru

96

going out from her and Tom's joint account on their last statement. It had been neatly sandwiched between the life assurance and home mortgage payments.

She bundled a squealing Nathan into the back of the Range Rover, climbed into the front with Jemma and they were off. The drive did not improve her, nor Jemma's nerves, for these roads had been put down long before the internal combustion engine was ever invented, and often, as they rounded yet another tight bend, unable to see anything approaching from the other direction due to the great height of the hedges on each side of the narrow lane, Jemma closed her eyes and prayed.

Luckily, as often happens on country lanes, nothing chose to approach, and the three of them arrived at Carnal House in one piece, so to speak, where they saw a queue forming. They parked the car, tagged onto the end of the queue and, after a few minutes' wait, were nearly at the front. There they saw Ma Anna Poona (with a peculiar smile on her face) and two burly male Peace Corps Devos vetting all and sundry. Jemma was shocked. They were not asking for tickets, nor invitations, but were sniffing each person that came up to them. Everyone in white was let through with no problem, but it was clear that non-Devos were not that welcome – certainly not on their own.

"Hello, Anna," said Pippa, reddening slightly, as their own sniff test commenced.

"Woof, woof, sniff, sniff," said Nathan, making his presence felt.

"Nathan!" snapped the beleaguered Pippa. "Er ... Anna, my friend Jemma – you met the other day – could we have a good seat, Anna? We so want a clear view."

"Well, dearie," replied MAP, sniffing loudly,

moving her nose all over Jemma's quivering body, "bit of a prob. I'm afraid it's the back of the hall for you three – it's the child, you see. I am so sorry. Next!" And she ushered them through with a bank manager's smile and a dreaded grey ticket each. "But ... Anna?" Pippa was so upset. Luckily, no-one she knew had seen them fail the test.

They sat down at the back of the hall with the other non-whites. She had tried so hard. But then, if Guru was that sensitive, he had to be protected from the unclean; and his Satsang at Carnal House would be a very special occasion. With Guru himself giving it, she thought, MAP was probably in an extremely expectant and highly strung mood. It was He who always insisted on everyone being vetted by smell; only the purest could approach Him. The big woman was only following orders. Pippa, for the moment, relaxed slightly.

After some time, the great doors of the hall were slammed shut, and she knew no-one else could gain admittance. At least they had got in – but it was so uncomfortable on the floor, cross-legged. Jemma was not happy, she could tell, and Nathan – well, he was already squirming. Most of the Devos were simply sitting, quietly waiting, cross-legged, attempting to relax. Some tried meditating, some sticking their tongues down their own throats, while new Premis nervously picked at their fingernails. Nathan, of course, picked at his nose. The more experienced Devos mostly just smiled. And smiled. And smiled.

Soon everyone was smiling, it was the thing to do, it was a replacement activity, and by the time the Guru was due to arrive all looked ecstatic. The effect was staggering. Everyone did feel happy, very happy indeed. The Knowledge was working.

Founded upon what is known scientifically as the

principle of the chicken and egg, it worked well, for the Guru had discovered early in his life that one could reverse the process of contentment. If one felt happy one smiled, and if one smiled one began to feel happier. And that was one of the basics of Knowledge – an idiotic, sickly grin that forced the poor unfortunate next to the grin to copy it, and so on. A room full of expectant people, some smiling widely, eventually created a room in which everyone was smiling; and, sure enough, the relaxed feeling of happiness and contentment soon enveloped all – that is, save for Nathan Throssell, who knew damn well that chimpanzees only smiled when scared to death. What a load of apes, he thought, as he accidentally, but quietly, farted.

Presently, Nathan saw the Guru enter the hall from the rear, a method of entry the great man often used (allegedly for security reasons, but some said unkindly it was something he had learnt from a lonely mountain shepherd from Attica who he had befriended many years before) and was being carried aloft in a throne-like chair by four Devos. Nathan heard nervous shushing noises, and soon after could have heard a pin drop. The Guru's face broke into a sickly grin, necks were craned and he made his way slowly and very regally through the seated mass of humanity.

"Bratavishnu, my golden ones," he said from his mobile throne, still giggling, in a voice as loud as he could muster.

"Bratavishnu, Guru!" came the reply from a thousand giggling mouths. And then the whole place broke into laughter. Jemma looked at Pippa. Pippa smiled back. Nathan once more farted. For nigh on five minutes the sound of mirth could be heard resounding around the great hall, and the laughter, nervous at first,

99

finally became almost genuine.

"Ve must control ourselves," came the mild instruction from a very tickled Guru, whose accent had become considerably more eastern for his audience, and had lost some of its mid-Atlantic twang. Slowly, the hysterical laughter subsided to a few titters, and eventually silence once again reigned. But Nathan could not control himself, and yet more wind was broken. A small gap had started forming at the back of the hall.

"Firstly," said the great Guru, not noticing Nathan, who was a long way off, "ve vill have five minutes' meditation." Not surprisingly, there was then five minutes' meditation. It was the Guru who broke the silence, coincidently as Nathan once again broke wind.

"Now, children of mine," he said patronisingly – which Nathan knew was the only way to deliver such lines, "ve have our Satsang. Ve vill start vith some qvestions. Who vill be first? Hmm ...? You?" he said, pointing at a spotty faced Devo, the proud owner of an exceptionally large piece of bird dung which appeared to have slithered in tramlines down from his forehead to a point midway between his eyes. "Vhat is your qvestion?"

"Guru, Bratavishnu," said the first Devo, who hailed from Delhi, "you have compared Hitler to Ghandi. How can this be? There were never two people more dissimilar."

"A good qvestion, and I vill tell you simply vhy they are similar," said the Guru, trying hard to sound more eastern than the Devo from Delhi. He looked around his audience. "Hitler vas a sadist who varnted to torment and then kill millions of people. Ghandi vas a masochist who varnted millions of tormented people to live. He vas more devious than Hitler. Next ..."

"Guru," asked a Devo, this time from Dublin, "you have said that Mankind has complete control over its own destiny; but how can this be? What about natural disasters?"

"A good question, my child, and one that I vill answer ... just give me an example and I vill show you vhart I mean ..."

"Well," asked the questioner, "for instance, what caused the Irish Potato Famine that wiped out a generation? It wasn't just the English ... or was it?"

"My child," squealed the Guru, thinking quickly, "no, no. There may have been some political reasons and bad decisions made at the time, but the main reason vas simple. The Irish used all the available fertilizer to make bombs to blow up the English!"

There was a stunned silence in the hall. Had Guru's mind been twisted in some sort of illogical time-warp? Quickly, realizing he may have spoken somewhat too contentiously, he pointed to another Devo, whose raised hand was quickly lowered as his brain cranked into action trying to understand the concept just expounded. Nathan thought the answer, in his own words, a load of poo - fertilizer, indeed! Then that's what fertilizer was. However, he now knew that when he grew up he didn't just want to be an Engine Driver or a Postman - he'd become a Guru. That's where the money was. It was obvious.

Just as Nathan was discovering this secret of life, the beans he had eaten at breakfast finally and explosively made their presence felt by everyone in the hall, including a Guru who, when the effect finally hit his nasal passages, fainted and fell backwards off the raised dais on which he sat.

As Nathan's body once again chose to expel noxious gases from its rear, this time with as much noise and volume as was humanly possible, Peace Corps heavies moved in, white bandanas tied tightly over their noses, and he, a crest-fallen Pippa and an embarrassed Jemma were also quickly expelled – from the hall's rear. However, dear reader, they never returned.

Because, for once, Pippa Throssell actually agreed with her son. She had suddenly realized the Guru was nought but a confidence trickster, whose mouth spouted almost as much well-fermented rubbish as Nathan's rear, and she was at her bank first thing Monday morning to cancel the standing order payment to him. Fertilizer, indeed! What a load of manure.

A red-faced Pippa dropped off Jemma in Stoke Gabriel, and made her way back to the cottage in Dittisham. She went upstairs to talk to husband Tom (still in bed), while Nathan busied himself squashing a caterpillar in their narrow hallway. At that moment, Mr. Hughes the newsagent pushed the Sunday *Bugle* through the door. The paper fell right side up, and huge banner headlines screamed out from it, but Nathan had more pressing commitments than reading the news. He continued squashing the poor ex-caterpillar until it had finally stopped quivering, and then his eyes obligingly wandered over to the paper.

"Bloody 'ell," he said. "Cor, lummie!" His English language schooling came almost exclusively from certain periodicals published in the vicinity of the River Tay in Scotland. He continued on the same tack. "Looks like a good one t' me." He picked up the paper and wandered into the kitchen.

Within a minute of finishing the article, he was prepared, if one would call it that. He had packed a tin of cake and biscuits, taken a can of sticky fizzy liquid from the refrigerator, borrowed his dad's camera (without permission), and was off.

"Nathan!" his mother had called from upstairs,

102

but he had gone. She continued pottering about the nether regions of the cottage and when, much later, she picked up the *Bugle*, she realized where Nathan had probably gone. He would be down by the river, looking for monsters, for the front page of that Sunday's *Bugle* said it all. A huge reward was being offered for certified proof of the Totnes Monster, and in banner headlines the amount leapt out of the page ...

MONSTER REWARD!
FIFTY THOUSAND POUNDS

13. A Totnes Monster?

An ancient station-wagon sped towards the river at Dittisham as fast as its old wheels could carry it. One Ivan Gold was at the wheel, his girlfriend Estelle tutting by his side. Ivan was nervous, and driving much too fast, for if what he was now intending to do was discovered, it could cause the failure of his degree course on aquatic dinosaurs. That would be so unfair. But when he too had seen the Sunday *Bugle*, he knew he could not ignore it. Fifty Thousand Pounds! His eyes had lit up like a fruit machine on heat. All that money!

Since that moment, he, Estelle, and his pal from engineering, Eddie Kotowski, had been hard at work all morning in the university wood workshops. Now Eddie was squashed in the back of the estate, horizontal, slowly chipping away at a large piece of expanded polystyrene with a blunt knife stolen from the students' union canteen. On the roof of the car was the large wooden frame they had made, and a rolled-up sail which had been purloined from the University sailing club on their way out of Exeter. They were transporting, in kit form, their very own Totnes Monster.

"How's it going, Eddie?" said Estelle, looking round. "Hey, you do look squashed."

"I'm OK," said a muffled voice. "Would it have a – nose, Ivan?"

"Er ... well, yes, but we haven't time, Ed. Just give it a long neck, two eyes, and, well, a sort of bump in the middle of its head. That should do it. Oh, and one on top of its head too. That'll confuse the scrutineers. We'll be at the cove in about ten minutes. Think you'll be ready?"

"Sure," said the encapsulated Eddie, "but do we

have to drive so fast?"

"Sorry, Eddie," said Ivan, "but we've got to get there as soon as we can. Then maybe we'll catch the scrutineers off-guard." He put his foot down further. Soon the terrible three and their bits of monster arrived by the river just outside Dittisham and parked their car away from prying eyes by Folly's Cove. A shaken Eddie emerged horizontally from the back and then the two lads set to, sorting out the roof rack, while Estelle went off to find a telephone.

Two sub-aqua divers, vital to their plan, had failed to turn up.

"So where are the divers, Estelle?" said an aggravated Ivan a few minutes later as his girlfriend arrived back from the telephone box. "You arranged them. Where are they?" He nervously pushed his glasses back up his nose, for arguing with Estelle was something he had learnt not to do.

"I don't know, Ivan," she whined. "They said they'd be here at twelve. They're not at home. I told you not to trust yoks. It's Sunday. They're probably pissed somewhere. I don't know." She whined on for a few moments more.

"Maybe we should give up," said a tired Eddie, interrupting her, something not totally recommended.

"Give up!" she shouted back.

"That's what I said," said Eddie the engineer timidly. "If they don't come we won't be able to attach the head to the rest of the monster; anyway, not with the bags full of stones to balance it. It's got to look right. I mean, the head has got to bob up and down, to articulate from the neck. Without the divers we're sunk ... well ... the monster will be."

"He's right, Estelle," said Ivan timidly. "Unless we can ring up that number in the paper and provide something that looks right from a distance, and we are as far from the observation station as possible, then we've got no chance of the reward."

"OK already!" she screeched, and then as usual took charge of the situation. "Look, get everything set up. Open up the frame, get the sail over it loose to simulate the hump back, attach the head to the frame so it wobbles anyway, and push the damn thing out. I know, Eddie, that it won't be balanced, and will probably sink, but so what? If it looks good, we'll ring them up. If it does not – we won't. We've nothing to lose ... and everything to gain."

The lads set to work. Soon, they were ready to launch their 'monster'. They threw the frame onto the water so that the sail filled with air to form the hump, tied the head on with wire, then pushed the whole thing into the river. It went out a few yards and stopped. The three watched sadly as the hump slowly deflated until all that was left was a huge polystyrene head, anchored to the spot by a waterlogged frame of wood and sail. They too were somewhat deflated, very tired, promptly gave up, and left the scene as swiftly as they possibly could.

Nathan Throssell strode purposefully down to the river, his dad's prize camera hung around his neck, whistling a happy tune. The sun was shining, the birds singing and one or two cotton-wool clouds as usual drifted lazily eastwards. Suddenly, he spied his quarry, just fifty yards out at Folly's Cove: a great white head bobbing up and down. It had to be the monster! He raised the camera. He couldn't focus it. Grrr! But it must be the monster! He was rich! As he rushed down to the cove, he thought of all the Action Men figures he could now afford, all the chocs and sweets, besides all the caterpillars and spiders he could kill. No-one would stop him now. No-one!

Not bothering to strip off, he rushed headlong into the water and right up to the monster. Then he looked up. The lump of polystyrene looked down.

"What the ... Grrrr ... Aarghhh!" cried Nathan, "Someone will pay for this!" Then he noticed his dad's camera, still attached to him, and now very wet indeed. "Grrrr ...," he said again. He realized he was now up to his neck in more than just water. Dad would not be pleased. As he turned to get back to the shore, something caught his foot. He tugged, he tugged harder. He was stuck. "What the ... Aarghhh!" he said. He could not move.

And the tide continued its inexorable push landwards.

From the middle of the Dart, Big Dirk sixth-sensed a soul in trouble. He swiftly swung his considerable bulk into action, turned to the direction of Folly's Cove, and with two powerful beats of his tail flukes, was off. As he neared the cove, he turned sideways on so that he could see what the problem was. It was damned annoying having such a big head; having to use one eye at a time was a nuisance and nothing he looked at had any depth – except, of course, the ocean, but then he couldn't see that either, depth only really being a concept. Not even Dirk's enormous brain could visually fathom out such theoretical concepts in depth.

Nathan was beside himself when he saw Dirk approach – not that he had actually jumped out of his skin, though after first assuming he was about to drown he had wished he could. It looked like he really had now found the monster, or at least it had found him, and in the nick of time, for the water was just beginning to lap at his face.

Dirk came up close. His big right eye slowly looked Nathan up and down.

"Oh, come on, monster," said Nathan quickly in his best voice, "be a good monster and save me. Please. I'll be ever so good from now on. Promise!"

Dirk realized the problem. He ducked under the water to have a look. It was very shallow here, a bit dangerous considering his bulk, but he could probably help. He could see Nathan's foot caught in the wire attaching the 'monster's' head to its body. He vowed to be careful. He must not break bits off *this* boy.

Grabbing the framework in his teeth, he pulled at it hard, shook it once, twice, once more, and then with extreme good fortune a happy Nathan Throssell floated free. Without even a 'thank you, mate', Nathan was out of the water, onto the shore, trying to focus his dad's camera to get his monster picture.

Though somewhat piqued at the lack of gratitude shown for obviously saving the boy's life, Dirk put on his best face. Nathan did what he could with the focusing, then pressed the shutter; but instead of a click there was a small squelching noise and a dribble of water appeared from the edges of the lens.

"Grrr ...," thought Nathan. "Just stay there," he ordered Dirk, as he scampered up the hill back towards Dittisham. He had to tell someone about this. He'd found the Totnes Monster! He really was rich! Filthy Rich!!

Hughes the News was just locking up his shop to do some monster hunting of his own. He too had seen the headlines – he couldn't have missed them. He had just put the 'closed' sign in the door, when he saw a very wet boy running up the hill, screaming at the top of his voice, "I've found the monster. The Totnes Monster!"

"Where? Where is it?" screamed Hughes, quickly grabbing his camera, hoping to get the picture that would qualify for the *Bugle*'s reward.

"Not telling you," yelled Nathan over his shoulder. Hughes followed him up the hill. Nathan reached his home, ran up the path and into the cottage, leaving the front door wide open. "Mum, MUM!" he yelled, as he hid the camera under a cushion on the floral sofa. "MUM!!"

"And where have you been, Nathan?" said his mother, coming down the stairs. "You know you must not go out on ... you're soaking wet! What's going on?"

"Mum, I've found the monster, and there's a reward. I found it! I'm – er ... we're rich, Mum. Have you seen the paper. Fifty thousand quids, Mum."

"Oh, Nathan, is that all you can come up with? Come on, let's get some dry clothes on you."

By now a small crowd, egged on by Hughes the News, had gathered outside the Throssell home. Much murmuring was taking place, most of which sounded like 'murmur, murmur, monster, reward, murmur, monster' – that sort of thing. Inside the house, Pippa Throssell had agreed, reluctantly, to accompany Nathan to the river to witness his monster vision. Of course, the real reason she had agreed was the large reward, for even she had her price. "But I tell you, Nathan, if this turns out to be a hoax ..."

"Oh, Mum ...," said Nathan, trembling slightly.

They left the house presently, but only after Pippa had quickly searched for the family camera to record the great event for posterity (and of course for evidence). "That's peculiar," she said, as they emerged without it, "I'm sure it was – oh well."

The crowd that had gathered outside her house surprised Pippa, but when she realized they could all act as witnesses to the great event, she was glad for them to follow her and Nathan down to the cove. The crowd in the meantime had armed themselves with their cameras, telescopes, tripods and all manner of optical recording apparatus. The happy throng swiftly made their way down the hill to Folly's Cove.

I am not happy with that boy! What a rude, ungrateful varmit!

I save his life, I pose for him – smiling like, give him my best side, no fee, no agent, no middleman ... and what does he do?

He keeps me, BIG DIRK, awaiting!

I am turning right round, and heading out to mid-rivah, where there are NO nasty little land urchins like him to mess me about ...

I am gone!

The crowd arrived at the cove. Nathan pointed. "There," he said, "just there – oh blast!" he said, noticing an obviously missing monster. "Grrr ... Aargggggh!"

"Well, Nathan," said his mother, "show me ..."

"Er ... Mum, I think he's gone. The monster was just there, by that bit of polystyrene that looks like the head of a monst ... Oh! ... Aarghh!! ... Er ..."

Hughes the News and three strong men had gone into the water, and were dragging the remains of the students' mock monster out of the river. People started laughing, and continued laughing until they could no more, till they were bent double with mirth. Everyone thought it the best joke since sliced bread; everyone, that is, except Pippa Throssell, who felt she had suddenly become the laughing stock of the whole village.

110

"Nathan!" she shouted. "NATHAN! NATHAN!?!"

But Nathan had disappeared into the crowd.

Back in their cottage in Dittisham, Tom Throssell had just risen from the matrimonial pit, had sat down on the living room sofa, and was pulling out a very damp camera from under a floral cushion. He looked round, lifted his head and angrily roared.

"N A T H A N!"

GRRRR .... AAARGGHHH!!!!

14. The Parish Council

Several editions of the Totnes *Bugle* later, Frederick Lukes, Esq., proud but embattled Parish Council Chairperson, was still coming to terms with having to purchase his local rag each day. In an unusual fit of pique, he had cancelled his subscription after the oil 'leak', but as chairman of the Council knew he had to keep in touch with all local goings-on; and besides the story of the discovery of Totnes' own black gold, the monster story was continuing to run, and run. So each morning on his way to the council offices just off the High Street, he would stop at Bert Hughes's newsagents in Dittisham for his morning edition. This Monday was no exception.

"Morning, guv," said Bert, touching his forelock with one hand and none-too surreptitiously adjusting his foreskin with the other. "Here's your copy. Thank you very much! Had a good weekend, did you? Funny business that, yesterday ... Monster made of plastic ... that's what! Good morning!" And then at 110 decibels, "PAPER! Get your PAPER!" Fred Lukes had no time to waste perforating his eardrums or watching Bert Hughes continuously adjusting assorted bits of his person. As he left the vicinity of the shop, Bert was behind the counter slowly disappearing vertically downwards, knees bent, presumably to remove bits of ancient holy cotton stuck far up his rear.

Fred looked at the front page ... Oil again, damn it! But pages two and three concerned the 'Monster'. What a load of monster poppycock, thought Fred; so it was only a student prank ...

He made his way into town, happy to get away from the noise of Bert's ancient sales technique. Puffing up the steps of the Town Hall, he didn't want to be a moment late for what promised to be a long and contentious meeting. As he entered the council chamber that warm and sunny morning, there were many more white-clothed people than he'd expected; the sound of argument hit him and he wished he had left home earlier.

The room was in uproar, the volume was intense and he had trouble calling the meeting to order. Even Councillor Frank Lee from Dittisham, his staunch ally for many years, had changed from his usual dark suit to a rather sharp white one.

"Morning, Frank," Lukes said, hoping for a smile, a handshake and a few friendly words before the start of the meeting. "What's this all about the monster being seen off Dittisham?"

"Fred, good morning," Lee replied, ignoring his question, and added, in Lukes' opinion much too brusquely, "and my name is now Premi Lax Sativa, so I would appreciate you using the proper form of address." And he then turned back to continue talking to another white-clad councillor. Fred was shocked.

Fred Lukes looked round the room and noted the numbers. Though white versus normal now seemed fairly even, he felt that councillors themselves might be fast becoming somewhat unbalanced. Looked like they'd got Frank – what next? The cacophony of sound rose to a crescendo.

"We must close the beaches – who knows what this monster can do! Yes, close the beaches!" came the cry.

"This meeting WILL come to order!" Fred Lukes had to shout above the din to make himself heard. He had never seen or heard disorder such as this in all his many years on Totnes Parish Council. There seemed to Lukes to be quite a few white-clothed people standing around the large oval boardroom table, waving their arms in the air and screaming to their hearts content. Bert Hughes had but been whispering in comparison. Obviously, the councillors had not heard the latest news about their monster. Gradually the room quietened, heeding his request, and they all sat down.

"Thank you, ladies and gentlemen." Fred took a deep breath. "Let us start. Good morning. Item one on the agenda ... er ..." He paused a moment to look pensively at his notes.

"Now, Council, we shall discuss our monster in due course. But we must stick to our agenda. Item one ... Councillor Lee has tabled a motion as follows ... 'That if it is the feeling of the meeting that officers be appointed with responsibility for various minority groups, then they shall be so appointed.' Do we have a sec...?"

"Premi Lax Sativa," interrupted Lee. "My name is *not* now Lee."

"Yes, er, Councillor Sativa, or is it Councillor Lax – which, Frank?"

"Councillor Lax Sativa, and please remember, Councillor Lukes, my name is NO LONGER FRANK!" replied the bristling Lee/Sativa.

Fred Lukes eyed his old friend sadly. Was it possible that soon the whole council would be in white? He continued, "As I was saying, do we have a seconder?" Another white-clad councillor raised his hand. "Very well," said Fred, "seconded by Councillor Phall. Councillor Lax Sativa, please propose the motion."

Frank Lee/Lax Sativa rose slowly, smiling at all the other Devo councillors who unexpectedly applauded him. "Thank you, my friends, thank you. Bratavishnu."

He held up the four-fingered salute.

"BRATAVISHNU!" came the reply in unison. Fred Lukes groaned inwardly as fourteen hands rose. Lax Sativa smiled.

"My friends," he looked around, waiting for his audience to settle, "we have in our community here more and more people who are not native Devonians, who are not of normal persuasions, who have 'unusual' ideas. There are those from other countries, whose religious beliefs vary, and those whose – for instance – sexual tendencies are not – how shall I say – 'run of the mill'. And not only people. Out of town, but still within the council boundaries, are many farms. Now, we must look after the rights of the animals on these farms ..." Fred could not believe his ears. Up to what was he leading?

"Point of order, Mr. Chairman," a cry came up from Lorraine Simpson, the wife of a farmer and long-time member of the council. Chairman Lukes allowed the point. At that moment he would have allowed anything. The lady rose. "I am a farmer's wife," she said, "and I should like to make it very clear indeed that my husband and I have no animals on our farm with strange sexual tendencies. I am, on their behalf, very upset at the suggestion. However, I will admit to one or two black sheep – but there is nothing you can do about that sort of thing, is there ...?" She droned on, to be swiftly interrupted by a tetchy Councillor Lax Sativa.

"Mr. Chairman, I fear Mrs Simpson has missed the point," he said forcibly.

"I fear she has," replied Lukes sadly. "Please sit down, Lorraine. Councillor Lax Sativa ..." How she had ever been elected ...

The newly named Lax Sativa continued. "I am simply talking about minority rights – the rights of the individual to do, within reason, as he, she or it pleases. And to this end I propose that if it be the feeling of this duly elected meeting that an officer be appointed to assist any particular minority group, then council funds should be provided for this purpose. That is my proposal." Lax Sativa sat down.

Fred Lukes feared as much. So the loony left had reached Totnes. "Who would like to start," he said, generously opening the discussion. Scanning the council, he realized that for the Devos the matter was cut and dry: all obviously wished to vote and be done. To stop an unrequited Lorraine Simpson – who was about to speak again – Lukes himself spoke.

"I speak now as a long-term member of council," said Fred, "and not in my capacity as Chairman. Just a bit of advice, really; I object to your proposal, Councillor, as it could very swiftly bankrupt the town. Your idea is so broad that we might end up with 'rights officers' for sewer rats."

"They play an important part in our eco system," interrupted Lax Sativa. Various Devos nodded their agreement. Lukes politely continued.

"Where do we draw the line?" he said. "We only have limited funds and if we create job after job like this, we will have no money left for the normal running of the town ..."

"Increase the rates ..."
"The rich could afford it ..."
"Communalize the farms."

"Order, order, order," cried Lukes. As the meeting calmed, he spoke again, trying to rescue the situation.

"Friends," he tried, smiling sweetly, "last year we made Totnes a nuclear-free zone. We all now agree that

116

to implement the suggestions made then would have been foolhardy. Never in a thousand years would we have been able to build the impenetrable geodesic dome that was suggested. Certainly we paid for the architect's plans, and for the initial survey of the capacity of the rock strata to protect us from nuclear attack or mistake. But the dome itself, and the anchor points and their inherent podia problems made us all realize that, not just for economic reasons, but also for practical reasons, we would have to abandon the idea of the protective dome. So we wasted some money and yet, legally, we are still a nuclear-free zone."

He continued. "If, however, some enemy state decided to attack our country, or if Hinkley Point power station up the road had a melt-down, we, like all the towns around us, would most certainly not be nuclear free. We too would be somewhat melted down. 'Nuclear Free Zone' means nothing in practical terms, and in economic terms it would have been a disaster to follow it through. Now you are suggesting an officer for any minority we feel needs one. What if the Crumbleigh bell pullers felt threatened by the introduction of tape recorded church bells – I know the Vicar is thinking of it as a belt-tightening exercise – would we provide a co-ordinating officer to help them? And would he have to be an accredited bell puller? If we did this, we would be creating chaos in our community by increasing its bureaucracy to an unacceptable level. Nothing would ever get done. Nothing could ever change the status quo. The town would stagnate. These are my feelings on this matter." He brusquely sat down.

Whilst he had been talking, Lorraine Simpson, the farmer's wife, had been itching to talk. And not just to talk. She had recently caught a rather nasty rash from one of her husband's prize Jersey cows. Well, that is where Farmer Simpson told her she must have got it. Now, whilst surreptitiously scratching herself under the council table with one hand, she was requesting permission to speak from Fred Lukes with the other. What on earth was she going to say this time, thought Lukes. He was nodding his assent as she rose to speak.

"Ladies and gentlemen," she droned, like a Douglas Dakota on take-off, "I have listened to what has been said. As you may know, I live on a farm. I am married to a farmer. Itchily, pardon me, initially these proposals seemed spurious to me, but I have now reconsidered the position and am willing to believe that, up to a point, Councillor er ... Lax Sativa is right. I have seen what happens to animals cooped up all day, bred artificially, with no life of their own." Fred Lukes leaned forward in amazement. Was this really Lorraine Simpson talking, the Mrs Simpson who even in the height of summer donned twinset and pearls for the weekly council meeting? He looked at the numbers in the room. Traditional loyalties were shifting. If she was siding with the Devos in white, the proposition might pass through. He listened on, frowning all the time.

"Why," La Simpson continued, "only the other day one of our prize Jerseys caught a very nasty little illness – I'm sure she was run down." The urge to scratch was simply awful. One hand surreptitiously moved down her body. "I think being cooped up in the cow shed with all those Friesians" (she was referring to the cows, not herself), "and Tommy the bull didn't help; all these things gave her the rash – the illness." Her hand gently rubbed the spot. "So I say my Jersey could jolly well do with a chap to look after her affairs."

To 'Hear Hear!' from the gruff Colonel North and applause from the Devos, Mrs Simpson sat down with all hands scratching. Lukes nervously looked at the

118

Colonel. Not him too? "Can we vote or do we have further discussion?" he asked quickly. He had checked the probable numbers and things were, he guessed, still just in favour of sense, but it all depended on the Colonel. He looked around. "Very well, let us vote on Councillor Lax Sativa's proposition. Those in favour?" He counted fifteen. "And those against?" Fifteen. Lukes was happily about to use his casting vote on the side of sense, when Colonel North put down his pipe and raised his hand. "Are you voting against, Colonel?" asked Lukes patiently. "Good Lord no, Lukes, voting for; forgot to vote, what, eh!"

"You are voting for the motion – is that right, Colonel?" said Lukes sadly.

"Yes, for the motion, Lukes, poor sods need someone to fight for them. Farmer's Wives. Poor sods. Have to protect them. Wouldn't marry a farmer for all the tea in China. Am one. Farmer, that is. Can't marry oneself, can one, what, eh?" and on he waffled.

"So," said Lukes, interrupting, "assuming we now have all voted – you may put your arm down, Colonel – we are sixteen for, and fifteen against. Motion, that minority rights officers be appointed as the council sees fit ... carried!" Fred Lukes could not believe it. Was the Council mad? He attempted to continue, sadness eating at his very soul.

"And now," he said, "item two on the agenda – Oil. A development has occurred which Councillor Lax Sativa has pointed out to me may well have a bearing not only on the possibility of test drilling for oil, but also on this 'monster' that I know you all want to talk about. In our last discussions I know we agreed that the River Dart was not the sort of place that would suit drilling platforms – not only due to the tourist industry, but also because of the beauty of the area. But if this monster

119

thing has any bearing on reality, then we must think again, or we will neither have the tourism, nor the oil revenue. Does anyone have any thoughts on this?"

Immediately, Councillor Lax Sativa sprung up to talk. "We must close the beaches," he said. "If this monster attacks just one tourist, we certainly won't have a good summer in any way." He seemed to be pretty sure of the monster's existence, thought Lukes.

"Very well," said Lukes, "let us discuss this damn monster – but, I add, only in the context of oil, and its bearing thereon. We cannot discuss anything that comes into our heads. We have an agenda to follow, and there are still two items to deal with. Councillor Lax Sativa, I presume that it is you who wishes to speak?"

"Thank you, Mister Chairman. Ladies, gentlemen ... friends ..."

Oh dear, thought Lukes, looks like a long one. Lax Sativa continued. "Most of us have seen the local television news reports concerning our monster. I believe now the national press has taken up the story. For many years we have been promoting the Totnes Monster as a 'possibility' – a fable, if you like; but now it appears to be a 'probability'. There is strong evidence that whatever it is, it does exist! We, as a town, therefore have a golden opportunity to capitalize on this remarkable find, but we must act quickly to keep up the momentum. Our first act must be to close the beaches."

There were murmurs of disapproval from the non-Devo half of the council. Ignoring them, Lax Sativa continued.

"For a town council to do that will imply to the outside world that they must be sure of the monster's existence, especially a town that relies so heavily on the beaches and river for its income. The reason for closing the beaches is obvious – we have to protect our townspeople and tourists alike from the threat of this deadly monster. The result will be twofold ..."

"Councillor Lax Sativa, please," interrupted Lukes, holding up the morning edition of the Totnes *Bugle* – the headline 'Totnes Monster – Vicar's Monster Vision a Prank?' was plain for all to see. "I fear Vicar Priestley may be mistaken, as he sometimes is. Our historic local legend of the monster and the mini tsunamis of the last few weeks may have combined to ... confuse ... his ... suggestible ... mind, er ... to bring him to the conclusion that he had indeed seen something large in the water. Apparently, it may be nought but a student prank ... this discussion must be relevant to oil, not the monster ..."

"Councillor Lukes, I am getting to it, if you would be so kind as to allow me," replied the Devo councillor tetchily. His monster train of thought clearly was not going to be derailed; by now the sound of anti-Lukes murmuring coming from the council Devos was fairly apparent.

"As I was saying, the result of closing the beaches and the river will be twofold. Firstly, people will flock to Totnes from all over the country, nay the world, to catch a glimpse of the 'monster'. Our hotels and guest houses will be full to bursting point. We will make national news headlines over and over again. And secondly, while the nation's attention is distracted searching for this 'frightening' monster, and while the 'River Closed' signs are up, we can instigate a thorough search for our very own liquid gold – oil. We now have geological surveys which show a good probability that there is oil beneath the Dart. I must emphasize that we would be unable to search for it if the river was full of pleasure boats, swimmers and the like. We will be keeping the town full of tourists, fuller than usual, and we will be looking for something that will turn Totnes into the richest town in England after they have gone. We must use the monster story, true or false, to enable the search for oil. Now, does anyone have any objections?" Lax Sativa looked around.

"What," said Lukes sarcastically, "will the monster think of the oil exploration, Councillor Lax Sativa? I cannot believe it would be very happy about it. What about its rights? Eh?"

One or two non-white councillors smiled at each other, but Lax Sativa would not be put off. "Councillor, you and I, and presumably most people here – and this is off the record, not for the minutes of the meeting – know full well that the chances of this monster really existing are low, as you rightly point out, Councillor Lukes. I am a pragmatist, and am merely suggesting we use this golden opportunity to put our town on the map. To reiterate, without the monster we would never be able to search, let alone drill, for oil in such an area of natural beauty. This is our only chance, and I say we vote for it."

"Seconded," said one of the Devos.

"Point of order," growled a voice from the back of the room. Lukes turned, as did all and sundry, to see the gnarled hand of one Captain Ayeup slowly rise.

"What about the fishermen?" he said threateningly in a calculated, low, north country voice (for that is from where he hailed: Whitby, they say), whilst polishing his nails noisily on the blackboard at the far end of the council chamber. "Ban t' boats, tek away our life. Tek away t' food from t' mouths of our little uns. Starving us, slowly, painfully, putting us aht t' grass." Never one to mince words, the Captain took a long pull from his even longer pipe, an act which cloaked him in a foggy cloud of smoke that smelled so evil Lukes thought

122

he might in truth be smoking something he should actually be put out to.

Ayeup leaned forward. "Now," he said quietly, "tha wouldn't do that, would tha?"

"I think we could allow the fishermen to continue using the river, at their risk, of course," Lax Sativa said nervously. All swiftly nodded their agreement.

"Then that's aw'reet," drawled Ayeup unhurriedly. He leaned back, taking a cloud of smoke into his well-pitted lungs. He just made people nervous.

"This would be a very bold step, Lax Sativa, to close the beaches," said Lukes, steering the discussion back on course. "Can we be sure beyond doubt that we are not cutting our collective throats?"

"We can never be one hundred per cent sure, as you know, Chairman," said Lax Sativa, "but I feel the risk is small. If we do not find oil, or the 'monster' finally disappears, or both, we will of course open our beaches immediately. This could even be done in time for the school holidays, so there is no problem." Lax Sativa searched the faces of the council members as a lawyer would a jury. "We must," he continued, "grasp this opportunity while we have the chance. Shall we vote?"

"Councillor Lax Sativa," said Lukes, "I am Chairman of this meeting – please remember that." Not for long, thought Lax Sativa. Fred continued. "Er ...," he said, "shall we vote?"

A nearly unanimous council then voted Lax Sativa's way, to shut off the river from all traffic save local fishermen, oil men and the emergency services, the only dissenters being two angry councillors who were directors of Dart Board Hire Ltd., who could only look forward to a summer of extreme leanness. There would be little windsurfing off Totnes this summer. The two men stormed out of the meeting on hearing the vote. The onshore traders, though, were very, very happy.

"Thank you for the vote," said the worried Chairman, "and the proposition that we close off the river to all but essential traffic is passed."

The Devos in the council seemed somewhat happy at the thought, and murmured their approval to each other. A concerned Fred Lukes looked at the agenda with trepidation oozing from his heart. With two more non-whites gone, any voting in council now would be without doubt dominated by those in white.

"One matter must be discussed which is relative to the matters on which we have agreed so far," he continued, delaying as best he could, hoping for time to run out before the next item. "We must decide what organization will undertake the oil exploration. Does anyone have any ideas?"

Lax Sativa was already on his feet. "I believe, Mr. Chairman," he said, "that the rights to explore the Dart are about to be purchased by, er, Randco Ltd., of the Cayman Islands, and naturally we shall, as a council, have to liaise with their local office."

"About to be!" said Lukes. "What do you mean?"

"Randco have," replied Lax Sativa, "a watertight option, if you'll excuse the expression, to purchase these river rights."

"You know it all, don't you, er ... Lax Sativa?" said Lukes. "Now, who is this Randco Ltd., of the Cayman Islands? I have never heard of them. And where is their local office? You seem to know everything, Councillor; please enlighten the meeting."

"I would be pleased to," he replied. He looked at his prepared notes. "I feel sure that I can recommend this company to Council as honest, upright and good for our books. Randco of the Cayman Islands have not actually been trading that long ..."

"How long?" asked Lukes sharply.

"Registered this year actually, Mr. Chairman," continued Lax Sativa, pretending to gain this information from his notes. "Randco are registered in the Cayman Islands, but of course have local onsite offices wherever they have an oil claim."

So that's why he hadn't heard of them, thought Lukes. "How many claims do they have?" he interrupted, by now exceedingly suspicious.

"At this moment, well ..." Lax Sativa once more ostensibly looked at his notes. "My goodness, only one. What do you know!"

"And where are their headquarters?" Lukes questioned again, knowing full well what the likely answer would be.

Lax Sativa pretended to look at his notes again. "Well, gosh," he said, now almost mockingly, "Randco (UK) Ltd., is registered at, um, Carnal House, Totnes. What a coincidence! So near – how convenient ..."

The rat that Lukes had been smelling was fast becoming a rodent out of all proportion and the reason the river closure was so imperative to the Devos was becoming all too clear. "I suppose," he said, "you would want to set up a liaison committee with 'Randco'. Am I right ... er ... Lax Sativa?"

"A brilliant suggestion, Mister Chairman, shall we vote on it?" said the Devo Councillor, now secure in the knowledge of a Devo majority due to the early departure of the Dart Board men.

"I shall ask that question, Councillor. Shall we vote on it, ladies and gentlemen?" Lukes realized the expression conflict of interest was one too polite to describe what was now happening. But he still had to do his duty. "Very well, those in favour?" Fifteen white-clad hands rose swiftly. "And those against?" Fourteen other mits lifted half-heartedly. "I see," said Lukes, whose casting vote was again of no use. "Motion carried. Those wishing to serve on said committee please raise their hands." All fifteen Devos did, as did Lukes himself. Lax Sativa interrupted.

"Excuse me, Mr. Chairman," he said evenly yet firmly, "I'm afraid standing rule 7 specifically forbids the council chairperson from attending liaison committees. You will have to withdraw."

"So be it," an angry Lukes reluctantly agreed. It had been worth trying to keep some sanity on the committee. "You sort out the damn committee, Fra ... Councillor. Looks like you'll be liaising with yourself. Good luck – you'll need it."

Fred Lukes was not at all happy at the way things were going and felt very lonely on his beloved council. On one side was arrayed crazed religious nuts all in white and on the other were the likes of Lorraine Simpson, Colonel North and Captain Ayeup. How was he meant to run the town? He looked round the room and thought back over the years. Perhaps his days were numbered. "Chairman ... MR. CHAIRMAN!" Lukes jumped at the sound of Lax Sativa's voice again breaking into his reverie, always that damn man Lax Sativa.

"What is it now, Fra ... Councillor?"

"We still have two items on the agenda," the man in white said, "can we proceed?"

The wind had definitely left Lukes' sails. He was in the doldrums, though being quite aggravated he was certainly not dead calm. In fact, he was angry, storm force ten angry. "Look ... Lax ... whatever your name is now," he said vehemently, "you run the bloody meeting.

126

You've got the majority now – do what you want. All right? I can't be bothered ... FRANKLY!"; and his fist hit the table as he sat down on his chair in a considerable huff.

"MISTER CHAIRMAN! I have told you my name is now LAX SATIVA!" The former Frank Lee growled aggressively at Fred. "Please do not refer to my former name. IS THAT CLEAR?"

And that was the hair that broke Fred's camel's back. Frederick Lukes, Chairman of Totnes Council for four years and Councillor for ten, had had enough. He stood, shook his head sadly and followed the Dart Board men out of the chamber. Enough had indeed suddenly become enough. Councillor Lax Sativa, Fred's former good friend Frank Lee, looked at the meeting, then the agenda, and took over.

One more item. No Problem!

Ah ... SLIM!

'Dreaded Disease Marches On!'

'Government Contingency Plans'

'Quarantine Regulations'

To be sure, those illustrious purveyors of British Standard Tested appliances, the Randi Rubber Co, makers of the famously reliable Randicond, would supply the town's needs.

They were in for a very good year.

(Passed Unanimously)

15. Knowledge

Some days later, our great and glorious Guru was once again attempting to relax; this time newly installed in his private rooms in Carnal House. He was still recovering from his extraordinary welcome at the hands of Ma Anna Poona, and though pleased that he now owned a river with oil in its bedrock, and that the 'River Closed' signs now going up meant that the exploration would be starting in earnest, things had not, for some reason, gone quite as he would have liked.

His Nurse was reluctantly attending to him, wishing she was with the Swami. Guru was as usual flat on his back in yet another bath. He was playing with various floating rubber toys and yet at the same time trying to read about himself in that day's Totnes *Bugle*, when his eye was caught by a story about some monster or other. But with no time to read the article, he put the paper down, for he was scheduled to give Knowledge to two girl Premis in just a few minutes, and they would be waiting for him expectantly. One of them was the young Swedish stewardess who had helped look after him on his flight over.

The Nurse looked down at the prone, foam-cocooned man. She knew him well, too well, and had become used to his sudden whims. As she was about to scrub his back just one more time, he let out a squeal. She took a deep breath. "What is it now?"

"It's the vhale. It has bitten me," replied the Guru.

"It's only a rubber toy!" She looked down into the bath. But he was right – his inanimate whale had somehow become firmly attached to his most intimate of parts, head down, with only its tiny tail flukes visible above the suds.

"See," he cringed. "My little whale has bitten me. Oooh ... Nurse! Help! Get him off!"

She unconcernedly leant over, grabbed the toy rubber whale with her right hand, and pulled at it. "Well," she said, "I wonder how it came to be there?" Rows of small rubber teeth lacerated the Guru and he let out a cry of pain.

"This is an omen, Nurse. If my Little Dirk can do this, then so again vill *Big* Dirk. But vhy me!?" Randi blanched at his own mention of the awful name.

Nurse put down the toy whale and looked at the man in the bath. Her eyes went to where his right foot should have been. Only a stump stared back – that is, if stumps do stare – for, as you well know, one foot was missing, absent, gone. "Big Dirk," she said, referring to the whale who, she was sure, could only have bitten off Randi's foot by accident, "will not bother you again. Do not fear. He was only playing with you. He liked you. It was a chance in a million."

She helped the Guru from the bath, dried him down and for once left him to dress himself. She needed to get away from him quickly and couldn't help thinking it a shame that Big Dirk hadn't chopped off more than just his foot all those years before. Randi was starting to annoy her, she had had enough of his ways, for, like Swami Tikka Masala, and also Big Dirk before in a different way, she too had now nearly bitten off more than she could chew.

Presently, Randi too left his rooms and, as he started down the corridor towards the Great Hall, a great feeling of unease came over him, exactly the same feeling he'd had during the flight from America two weeks before. He spun around. No-one there! It certainly *was* an odd feeling. He entered the Hall, in the

130

centre of which two white-clad girl Premis were sitting crossed-legged, talking away excitedly.

"Will Guru be giving Knowledge?" said one to the other.

"Is he coming?" said the other.

The Guru overheard their chatter and for a moment forgot about his inexplicable unease, for Knowledge giving the Randi way was often very pleasant for the giver, especially with young, pretty girls, one of whom he recognized as Ma Prem Dansak, the flight attendant.

"Children," he said, holding his hands in the air as the same girl had done on his flight over when pointing out the emergency exits, "ve vill soon be on a higher plane. I shall give you Knowledge."

The girls looked up open-mouthed. It *was* Guru!

"This moment," he continued, "for both of you vill be very precious. Now you," he pointed to Dansak, "I vill give you Knowledge first. Come vith me."

The girl stood, and meekly followed him to a side room. The Guru shut the double door and motioned for her to sit down. He then followed her to the floor, sitting opposite her, cross-legged. His knees cracked. He reached out and held her hands.

"How larng have you been a Premi?" he asked.

"Three months, Guru."

"And how old are you?"

"Just ... seventeen," she lied.

"And you are sure now that you varnt Knowledge?"

"Absolutely sure," she replied.

"Very vell. Are you ready?" asked Guru, looking deep into her eyes.

"I am ready."

A pretty girl this one, thought Guru, with long

hair almost down to her waist and a body that went in and out in all the right places.

"Now then, now then ...," he said. "First, you must take arf your clothes."

"Pardon?"

"I said first you must disrobe," repeated the Guru.

"You mean ... ALL my clothes?"

"Yes."

"But ... I just want Knowledge."

"And by God ... er ... Guru you shall receive it. There must be no artificial barriers betveen us. First, you must take arf your clothes. Then, you vill take arf mine. Obedience is also part of Knowledge. Now do as I said."

The girl hesitated slightly, stood up and lifted her long white robe over her head. She folded it and laid it on a cushion. Then she stopped, standing only feet from him in just a tiny pair of briefs. The Guru looked at her hard. A difficult one, but then she was *very* young. He'd show her. She turned around and quickly pulled them down to her ankles, bent and threw them onto her robe. She turned back towards him with her hands held demurely in front of her. "Now take arf my clothes," the Guru instructed as he stood up. She hesitantly walked round behind him and unwound the sheet covering him. He kicked off his sandals. "Good," he said. "Now ve resume our previous positions."

She sat opposite him as before, still trying to hide herself from him as best she could. He reached out, taking her hands in his again, feeling a certain amount of reticence on her part. "You must relax," he said, and unceremoniously clasped both her hands around his part, something she had not intended to be hanging on to so early in the day. She resisted initially, but soon was doing as instructed.

"But – I only want Knowledge," she said, as she gently caressed him.

"You vill get Knowledge, but ve must first learn to be relaxed, happy and loving with each other. Now," he said, extracting a limp Randicond from his bag, "you must put this on me. Ahhh, now you understand me, don't you. Aaahhhhh." The Guru moaned again. "Good, you're learning. Now come closer and close your eyes. This Mantra is for you personally. No-one else has it. Vhen you are meditating, you must say this over and over to yourself until you see the Light. Your vords are ... are you ready?"

"Yes, oh yes."

"Doo Wop Shoo Bop Wop. Now you say it."

"Doo Wop Shoo Bop Wop."

"Good," said Guru, "now keep saying that to yourself vith your eyes closed. That's it. Good. Keep your eyes closed. Keep saying the Mantra. Lie back gently on the cushion. Right, good! Now take me – keep saying the Mantra, keep your eyes closed – and – put – it – aahh – that's – aaahhhhh ... good. Can you see the Light yet?"

"I – think so ... I'm not sure," came the confused and breathless reply.

"Don't varry, you soon vill!" Gently, the Guru started rocking back and forth. "Now, carncentrate in the centre of your farhead," he said, suggesting the well-nigh impossible, considering what he was doing to the girl. "Keep calm, look for the Light." He started rubbing between her eyes with his thumb. "Can you see it yet?"

"I think I can," came the startled, panting reply. "It's a bright light – white-orange ... it's aaaahhh ... it's ... moohhh ... ahhh ..."

"Aaaaahhh ... Ohhh... OOOhhh ... AAAhhhh

133

...," replied the Guru, rubbing both her forehead and himself deep within her as fast as he could. "OOOOhhh ..."

"It's AAAHH! IT IS THE LIGHT! I CAN SEE IT NOW!" she cried. "AAAAAHHHHH", they cried in unison, and slumped onto the floor.

The girl had got the Knowledge.

When the Guru had composed himself, he gave her more instructions. "Now, girl, go to the stores and ask for your very own personal Knowledge kit. The kit is one short plank and a vooden rest on vhich to balance your hands vhen you are meditating, plus a dark blanket to cover yourself to keep out unneccesary light. You have money arn you? – Good. You vill also be given a packet of Randiconds – use them on your men – you can get more vhen you need them. Now, varne more thing." He held his fingers over her eyes. "Between you and me, here is a qvick vay to see the Light. There – jab your fingers into your eyes – see, Instant Light. Saves time. OK, I think that's it. Put your clothes on and send in the other girl. Bratavishnu!"

"Bratavishnu, Guru," said the confused, dazed, partly blinded and suddenly dismissed girl as she pulled on her robe and left his presence.

The other girl then cautiously entered to the sight of a naked, prone Guru, who had not surprisingly forgotten all about both the Monster and his 'little' problem, and was lounging on the scatter cushions lazily adjusting his personal equipment.

"Good day!" he said.

16. A Mantra Too Far

As the Guru was in the process of rearranging his bits and pieces, Swami Tikka Masala was sat at his desk in a state of shock, having just scanned the many CCTV security cameras installed in Carnal House for a sign of his beloved Nurse. His trawl through the rooms had stopped at camera 17, positioned in a side room next to the Great Hall, the room in which his mentor was giving Knowledge. From what Tikka could see, he was not just giving Knowledge, but a lot more besides. It seemed that Guru was taking great advantage of his position to make a very young-looking Premi take part in some pretty unsavoury acts.

Tikka recognized the girl! She was the Swedish one who worked for Randair. He was sure she was only fifteen, and had been admitted very young as a favour to her mother, who was a long-time Devo. Guru must know the rules ... no Knowledge sessions with under-age Premis! What was he thinking of? If this ever got out ...

He quickly removed the tape from the DVR and buried it in his bag. He would have to speak seriously to Guru, a task he would not delight in. Nor would the Guru, when he had finished with him! Little did Tikka know how soon his thoughts would become a reality.

His intercom buzzed. "There's a Mr. Jones on the 'phone, Swami," his secretary said, a touch agitated. Tikka reduced the intercom volume. "He sounds very angry – says Guru gave him the very same Mantra that he gave to his friend. He wants all his money back or he'll go to the papers – shall I say you're not in?"

"He says what?!" Swami Tikka Masala was most disturbed, for at that moment anything would have annoyed him. "Impossible – of course I'm in, girl – put him through ... Hullo, Hullo – ah, Mr. Jones, I believe. How do you do? Now what's all this about? Eh? Some story you've got there – I mean, you know as well as I that Mantras are unique to the person receiving Knowledge. And Guru gave you Knowledge, I understand, so frankly I just don't see it."

"I'm afraid it is true," said Jones. "To explain – you know me as Methi Aloo Bhindi, that's the name the Guru gave me – do you remember me?"

Tikka thought back – yes, he did. Fenugreek Potato Lady's Fingers had been a good name for the smelly, fat, green-fingered Jones – a real Mr. Potatoface, but he had been a good worker – the strong, sensible type. Most unlike him to stir things up. "Yes, I remember you. So you're Mr. Jones now, eh? Well, what happened?" Tikka drummed his fingers impatiently.

Mr. Jones started his story. "Ten years I worked for the Guru," he said, "ten long years, and then to find out by chance that all that time I had the same mantra – it was 'Shooby, Dooby, Wah' ..." Tikka winced "... as Guru had given to my closest friend. I was shocked to the core. One morning I was sharing his room, and I awoke to find him chanting it out loud. I nearly strangled him with his Mala. I know the rules and he shouldn't have been chanting with someone else in the room, but he was. That's when I discovered it. Later, we found others who had been given the same Mantra. I tell you, I was disgusted. The whole basis of our faith was knocked sideways – may I ask what Mantra Guru gave you, Tikka?"

"You may," said Tikka, bristling with anger, "but I won't tell you – you know they're totally secret." Tikka's anger was not caused so much by the impertinent question, but by the Mantra, his very own

137

Mantra, now whirling round in his brain. His too was 'Shooby, Dooby, Wah', but no way was he letting on to Jones. "What," he growled, "do you propose to do?"

"Well, Mister Tikka," said Jones, "I want my money back – my life savings, ten years salary from the advertising agency, and my coin collection. I gave them all to the Guru. And I want them back."

"And if," interrupted Tikka, "we can't oblige?"

"Then," returned Jones, "my friend and I shall go to the Sunday papers with the story. And not just about my Mantra. I know for a fact that the Guru grooms young female Premis under the cover of giving Knowledge! Don't deny it! He should be locked away ... charged with rape! I know for a fact we could get a tidy sum from the papers, and he'll get locked away for years ... my friend actually works for the *News of the World*."

"Not ... the *News o* ...," stammered Tikka in mock horror.

"So, Mister Tikka," Jones ploughed on, "I suggest you talk to your Guru, and sort something out. You have a week. Goodbye, Mister Tikka." And Jones cut the line.

'Shooby, Dooby, Wah', murmured Tikka. He always said his own mantra under stress, it usually calmed him down, but somehow the magic was gone. Angrily he hit the intercom. "I have to go out!"

"Yes, Swami," replied his secretary. "Bratavishnu!"

"Brata ..., see you later." The word had stuck in his throat. He checked the cameras again, this time finding his Nurse, and buzzed her, telling her to meet him at the main entrance with an overnight bag. He threw a few things in his on top of the tape, grabbed the keys to his new Rolls and strode purposefully down the corridor and out of the main entrance of Carnal House, where Nurse was waiting. A kiss and a few brief words, and then they were in the big car and away.

17. There He Blows!

Some few hours later, and now back in his room at Carnal House, Guru Shami Randi was looking in the mirror at another monster, this one receding. He lifted his turban and noticed the hairline. It had definitely moved from where it was last month, and the wrong way, too. There was a knock at the door. He swiftly replaced his hat.

"Vhat is it?" said the Guru when ready, a frog apparently taking up temporary residence in his throat.

"It is a knock at the door, Guru. May I enter?"

"Enter!" he squeaked. He cleared his throat. "Ummmmm."

Councillor Lax Sativa entered. "Guru, you look shocked – what is it?" he asked, seeing his worried face.

"Oh, it is nothing, no... thing." He pulled the front of his turban further down. "I was surprised to see you. Vhat can I do for you?"

"Guru," said the Councillor, "Anna had asked me to help out, as it seems the Swami has disappeared."

"Tikka, garn? Vhere?" cried the Guru. "No-one tells me anything!"

"My apologies, Sire. I thought you knew ... and Nurse too ... They have just ... gone, and I believe they telephoned Anna to say they would not be returning ..."

"You had me varied for a moment," said a happier Guru. "Anyvay, I never trusted Tikka ... at least *my* Nurse is still here ..."

"No, Sire, she is gone ..."

"But you said Nurse 2! Mine is Number One!!"

"We will find you a new, younger, prettier Nurse, Sire ..."

"Oh, good riddance anyvay," said the Guru, "she

was too ... rough ... and disrespectful ..."

"Now," said Lax Sativa, who knew he needed to change the subject-matter fast, "the TV news, you must watch it. They have mistaken the *Obtuse* for a whale. What fools – it's on now." He strode purposefully to the television and switched it on.

"The *Obtuse* is here already?" Randi asked, then added nervously, "A vhale?"

"Yes, Guru, the sub is in the boathouse ... Look," he said, pointing at the TV, where an announcer was relating some trivial news. "Our man at the TV station says its third item tonight. It will be on any minute. See – here it is."

And sure enough, with a scenic view of Totnes and the Dart, the reporter was explaining the true significance of the extraordinary discovery of the Totnes Monster. Even with skilful editing, clever camera angles, maps, diagrams and dubbed monster noises, the news item was ambiguous, almost tongue in cheek. But the Guru thought from the report that what he had seen really was animate. His stomach churned, for the few seconds of film actually devoted to the 'monster' reminded him of his very own monster, the whale that had horribly ripped off his foot all those years ago, and Lax had indeed said whale ...

Lax Sativa noticed the sudden change in Randi's behaviour from annoyance to fear, for he had become very pale indeed. "What is it, Guru, you look ... white?" he enquired.

"And vhat is wrong with that? White is good ... Ummmmm? I ... I ..." He pointed at the pictures on the screen. "It's that vh-vh-vhale. It has followed me all my days. Vhy do I deserve this?"

The Councillor tried to reassure him. "Nonsense, what whale? Oh – *that* whale! I am so sorry!

141

No, look at the sunlight; whales do not reflect like that. No, it's our submarine, Guru, do not worry." He put his arms around the now shaking wreck to steady him. "It is not the whale, Guru, it is not. You are too fearful. Please relax," he said, and he sat the little man down in a comforting armchair. There was a knock at the door. Randi was shaking with fear, but relaxed slightly when he saw who was entering his room. The door opened very wide, then wider, then wider still, and Ma Anna Poona squeezed in.

"Good day, Guru, Councillor – are you both well?" she said. Randi continued to cower in his chair, with Lax trying to bring him back to life. "What is it, Guru, you look – white?"

"Anna," said Lax, "Guru is convinced this Totnes Monster is the whale that attacked him when he was a boy. Talk to him."

"But, Guru, that's impossible. This whale is too ... loving." The Guru groaned. "He couldn't possibly be the one that ate your foot. Not my Dirk ..."

"VHAT DID YOU CALL HIM?" shouted an aggravated Guru.

"Well, I call him Dirk, Big Dirk – he's so ... big." MAP blushed, something Lax had never seen her do before.

"THAT'S HIM. THAT'S THE MISTER!" screamed the Guru.

"But he's left now, hasn't he?" said Lax, nodding vehemently at MAP, who finally understood.

"Oh, yes," she lied quickly, knowing full well that Dirk had not gone, "he's left, left the river ... He's er ... gone."

"So vhat is *this* monster," said the Guru, shaking and pointing at the television. "The reincarnation of Adolf Hitler? Do you think I'm mad?!"

"Guru," said a slightly confused Councillor, for it looked nothing like the man in question. "I have just left the boathouse. The *Obtuse* is there. I saw it – the 'monster' is just a cover we thought up. You see, the TV news director is a Devotee – now do you understand?"

"Ahhh, a cover ... Ummmmm, very clever, but the Vicar saw a monster ..."

MAP jumped in quickly to take up the story. "Oh, he must have seen the *Obtuse* at dusk; it was a lucky mistake for us, that's all." She looked at Lax and both nodded vigorously.

Randi relaxed again. Once more, there was a knock at the door.

"Who now?" cried Randi; the great though still nervous Guru could have done without these constant interruptions. Councillor Lax Sativa moved to open the door. A broken man slowly entered the room. The Captain of the *Obtuse*, our old friend Halitosis Kamakis, was reporting in.

"Hal – it is you!" cried Randi, happy to see his Greek Captain, yet stating the obvious, "Vhat has happened to you? You are stooping, and your arm ..."

"Yes, Guru, it is I," replied Kamakis, "and the *Obtuse* is here. But we had some problems – first, my chair attacked me and then I was swallowed by a whale, who broke my arm. Luckily, I ..." Kamakis stopped in mid-sentence. "What is it, Guru, you look ... white?"

To Randi, the echo was turning into a conspiracy. He certainly was not turning white, though maybe to jelly. "A vh-vhale," he moaned, MAP instinctively now wrapping her arms around him, "vh-vhat sort of vhale?"

"Oh, a Great Sperm Whale, Guru – a peculiar chap, seemed to know what was going on – very human," replied Kamakis. "At Vigo I thought we'd got

143

rid of him, but yesterday my number two saw him in the periscope. I fear he is still with us. Is everything all right?" Kamakis looked at the three other figures in the room; lifting his head, he noticed something out of the corner of his eye, and there in the distance through the windows he saw the subject of their conversation blowing and sounding in midstream. "Guru, look, there he blows!" cried Kamakis.

Randi shuddered and agonisingly looked up from his chair. He stared out to the river, rigid with fear.

Monsters don't blow that way. He was looking at a whale.

18. Two Admirals Rear

Near Totnes, Rear Admiral Henry Potts-Johnstone was in the back seat of his Jaguar on his daily drive to his place of work, speeding towards the naval dockyards in Plymouth. Recently promoted to Flag Officer and with a twenty-five-year career behind him – a career of which he was proud – he was quietly mulling over the headline story he had just read in the Totnes *Bugle*. Could there be any connection between this 'monster' and the telex he had received the day before from NATO HQ in Brussels? And just how could an old vicar be sure of a twilight sighting of a dark object half a mile off shore? It might, just might, be the submarine – what was it? The *Obtuse*, about which there was all the hoo-ha, the one that had, amongst other things, penetrated NATO's Greek flank. It was the first time Plymouth had been on amber alert since the Falklands, and whoever found that sub would be sure of great things to come – maybe even a promotion to Admiral of the Fleet, or at least what was left of it. The ambitious Potts-Johnstone vowed he would not let this one go.

As he entered the gates of the naval dockyard, he happily noticed the intense security. And for the first time he could remember, he was actually challenged. His driver parked his Jaguar in his reserved space, that day it was free, and Potts-Johnstone wasted no time getting down to the business of the day. Sitting down at his imposing desk of leather and oak, rumoured to have once been Nelson's (or was it Drake's?), he reached for the red telephone, the direct line to Brussels and his counterpart there, Hugo Horneyolde-Foxe. Both men had grown up together (in the same house at Eton), had trained as cadets at Dartmouth in the same year, and were now, at the tender age of forty-five, Rear Admirals both, with similarly responsible jobs, not to mention similarly peculiar family names.

"What ho, Hugo," said Henry on being connected.

"Henners, how the hell are you?" countered Hugo.

"Fine thanks, old bean ..."

"And Emilene, and the sprogs ...?"

"All ship-shape, thanks awfully, and yours ...?"

"Spick, span and Bristol fashion, what!"

The preliminaries having been disposed of, Henry Potts-Johnstone read the monster story in that day's *Bugle* to his friend and colleague in Brussels, who agreed wholeheartedly with him that the coincidence might be just too much.

"I say, if we have found the *Obtuse*, it won't do our careers any harm, will it, Henry?" said Hugo in Brussels. Henry smelt a rat. Not for the first time was Hugo jumping on a bandwagon he, Henry Potts-Johnstone, had started.

"Hang orn, Hugo," he said, "I made the connection, old bean, and don't you forget it!"

"Of course, old man, of course. But we did let you know it was headed your way. Would you like me to set the NATO wheels in motion? Eh?" Hugo was so eager to help.

"No, not yet thanks, Hugo," Henry said, thinking quickly. "I think we can handle it from here. We do still have a fleet here in Plymouth, you know – I don't think it's quite a NATO problem yet."

"Well, I don't know, Henry, it was a NATO base that the bits and bobs went from, and we did inform you ..." Henry was fast becoming hot under the

146

collar with the gentle pushing. He had experienced it before, when they had both been going for the same NATO job, which Hugo had unfortunately got.

"Look, Hugo," he said, "I said I'll handle it from here. This is internal at the moment, and I intend to keep it that way."

"Very well, Henry, I respect your wishes, but remember – the moment the affair gets into deeper waters, so to speak, it becomes a NATO affair."

"Goodbye, Hugo."

"Goodbye, Henry."

The click, as the line went dead, had been simultaneous. Henry Potts-Johnstone had stood up, patted his forehead with a handkerchief, adjusted his collar and strode purposefully to the chart room to plan his strategy. There he decided on a barrage of ships across the mouth of the Dart, with a small presence made up of a frigate and maybe a couple of MTBs, if they had any, right up it for the purposes of the actual search. He did not expect a long campaign, not if he could help it, so few stores were loaded, and the motley collection of ships – large, small, old, and very old indeed – had gently steamed out of the dockyard in mid-afternoon, one or two being left behind due to malfunctioning engines, unused for so long – some of the ships even faintly smelling of mothballs. At the entrance to the Dart, three of the smaller vessels had broken away to a flashing of rusty semaphore signalling, and had started up the river.

Rear Admiral Henry Potts-Johnstone, taking personal charge of so delicate a situation, watched events unfold from his flagship, the intimidating destroyer *Superfluous.*

Against his will, Admiral Lidl Shortass, Commander in Chief Allied Forces Europe, was seated in his Battle Room deep within the bowels of NATO headquarters in Brussels, for NATO was now on amber alert due to the larcenous pirate submarine, and someone had to be in charge. He felt it was time for someone else to join him in his Spartan hell-hole. Checking the day's duty rosters, he saw that one British Rear Admiral and two Captains – one Greek and one American – were on the schedule. He swiftly requested their attendance for a crisis meeting. Some time later, the three men found their way to the Battle Room, having been lost twice en route in the maze of passages that is NATO HQ, a journey that seemed to the three men as complicated as an arctic north-west passage. Thank the Lord they were not in a boat.

"Sit down, men," said the Admiral, as the three eventually entered. "You took your time. Are we, or are we not, on red alert?"

"With respect, sir," said Rear Admiral Hugo Horneyolde-Foxe, "I believe we are actually on amber alert, if I'm not very much mistaken, but a chart would have helped ..."

Shortass manically chewed at his huge cigar, ignoring their incompetence. "So, men, I understand we have found this submarine, the ... *Obtuse.* Right?"

"Right, sir," said the US Navy Captain, Dwight D. Enright. "It had surfaced on the Bay of Biscay when the U2 caught it. A beautiful picture, the way the sun was glinting on the s..."

"Thank you, Dwight," interrupted the Admiral. "Do you gentlemen have anything to add?"

"Sir, I think the submarine – Oberon class, I believe," said Horneyolde-Foxe, "was probably on the surface to charge its batteries, its ... new batteries, which came from Paleocastritsa; they were one of the many items purloined in Corfu ..."

"Rear Admiral, plis tell me," asked Captain Stavros Anastosopoulos, "why does it need the surface? Is a submarine, no?"

"Oxygen, old boy, oxygen," replied the British Rear Admiral, "but if they had been properly trained, they could have got this through the snort system."

"The what?" interjected Anastasopoulos, who had just begun to understand the Englishman. Admiral Shortass, eyes to the ceiling, took a deep breath and a long pull on his cigar.

"The snort system," replied Horneyolde-Foxe. "To reduce the possibility of detection whilst the diesel generators are recharging the batteries, the air needed for their engines can be drawn down through the snort system while the submarine remains submerged." He looked around the room in triumph. Shortass took another bored lungful of smoke. Evidently, he had his own snort system.

"And what is the pairpose of this?" asked Anastasopoulos, raising his arms and eyebrows in exaggerated wonderment at yet another British triumph.

"Well, dear boy," replied the British Rear Admiral, "by snorting thus, Oberon class submarines can remain dove for periods of more than six weeks!"

"Hell, men," snorted Shortass, "we're getting off the subject of this meeting. Anyhow, US subs can stay submerged until their crews die of old age, and then some. And they don't have to ... snort." Admiral Shortass looked hard at the three officers in his war room. "Men," he said, "what are we going to do about this *Obtuse*? Why did the Greeks let it have the *132* torpedoes?"

"And the deck gun," added Enright.

"And the new paint job," chipped in Horneyolde-Foxe.

"Because," replied a peeved Anastasopoulos, "the American satellite computer NATSAT said we could. And fairthair more, that is why we are on Amber Alert today! So don't blame the Greeks!"

"They invented democracy ... but he has a point," said Horneyolde-Foxe.

"OK," said Shortass swiftly, "so what are we going to do? We know where it was two days ago; where is it now?"

"Well, sir," Horneyolde-Foxe jumped in, "I am led to believe from my ... er ... source in Plymouth that it is probably holed up beneath the waters of the River Dart in Devon, and that the British Royal Navy is, how shall I put it, on the case. But I must say, I'd like to have a crack at nabbing it myself."

"Well, what's to stop us?" asked Shortass.

"British territorial waters, sir, that's what it's in." The British Rear Admiral was feeling a slight conflict of interests. "Technically, NATO cannot enter these waters without first receiving an invitation from the country concerned – in this case the United Kingdom of Great Britain and Ireland."

"Northern Ireland, to be sure," corrected Enright, of Irish-American stock.

"Yes, Northern Ireland," agreed Horneyolde-Foxe begrudgingly, for he didn't like to lose ground. "But the moment it gets out of the twelve-mile limit, I'll be onto it like a dose of salts, if, of course, it's my turn to be NATO Flag Officer."

"So we have to wait?" asked Shortass.

"Seems like it, sir," said Enright.

"Jeez, we sure could do with some action." A bored Shortass looked round the bland walls of his bomb-proof office, never yet used in anger. "Hell," he said, "this is a war room! So I'll tell you what to do ... do we have any ships?"

"Well, as a matter of fact, sir," replied Hugo, "unusually, at this moment there are two docked in Ostende under my command ... the *Valiant* and the *Victor*, and with your permission, sir, under NATO command, I could position them appropriately at the mouth of the Dart to await orders ..."

"Rear Admiral," said Shortass, without blinking, "permission granted!"

A very pleased Hugo Horneyolde-Foxe made his way as swiftly as he could to Ostende to get his ball, so to speak, rolling. NATO Flag Officer at last ...

And out on the Dart, Rear Admiral Henry Potts-Johnstone had searched the river's length and breadth. Twice. It had found nothing, not a thing. Where could that sub be?

19. A Crew Loose

Hidden away from prying eyes in Carnal House's converted boathouse, that's where the *Obtuse* was, and its crew were cleaning their shoes. Few had bathed, few had shaved, few had cleaned their teeth, but all would clean their shoes, for the crew had had enough of their steel-shelled prison and were going on the town, and that, for this bunch of Greek seamen, the Lord knows why, meant clean (squeaky-clean), shiny, polished shoes. Captain Kamakis was not in the sub, since he was ensconced with Randi in Carnal House, now watching slow motion and stop-frame videos of the Monster. In his present unhinged mental state, brought on by the close proximity of Big Dirk, Randi had actually given permission for the men to leave the *Obtuse* for a short while. Spiro Sporades had argued the need for security, but had been gently overruled by both Kamakis and the Guru, and their men had all agreed to keep a low profile and to return by midnight. Spiro was worried, feeling sure that some would never return. He watched them leave one by one up the ladder, shuddering at the thought of Kamakis' reaction if they didn't come back.

The happy men set off obeying Spiro's instructions. Keeping to the garden's lush borders, they left Carnal House unnoticed and made their way into Totnes to find some drink and hopefully some female company. Little did they know what sort of effect they would eventually have on the town, for what they had picked up from the Geishas of Paleocastritsa now had hold of their bodies, and in the close confines of a submarine where there were no girls and insufficient diversions, many unsavoury things went on. As a result, virtually the whole crew, save for Sporades and

Kamakis, were now riddled, if indeed one can be riddled by a disease, with SLIM. Kamakis had his own problems – luckily, the chair had not been infectious, having only just come out of its packing crate when it had attacked him, but the crew – that was something else.

Each of them had a considerable medical problem. Friday night in Totnes would never be the same and, when the crew had had their evil way, neither would Totnes. The men made for the first pub, had a drink, then another, and left. This went on all night, until the last orders' bell was rung, the crew all nautically jumping in unison at its chime. They were directed to the local late club, The Bucking Bronco, a dark place with some flashing lights, very loud music, a mechanical bucking bronco, a sprinkling of punters, and one or two whores. The men, some fairly legless by now, took their rides in turn. Some rode the bronco, some in a back alley the whores, then swopped. None of the men stayed on either ride for very long, what with the drink and the lack of practice, but by the end of the evening many were bruised, many had great gashes in their trousers, some even from the Bronco. However, all were very satisfied indeed.

As a result of this glut of satisfied seamen, all the whores in South Devon had now become riddled with every strain of SLIM known to man, for the few that had been in the Bronco when the men arrived had graciously contacted their colleagues in Torquay and Plymouth, urging them to get to Totnes as soon as possible, as taxi drivers do on the arrival of the London train. The bored girls of the night had leapt at the opportunity, had jumped into cars and sped to Totnes, only to then be jumped on by the filthiest and deadliest group of men that had possibly ever existed. But at least the men's shoes were clean.

The crew were thrown out into the street, for the Bronco had closed. They staggered around, and around, and around, one by one succumbing to the effects of too much alcohol. Most made it to the shores of the Dart to sleep where they wouldn't disturb anyone, but none reached Carnal House or the *Obtuse*. Kamakis had stayed in Carnal House, thus prolonging Sporades' life by at least one day, for Spiro knew that, though not his fault, he would be blamed. It was to be a long night for Spiro, and a very lonely and worried First Mate went to his bunk that night not sure whether or not to lock the hatch.

For there was definitely a crew loose in Totnes.

* * * * * * * *

The next morning dawned, as mornings tend to each day, and it also dawned on the awakening Greeks, one by one collecting their thoughts, that it wasn't just the alcohol and lack of sleep that were making them feel so ill. Something else was wrong with their bodies. After a quick discussion, and a bit of sensible conclusion-jumping, they set off en masse to find The Clinic.

And some time later in Totnes Police station ...

"What sailors? You sent them to the telephone exchange!" said the Sergeant, for a moment putting the preparations for the forthcoming visit of the Duke to the back of his mind. "What on earth for? And they couldn't speak any English?"

The Constable looked sheepish, looked down at his boots, looked up. "I assumed, Sarge, that they wanted to 'phone home," he said at last.

"You assumed – you're not paid to assume, lad. Explain yourself!"

"Well, Sarge, they kept saying S.T.D. over and over – it's all they said, so I looked it up in the book, and the book said, 'Subscriber Trunk Dialling'. And that's why I sent them there. Was I wrong?" The Constable, a novice with only two weeks and not much else under his belt, looked worried.

"Wrong? WRONG! Of course you were bloody wrong. The 'book' you looked in was the bloody telephone directory, so of course it said Subscriber ... - whatever. Firstly, lad, if a large group of foreigners suddenly appear in the locality, none of whom speak the Queen's, God bless her, English, when it's not the football season, and when we have just received a Special Branch red notice suggesting that it might be advisable to detain or follow any such group found in our locality, and when the Duke is about to visit, you don't just send them off to the bloody telephone exchange to 'phone home to MUM! Now do you?" The Sergeant had a point. "And secondly, S.T.D. in MY book stands for Sexually Transmitted Disease – something foreign sailors often have. They wanted the bloody Clap Clinic!"

"Sorry, Sarge," said a despondent Constable, "I did my best."

"Where were they when you saw them, lad?"

asked the Sergeant.

"Right by the castle ruins on High Street, Sarge."

"Get on to dispatch and have all cars scour the town. I want every post office covered, right? And don't forget the one in Bridgetown – or the Telecom Exchange – and, just in case, get them to check out the hospital on Harper's Hill." He looked at the confused Constable. "Second thoughts, lad, I'll do it. All right? Then there won't be any more mix-ups now, will there?"

"No, Sarge." The Constable was crestfallen.

The overweight Sergeant ran as fast as he could to the radio room, hitching up his trousers as he ran, stopping momentarily to adjust them further when he had painfully pulled them up too hard. He barked out instructions to the W.P.C. behind the microphone, and then proceeded in a more orderly manner to the Superintendent's office to report the incident. He knocked on the door. After a moment's hesitation, the all clear was given and the Sargent turned the knob, pushed the door and entered. The Superintendent's secretary, Dorothy Meaner, unmarried, was smoothing down her very tight skirt.

"Afternoon, Super," said the Sarge.

"Hullo, Lovely," replied his boss from his armchair.

The secretary tittered, the Superintendent, suspiciously out of breath for one in so sedentary a position, guffawed mercilessly at his own razor-sharp wit and the Sergeant frowned whilst attempting a faint smile. He hated that old joke. "Fr ... Super," the Sergeant spat it out, "... um ... there's a large group of sailors, I think that's what they are, not Brits, wandering town looking for the clap clinic, if you'll excuse my vernacular. Most peculiar ..."

"Isn't there a Special Branch red notice about

157

them?" asked the Superintendent. "Are they under lock and key now?"

"'Fraid not, boss. Constable sent them to the telephone exchange."

"What is the ...," bellowed his boss, "telephone exchange?!"

"Yes, you know, big building in Bridgetown, lots of wires ... Anyway, there's an 'All Persons' out for them already. We'll have 'em in no time! I better get to the control room quick ..."

The Sergeant turned and ran ...

20. Squid!

Jeremy Fortesque-Smythe was in the Jot and Tittle, a public house on the Kingsbridge road, waiting to celebrate the Duke's arrival, and was on his fifth pint of frothing brew, which he slurped from his personal pewter tankard. Having once again explained to landlord Bert the intricacies of the internal combustion engine, he was momentarily at a loss for words. He leaned against the bar, one elbow taking most of his body weight, resplendent in his peaked cap, green wellington boots with a tie at the top and his favourite waxed gamekeeper's jacket, recently purchased by mail order from the London *Times*. Unbeknownst to Jeremy, the self-same jacket was also simultaneously offered for sale at a more advantageous price in the Manchester *Guardian*, though in that august organ of the people it was termed a poacher's jacket. Evidentially, the status of people north of Watford was somewhat questionable.

Landlord Bert had moved away to polish his multitude of brasses liberally scattered on every beam of black distressed wood which carefully concealed a further plethora of reinforced steel joists that in reality stopped the ancient watering hole from collapsing. There were only two other customers besides Jeremy, most of the regulars being outside awaiting the royal arrival, and anyway the two made it very clear that neither wished to actually be beside or communicate in any way with Jeremy, both by now knowing the internal workings of the internal combustion engine backwards, forwards and every which way the engine chose.

As he was about to sup up and leave, there was a commotion in the doorway, and a herd of very pale yet swarthy men burst in, looking for a lunchtime drink, gabbling away incomprehensibly. They had given up their search for The Clinic, sensibly thinking 'the hair of the dog' might improve their lot. The pub's lounge bar filled with the smell of garlic-laden sweat, the two other customers swiftly upped and left, leaving Jeremy looking at his pint, which suddenly seemed to have a long way to go. Then he looked at the men. In his opinion, they certainly looked in need of some education and a hot bath. "I say," he blurted out, "how d'y do?"

The men looked at Jeremy. "Ti?" they questioned.

"Tea? No chance, matey. This is a pub. P.U.B. Serve beer here. But no tea. Sorry."

"Ti?" they reiterated.

"Oh, I say. Look. Watch my lips move. NO TEA. TEA ROOM UP THE ROAD. TEA AND CAKES. SAVVY? P.U.B." Jeremy spelt it out. "STRONG DRINKS HERE. YES?" Bert had heard the commotion in the back room and presently returned from his brass-rubbing to investigate.

"Can't understand the lingo, Bert. Typical! Come over here and don't have the decency or brains," announced Jeremy, "to learn the Queen's English. V. bad show, don't y' know."

"Right, gentlemen," said Bert, ignoring Jeremy, "what can I get you?" The questioning inflection in his voice was obvious.

"Biera," replied the first one, looking around his mates. "Allo biera." He made a circling motion with his hand.

"Hullo Vera? – the man's called Bert actually," said Jeremy angrily. "The cheek of it, eh, Bert?"

"Ti?" said one.

"Not again," said Jeremy. "Look, if I've told you

160

once, I've ..."

"So that's beer all round – correct?" Bert cut in, and got on with pulling the hand-drawn pints. From the state of the men, he was glad it was nearly closing time. They had obviously been at the amber nectar for quite some time. "That'll be nine-ninety, gents, many thanks." Bert put the proffered ten-pound note in the till and returned the correct change. "Where are you from?" he asked. "What country?"

"Hellas," said one.

"Now you've upset him," piped up Jeremy.

"Alas?" questioned Bert.

"Hellas, ne."

"Now where the blazes is that?" Bert shrugged his shoulders.

"Hellas – ah! ... Espana, Italia ... Hellas," said one, pointing at different bar mats.

"Ah ... Greece!" Bert was quick off the mark. "You're from Greece. I was in Crete in forty-five. Kriti. Lovely place. I'll always remem..." Bert's words were drowned as the men hurled themselves over the bar to hug him, for someone who had fought for Greek freedom was a friend for life. As Bert disentangled himself from the men and Jeremy, who had been summarily squashed, the door opened and Captain Ayeup came in for his swift lunchtime snifter. "Ayeup," said Bert, "you're late, we're almost closing. What'll it be, your usual?"

"Aye, Bert, pint o' Natch. What's going on 'ere?" Ayeup eyed the Greeks suspiciously. As he did so, the door was flung open once more, this time to reveal the dynamic duo of Spiro Sporades and Hal Kamakis, who both looked extremely angry.

The crewmen hushed. Kamakis yelled at them; yelling, of course, that was totally incomprehensible to

161

the three Englishmen, though the gist was obvious. They should not have been there, for the by now extremely worried Guru had told Kamakis to get the men back to the confines of Carnal House forthwith or even sooner. They had searched the town and were about to give up, not believing for a moment that a small town such as Totnes could have so many pubs.

Kamakis instructed Spiro, who was not in his good books at all, to escort the men back to their ship, whilst he stayed on to check out just what beans had been spilled. As the men downed their pints, shook Bert's hand and left, Hal Kamakis smiled and ordered a pint in his best English. "Sorry for our men to invade your pop. They are very, how you say, lively. Thank you, sir," he said to Bert, who handed him his pint. "They do not speak much English. Did you, er ... comprehend them?"

"Couldn't understand a word," said Jeremy.

"Good, er ... what a pity," said Hal Kamakis. "So you could not converse, no?"

"Not a word, old man. Tell me," asked Jeremy, "do you drink a lot of tea in Greece nowadays?"

"Tea?"

"Yes, tea – they kept asking for tea, just like you did then; most peculiar." Jeremy was not satisfied.

"Oh ... Wod!" said Hal.

"I said ... they kept asking for tea just like ..."

"They were saying 'wod'," explained the Greek; "in my language 'ti' means wod."

"Wod? Aah ... you mean what!" said Jeremy. "Anyway, stupid bloody word for it if you ask me." Bert and Ayeup looked at each other and then to the heavens. "I mean to say," he continued, droning on, "isn't it confusing? How d'you know when someone does want a cup of tea? Nation drinking what ... what?"

Halitosis Kamakis looked at Jeremy Fortesque-Smythe: they were worlds apart. He opened his mouth to explain, but changed his mind.

"I was in Crete during the war," said Bert, diplomatically changing the subject. "Your men seemed pretty pleased to know that."

"Oh yes, they would," said Hal. "We are a proud nation. You are our friend for life." He shook his hand.

"Nice to know," said Bert. "What exactly do you all do, if you don't mind me asking?" Kamakis did. Luckily, Guru had provided him with a reasonable cover story. "They are all cadets at Dartmouth Naval Academy on an exchange," he said. "We are from the Royal Hellenic Navy." Bert and Ayeup exchanged glances. The men had looked filthy and couldn't understand any English. The story seemed tall in the extreme, especially as the Hellenic Navy was no longer quite that Royal.

"I'm a seaman," said Ayeup; "where's your boat moored? Dartmouth or Totnes?"

"We are not on a boat. We study at the college," replied an uneasy Kamakis, fast swallowing his beer in order to beat a hasty retreat.

"I see," said Ayeup. He did not.

There was a lull in the conversation, unfortunately broken by friend Jeremy. "I say," he said to Ayeup, "you know all this 'monster' thing that's in the papers and on the television – what do you think, Captain – is it real?"

"Dunno, lad, but what I do know is that there's no squid left in't river, and very little fish. Suddenly been fished out. Something, or someone," he said, looking at Kamakis, "is teking it all. Might be the monster, but then again ..." Ayeup was thinking of the Spanish fishing boats constantly hovering just outside the twelve-mile limit. "You sure you're Greek?" he said pointedly to Hal, sensing something very fishy.

"Of course I am Greek," said Kamakis, downing the last dregs. "I would not lie about my country. Well, I must go," he said, wiping his mouth. "Thank you for your hospitalizations."

"Nice to meet you," said Bert.

"Good sailing," said Ayeup.

"I say," said Jeremy, suddenly remembering something from his last year's holiday on the island of Rhodes, "so something is eating all the - 'Kalimeras', eh!" He drew himself up to his full height, proud at having remembered at least one word of Greek.

"Eating all the .... good mornings?" said Kamakis, who was at the door. "Wod do you mean?"

Jeremy persisted. "Eating all the squid - Kalimera ... Greek for squid, eh!"

"Excuse me, but Greek for squid is Kalamari," said Kamakis. "Kalimera mean good morning. But I must go now. Thank you so much, and goodbye." He shot out of the door before anyone else could say anything. Bert and Ayeup looked at Jeremy, who was reddening with embarrassment.

He must have been the laughing stock of Rhodes that summer past. Never mind his sandals, knee-length socks, shorts and ancient shirts, for his morning greeting in the breakfast room to all and sundry, so lovingly rehearsed in front of the mirror in his hotel room, 'Learn Greek in One Week' at the ready, had been one simple word ...

Squid!

Oh, yes ... Squid!

I am so tired and angry, and verily hungry!

I have scoured this one-way street of a river, and I have not seen even one big squid for days. Not one! Just small fry. I cannot think of ought else. My gigantic tummy has been rumbling gigantic empty rumbles. I am so ravening and losing weight, rapidly.

Maybe I should leave and head out to the ocean; for I have not seen my friend in his strange submersible for days, never mind no squid.

I have looked for my friend. I did NOT mean to break his arm! I have looked in every inlet and cove I can find and I no see. All right ... I am willing to believe that there being no squid may, I say may, be a problem of my own making, for I munched my way through a multitude when I first get here. But where be my friends? I must say sorry! Them I have not eaten ...

But river is deserted ... There was that big woman, ah yes! And a horrid little boy, but now no-one. No-one on the water, no-one on the shore. No food, no company, no nothing ...

Very big empty tummy.

Very big yawn ...

165

21. Liquid Gold

Big Dirk had still found no food. He was starving. As he headed back up to the surface, searching left, right, up, down, he decided. Enough was enough – or rather, in his case, not enough was enough. He would head for the open sea and lunch.

As he surfaced, he spied a fishing boat heading his way. Captain Ayeup, for it was he steadily chugging towards Dirk, thought he was damned if the Greek or Spanish fishermen, or whoever it was that had emptied the river of fish, were going to steal his livelihood from right under his nose, and had ventured out in his ketch *Squalus* on the quiet river to try at least one catch that week. To his great amazement, he had been successful in his endeavours, and was pleased now to see quite a few boxes of freshly caught squid on deck. The squid were none too pleased about this as, of course, they were now ex-squid, but Ayeup at least was satisfied with his day's work.

He was happily weighing up his catch when an enormous head suddenly appeared beside him and looked into the boat. Dirk covetously spied that day's catch of squid lying in the ice boxes. Ayeup, whose first catch for a week this was, looked at Dirk and froze. Of course, the squid too was now packed in ice and was also pretty frozen, but Dirk, the only truly cool one there, didn't care. With a flash of his tail, he hit the side of the *Squalus*. The boat lurched alarmingly. He hit it again – not surprisingly, it lurched some more.

Ayeup ran to the fo'c's'le, grabbing a gaff as he moved forward and tried to fend off Dirk, who hit the boat again, this time holing the side, throwing the *Squalus* this way and that. The squid in the remaining boxes started sliding towards the hole. Ayeup tried to stop his valuable catch of the day getting away from him and so stuck his foot out. As luck would have it, by doing this he managed to tip the boxes over. The unhindered squid then slithered towards the hole the whale had created. Dirk was ready.

The squid slid forwards, gathering speed. Ayeup tripped over his aptly named gaff and went flying on the ice. Dirk opened his mouth and all the boxes of squid neatly plopped in. The frightened Captain cursed as he himself then slid towards the whale, but Dirk took one look at Ayeup and firmly closed his mouth. No way. Not again. He licked his giant lips, smiled with satisfaction at his day's catch, and dived.

Oh, he was so happy: if he had been able to, he might have pirouetted with glee. He munched away, tentacles, beaks and all the other squidy bits swallowed in great gulps of hunger. He circled, dived, did a figure of eight and finally, in so euphoric a state, shot vertically upwards to break the surface with force, leaping high out of the waters of the Dart. *Squalus* and Captain Ayeup had no chance.

Once again, Dirk totally misjudged his awesome power. He realized as he landed back onto the surface and blinked away the water from his eyes that he had chosen just the wrong place to come up. Either side of the boat would have been acceptable. Coming up from directly below it was not recommended. The little boat had turned turtle, throwing everything in it into the waters of the Dart. But there was no stopping Dirk now, delirious with joy as he was, and once again he dived.

Now, when a large sperm whale – such as Big Dirk – sounds, one or two things happen. Firstly, huge tail flukes shoot up in the air, and then they splash down on the water with much ferocity. This dual action in turn causes two things, though these two things are the same. They are waves, big waves; and, not to put too fine a point on it, they also come in waves.

Ayeup had managed to scramble onto the boat's hull, when he was immediately knocked off by Dirk's tail going up a second time, and the laws of gravity being what they are – to be precise, what goes up must come down (the situation was grave, but the old seafarer was at that moment hoping to avoid a watery one) – he was once again sent flying.

Slowly but surely, the *Squalus* started sinking. As it filled with water, it naturally went down faster and faster. When Captain Ayeup had finished cursing and swearing, he took stock of the situation. In a few minutes he'd be under water. All his emergency flares were sinking with the boat. Even the skiff in tow had sunk due to all the commotion. He'd just have to swim.

Now Dirk was not the only one on the Dart in paroxysms of delight. Half a mile away, up river from the sinking *Squalus*, there had also been hoops of joy and much thigh slapping. On a platform operated by Texmex Prospex Inc., the men were cock-a-hoop, all looking forward to some substantial bonus payments, for on only the second day of drilling they had actually struck oil. Gallons of the shiny liquid were shooting up the drill pipe, and the crew were struggling to put a retaining cap on to prevent a very nasty ecological disaster.

As a result of this distraction, the safety look-out had failed to see the *Squalus* sinking into the waters of the Dart a short distance away, nor had they noticed the sight of the over-excited whale. They also, initially, failed to spot that the liquid shooting up the drill pipe was not the usual black colour of unrefined oil. What they were extracting from the depths of the Dart was more of a true golden hue – maybe white gold, but not black gold at all.

After the men had finished leaping and a-hollering, and as the sounds of Mariachi music drifted slowly away down river, the rig boss was drawing breath when he noticed that the product they had just stopped spouting did look somewhat clean and refined. Not really what he was expecting, for in all his years working on rigs in the Gulf of Mexico, he had never seen such a clear, sparkling liquid come up any of his drill pipes. It rather put him in mind of the product he used to fill up his SUV at his local gas station ... it looked remarkably like ... petrol!

"Slim!" he hollered to his weight-challenged drill captain. "What the hell is this? We've hit something here, but what is it? Smells like, looks like, and tastes like ..." (he spat the product out), "damn it ... gasoline!"

The aforementioned Slim moseyed over. "Sure does, boss," he drawled. "Ain't that something! Struck gold! The purest, cleanest, clearest crude I ever did see!"

"Slim, that is the problem. It is also the most refined-looking crude oil I ever did see too. No oil comes out of the ground that colour!"

"Maybe river oil is different, boss," suggested Slim. "We ain't never drilled in a rivah before ..."

"Have you taken a stupid pill, Slim? This ain't come up from no rivah! We've done gone and hit something down thar! Get a diving team tooled up and ready. I'm going down with them."

Twenty minutes later, a team of divers, led by one very confused and worried rig boss, started down the drill pipe to investigate. As they neared the river bed, the water became more and more cloudy and oily, until they could hardly see through the murk of churned-up mud and oil. Finally, the awful truth dawned on them.

169

There was no dispute about what they had done. They had indeed struck oil. But it was obviously someone else's oil, and refined at that, for there in the gloom at the river bed a pipe came into view with their drill stuck right in it. Where the pipe came from, where it was going, at that moment they did not know. What they did know was that the pipeline was about 24 inches in diameter, a significant one, and that barrels and barrels of oil were now leaking out into the, until then, relatively clean waters of the Dart. The rig boss quickly calculated that petrol would be escaping at the rate of about one thousand barrels per day. There was a major problem, and it could become yet another monster.

Back on the surface, the rig boss and his team sprang into action to contain the problem as best they could. Heavy equipment was lowered to the river bed to detach the surface pipe from the drill bit and weld the bit to the pipeline to affect a temporary repair. Environmental agencies were contacted. Miles of floating booms were shipped to and positioned on the Dart to stem the possible tide of pollution, and Big Dirk looked on in wonderment from down-river at the sudden unexpected activity. At least he now had a cabaret of sorts to keep his mind active. Humans did do the strangest things ... And an exhausted and somewhat incendiary Captain Ayeup climbed ashore smelling strongly of petrol. He pulled out his pipe as he collapsed onto the beach at Folley's Cove, hoping to calm himself with a smoke. Though he knew it not, fortune had at last smiled on the good Captain that day, for if he had been able to light his pipe with his sodden matches (and by Jove he tried), he really would have been incensed.

The very next day, an emergency meeting of the Totnes Parish Council was convened, with Councillor Lax Sativa now ruling the roost, to discuss what could become a huge environmental problem, for an oil slick, though substantial but thankfully not the size of Wales, was heading up river towards Totnes from near Dittisham, threatening an imminent landfall in the town.

"This will become our new Totnes Monster!" cried Councillor Boti, on hearing the news. "Thank Guru we closed the river! What can we do?" The usual muttering and noises off started from the members, building in volume.

"Councillors," announced a surprisingly self-satisfied Sativa, "please be calm, everything is now under control. You will be pleased to know that a floating barrier is now encircling the oil that has escaped, and I am told that the surface of the Dart is being skimmed as we speak. The broken pipeline has been plugged, and appropriate legal action is being taken against Texmex Prospex Inc. to recover the costs of the clean-up. Why did they drill just there, you ask? Well, it appears that the company had information that at that point on the river bed was the best position to find oil, and the tests were technically correct. A robot submersible had detected an oil flow. The tests were right, there was oil there, but it was in a pipeline feeding the distribution depot for the Torquay area, and apparently no-one checked the pipeline maps. A school-boy error, for which they will pay dearly. I am told the search will go on, but the original optimism that there is oil under the Dart did come from the robot submersible's report, so there is now a probability that there really is no oil."

"But didn't we ... er ... Randco buy the river rights?" asked Boti.

"Yes, Boti, we ... they did. Perhaps the rights can

be sold back, but that is for another place," he reminded the Council. "In any case, I shall have a word ... Now," he continued, "to the matter in hand. I have here," he held up a piece of paper, "a letter of resignation from Councillor Lukes. As you know, I have been standing in as Chairman since he stormed out of the last meeting he attended, and he needs to be replaced. I would be willing to stand ... any proposers?"

"I propose you," shouted Boti.

"Seconded," said Phall quickly.

"Any objections? Passed. Thank you, ladies, gentlemen, Devotees, I shall be happy to undertake the Chairman's duties diligently. Finally, as you know, the Duke is coming to Totnes tomorrow. Is the town prepared for this Royal visit, and what programme shall we prepare for him?"

A discussion subsequently followed and the next day's festivities were planned in detail, the upshot of which was that the Devos on council democratically agreed that they would look after him right royally, welcome him to Carnal House, show him their way of life – the clear and only true way. Who knows, he could be the first royal convert. What a coup that would be!

(For the town, of course ... Meeting Ended.)

22. The Duke

The Queen was in the counting house, counting out her money – but where *was* the Duke?

Was he riding a cock horse? Was he marching to the top of the hill and marching down again?

Was he putting Humpty together again?

In a manner of speaking, yes. He was in the business of furthering peace and international understanding, and these honourable intentions were often taken to their logical conclusion with as many as possible in as many places as possible – now that the government had kindly supplied him with his diplomatic anti-SLIM kit. And diplomatic it was – neatly housed in a standard-looking thermos flask towards which no one would bat an eye, it contained a selection of rubber appliances that Guru Shami Randi had already been issuing to his staff for years, though thankfully for the Duke, not of the same make. There was, however, one additional important item – sterile blood plasma. This was housed, in consideration for the Duke's status, in a royal blue container which fitted neatly in the thermos.

Though intended for use in the royal vein, the plasma itself was not blue; that was clear, even to the Duke, but neither was it red in colour, being only a substitute for blood should the royal personage in question need an emergency transfusion in some God-forsaken corner of the globe.

Beside the plasma were housed the rubber appliances: one pair of re-useable marigold mittens and a 12-pack of once-only spermicidal condoms. In their wisdom, the government had decided to try to prevent the creation of any more royal bastards than absolutely necessary, and so the spermicidal ingredient had been added.

But the Duke had a problem, though in his case it was only a little one, so a packet of little blue pills had been generously added to his kit. The instructions said he had to put on the rubber as soon as 'it' was hard, but 'it' didn't do that often these days. He was not a big man in so many ways. His videos, his books, his magazines tickled him to the bone, but it was usually a pretty soft one, and he was worried. Thank heaven for the pills. Was he past it?

He looked hard in the mirror. No – he wasn't! Though the thinning grey hair, the seadog wrinkles around his eyes and the multitude of moles liberally scattered like sheep droppings over his face were in no way this year's spring chicken look. There was a knock at the door. He splashed on the last of his duty-free cologne, thanked God he travelled a lot, then cleared his throat. "Come!" he announced – a nice, aggressive word.

The door opened to reveal the face and person of his **PPS**, the Honourable Montague Archibald Arbruthnot, Eton and Balliol, God knows how or why, who also cleared his throat.

"Good day, sir," he said.

"Good day, Monty."

"We must be gorn soon, sir," continued his **PPS**. "The horses are fed and watered, and I am pleased to say the coach did pass its MoT test. Also, the MoD have had a butchers and insisted on plating the interior ..."

"Butchers ... plating ...?" asked the Duke.

"Yes, sir," said the brillianteened though far from brilliant Monty, "armour plating – for your protection. Also, they inserted new glass in the windows. Had to change the springs, though. Too much wait – I mean weight, sir. The wheels are greased and ready to roll, as they say, sir."

Monty Arbruthnot sounded eloquent, yet was in truth irrationally homophonic ... may I offer an example? A 'for instance'? Well, the difference between weight and wait was surprisingly obvious within his archaic speech patterns; that said, though, he would spoil it all, time and again, by using the incorrect word from a homophone pair. Thus, he himself, let alone his listener, could often not comprehend what he had just said. Nor, for that matter, could anyone else. You see?

His chin had gort into the habit of receding even faster than his noble hairline, and his many friends, amongst whom he numbered the Duke, were in the habit of wondering if the race was on. Was his chin trying to beat his hairline at the receding game? Would they meet at the back of his neck? And where would Monty be then? If they didn't get a move on, nowhere.

As they only had a short journey from his country seat at Meltdown Manor to Totnes, the scene of that day's royal visitation, the Duke had decided to drive himself there using his favoured method of travel – the coach and four. This decision had thrown his security men into utter disarray, their well-laid plans having to be suddenly redrawn. Lightweight armour plating was ordered from Chobham, armoured glass from Aldershot, and then the lot was unceremoniously stuffed into the coach – Lady Sarah-Jane. The security men now felt reasonably secure. They were aptly named.

"Come on, Monty – let's proceed." The Duke rarely went, he usually proceeded.

"After you, sir." So the two men proceeded down the corridor to the great hall and the front door of the manor. "Our ETA is noon, sir," continued Monty, "and there is a change of plans. Apparently, the chairman of the council has resigned, though there is some doubt about this, and we are to be met by someone called, er ... Lax Sativa. Odd name, don't you know. He's sort of taken over the council chair; spoke to him by telephone this morning. Promises quite a welcome. Belongs to some group connected with the submarine there's all the hush-hush flak about. Got to keep our eyes on him."

"So what is it one has to do, Monty? Eyes right for some rogue sub, what? Can't MI5 do their own cloak and dagger jobs these days? Too many Ministry of Defence cut-backs; one having to do their spying for them is a bit steep, don't you know. One's meant to stay out of politics!"

"Well, sir, the request from the chief of staff was for you to reccy their HQ – Kernel House, or somesuch. That's first stop after your grand entrance on High Street. MoD think's the sub's concealed somewhere nearby. I believe the thinking behind the request for your assistance is that no-one would suspect you of spying. As you say, non-political business royalty, what?"

"I see, Monty," said the Duke. "Good ruse. Have to give it a try then. King and country, eh?"

They had reached the coach and horses. The Duke creaked up into the driving seat and grabbed the reins in his painfully arthritic hands. Monty Arbruthnot followed into the passenger seat. He thanked God the weather was warm. Then, flanked by motorcycle outriders and followed by one of the family Rolls, crammed to the gunnels with security men, the Duke smacked the reins, whipped the horses, adjusted his trousers and they were orf.

Two days later, Lady Sarah-Jane once again underwent major surgery when she was stripped of her newly installed metal plating, its efficacy having been called into question by some recently graduated clever sausage from MI5. He'd noticed the relevant requisition on his in-tray and had pointed out to his superiors that Dick's Sheetmetals of Chobham did not supply armour plating of quite the same quality as Cobham armour from the MoD quartermaster's stores at Aldershot. Luckily, that day no-one decided to take any pot shots at the Duke.

A clerk from the MoD stores, who appeared to be related by marriage to this Dick, was, however, almost introduced to his very own firing squad when it transpired that all the Chieftain tanks in the British Army had also received their armour from the very self-same Dick. And to cap a bad day for the Ministry of Defence, a vast hangar in Aldershot, which should have been emptied years before, was later discovered still bursting at the seams with the real Cobham armour. But I think perhaps we are deviating a little ...

The centre of Totnes was heaving. Hordes of white-clad people crammed the streets that Saturday morn, spilling out of the pubs, restaurants and cafés. Flags were waved, bunting was out, the sun was shining.

Councillor Lax Sativa waited on the steps of the Town Hall with his lackeys from council, but Colonel North, Mrs Simpson, Captain Ayeup, and even the men from Dart Board Hire were not with him. They had formed their own small group a short distance away and were patriotically holding their Union Flags in their hands. To an uncultured observer, most of the rest of town appeared at first glance to be surrendering, for all and sundry held white flags, pure white save for the small four-fingered Devo motif in one corner.

Even the sailors from the *Obtuse* were there, having still not returned to their ship. They had heard of

178

the Duke's visitation and, as he and the Duke's family had hailed from their neck of the woods, the men had tarried in Totnes to welcome him. Spiro had reluctantly allowed them one more hour of freedom before locking them up in the *Obtuse*. Surreptitiously, they had taken a Greek flag from it with which to show their patriotism.

And this was the scene that awaited the Duke. Councillor Fred Lukes, though, did not, having been removed the previous day as chairman of the council by the extraordinary meeting convened by Lax for a purpose partly but not totally unconnected with the self-same removal. The Devos now had the town in their grasp; most of the real locals were staying indoors and would be watching the festivities on TV, as would the former chairman. Fred Lukes was not a happy man.

The right royal hand hauled on the reins again to slow down to a trot. The left one replaced the whip in its holder and started waving the royal wave at the increasing numbers lining the route into town. It had been an easy half-hour drive for the Duke, not too difficult for Monty Arbruthnot, hard for the horses pulling a lot of extra weight, and extremely manure-splattered for the security men following in the Rolls, for every few minutes at least one of the horses relieved itself at speed, the relief product being temporarily attached to the large rear wheels of the coach they were pulling, to then be hurled at a great velocity towards the front of the previously gleaming Rolls. On arrival in Totnes, the windscreen was totally covered with nitrogenous fibrous material, save for a *'window'* in the centre, kept clear with vigorous applications of water and wiper.

Not only were the security men now very smelly, they had also received the news about the Cobham armour over the airwaves and had managed to halt the

Duke's progress just before Totnes itself. The Duke, when told he would have to travel into town in the much-safer Rolls, had taken one look at the manure-splattered car and had refused to travel in something so akin, in his own words, to a shit heap. He had also pointed out that, as he was outside whilst driving the coach, whether the armour plating was from Cobham or Chobham would not matter a jot or tittle, a fact which till that moment had failed to materialize in the minds of the men from the ministry.

The Duke remounted his coach and was able to ride into town in his intended grand style. He had been in Totnes once only, years before with his wife, and he was sure that then the townspeople had not all been in white. And why were they nearly all waving white flags – what on earth had happened? Monty shouted something in his ear about Randi; the Duke missed the exact meaning due to the commotion all about, but anyway shifted a bit away from Monty. Keeping one eye on him, he carefully steered the coach through the thronged narrow streets and brought it to a halt by the steps of the town hall, peeled his right hand from the reins and painfully clambered down.

To his left were a normal-looking small group of people with normal clothes, a normal flag and normal faces; to the right appeared a group of, well – though pale through lack of sun, they had to be Greek. There was the blue and white flag, and, yes, he distinctly heard them shout 'Yassou Principopoulo!'

And then everywhere else all around were people in white, waving white flags. An explanation was needed. Monty also had a look of flumoxedness about him, though this was fairly normal. A man in a white sheet complete with a bird dropping between his eyes came towards the Duke and shook his hand. Behind

180

him were a group of similar-looking people, also in white. What on earth was going on? Had he gone to Heaven? Was he off his royal rocker? The apparition, one Councillor Lax Sativa, then spoke.

"Your Royal Highness, on behalf of the town and people of Totnes, the first Devoconscious town in England, I wish you a warm and hearty welcome. We have planned for Your Highness a quick drive through the town, then a visit to Carnal House, our headquarters in the West Country ..."

At least the man was suitably humble, thought the Duke, but what was all this Devoconscious stuff? And pale Greeks in midsummer – but, of course, the submarine crew! So, it *was* near here! Now he would be heading for Palm Kernal House – whatever it was called. The plot thickened.

"... and so, Your Royal Highness, we ask you to accompany us to Carnal House to meet its staff and our beloved leader, Guru Shami Randi. Please follow me." Lax stuffed his prepared speech into the folds of his white sheet and waved a hand in the direction he wished the Duke to go. To a multitude of cheers and much flag-waving, the Duke, Monty and the security men, near whom understandably no-one would go, followed Lax towards a line of clean, shining white Rolls Royces.

In Carnal House, MAP was arranging her very own special welcome for the Duke. His capacity for indulging himself was known the length and breadth of the land, and she was preparing a special session for his good self. One hour of relaxation in a private room had been requested by his staff and that was just what he was about to receive – and he would be truly thankful. As she laid out the rubber appliances of various shapes and sizes, she planned the order of the Duke's relaxation. First, she would allow him ten minutes alone to wind

181

down from his journey; then fifteen minutes in the private whirlpool, during which time she would personally offer any assistance he required; and finally she would massage his tired old frame from top to toe. Of course, if he had any 'body' problems, she would be happy in her capacity as sex therapist to try to sort them out. She was just doing him a service, and from recent pictures she had seen of the old royal, what was required was a pretty major one.

Whilst MAP was inside Carnal House preparing her own welcome, Guru Shami Randi, who had for the last few days been locked trembling in his room, afraid to emerge for fear of somehow meeting his old adversary, Big Dirk, was tentatively standing on its steps with the redoubtable though unimpressed Halitosis Kamakis. They were surrounded by Devos, all awaiting the arrival of the Duke.

"Hal," Randi announced with a tremor in his trebly voice. He really was very confused with the proximity of Big Dirk. "The vale will get me, he vill, I know it. What can I do, ummmm?"

"What will get you, Shami – the veil?" Hal appeared to have misheard him.

"The vale, Hal – Big Dirk. I know somehow he vill. Vhat can I do?" whined the little man from Nepal.

"Guru, have no fear, Hal is here," said Hal, who rubbed his own broken arm. "If you stay in your room, quietly, watch your videos, listen to the tapes of your Satsangs, everything will be fine. I promise. Your Devos will all look after you, you know that."

"Thank you, Hal, I will not forget this."

"Er ... Guru," replied Hal (this was the moment), "when can we start to explore for the oil? We have been here too long already. We will be discovered before the oil is! When can we start?" But just as Halitosis thought he was at last getting somewhere, the first car of the Duke's motorcade entered the driveway, and the Guru was once more distracted.

Soon the trail of Rolls stretched from the mansion's steps up to the main road. Randi stepped forward as four burly men, all wearing earpieces, leapt from the third car and ran to the second, in which the Duke sat. One man opened the door, two grabbed the elderly royal and unceremoniously yanked him out, and the fourth dusted him down while adjusting that day's royal clothing – a rather outdated, overcut suit with enormous lapels.

Unsteadily, the Duke gazed around, noticing an obviously important sub-continental man, seemingly similar in import to his own royal personage, coming towards him with arms outstretched. He glanced at Monty Arbruthnot, who was at that moment emerging with difficulty from the lead car. Monty gave a little nod of ascent or permission, depending on one's point of view, and so the Duke stepped forward to shake the man's hand. Another damn welcome speech, he thought.

The Guru did welcome the Duke, amazed everyone by making a sort of curtsy, the Devos cheered, the Duke smiled, gave a little wave, and within minutes all were thankfully inside the cool great hall of Carnal House.

After a few minutes of conversation had been attempted, the Duke was shown to the room MAP had prepared for him, but not before the famous four from MI5 had undertaken a full security sweep. He was then, though not quite ready to meet his maker, left to rest in peace. Monty Arbruthnot and Councillor Lax Sativa were shown to an office where they were able to discuss the day's proposed programme. Guru Shami Randi returned to his own room to watch himself on video, and, as would a flamenco dancer, basically to look up his own rear end. And the famous four minders smoked cigarettes, talked cricket, all the while like expectant fathers pacing up and down outside the room where the Duke was horizontal on that oh so convenient couch.

The Duke was now thinking and pondering. He was in a room with couch, whirlpool bath and a dresser covered in various bits of rubber. He lowered himself off the couch, walked over to the dresser, picked up one of the gloves, looked at it quizzically and tried to stretch it over his hand. Dear God, his arthritis was painful. He tried again, but his hand wouldn't go. He pulled open a drawer to see hundreds of packs of twelves staring up at him. He slammed the drawer shut, thinking he had had enough trouble getting on the rubber gloves, never mind those things. It all reminded him of his new SLIM kit. Maybe there was some truth in what he had heard – that it might be the new Black Death. He sincerely hoped not. These days he always had short rests after a journey, but none of the rooms in the last few years had ever been quite so peculiar. He lay down on the couch, closed his eyes, and drifted off to sleep.

Some time later, there was a noise at the door and he awoke with a start, right in the middle of a dream about Totnes monsters, submarines and Greeks. Of course – those Greek sailors – he had forgotten to tell the security men! As he was about to get up to find them and reveal all, a large hand steadied him, gently but firmly pushing him back onto the couch.

He looked up.

Aarghhh! So Totnes had two monsters ...

184

Ma Anna Poona's laying on of hands had done the Duke the world of good. Even his arthritis seemed better. The one hour's administrations allowed in his schedule had expanded into a few, and his security men were tearing their hair out, pacing up and down faster and faster, smoking almost a year's production of Virginia tobacco; for, each time they knocked on the hospitality suite's door, all they heard in return were moans, groans and a short and extremely rude admonition to go forth and multiply – or words to that effect.

Monty Arbruthnot, whose chin and hairline were once again uniting in sympathy, both having to be attached to someone so totally ineffectual, did try to communicate with the Duke, but he failed, his superior's admonitions becoming fierce commands that turned Monty's knees to jelly. When the Duke finally did emerge, he was glowing from head to foot. His hair seemed fuller and less grey, he was taller and was smiling from one ear to the other.

"OK, chaps," he said, as if satiated – which, of course, he was, "where to next?" Monty jumped forward.

"Well, sir," he said nervously, "we are due in Dartmouth about now. We had hoped you could tour the grounds here and see more of the work that goes on, but I fear we must leave now. What a pity. Well, we could pop in on the way back to the Manor if you wish ...?" The Duke's eyes lit up.

After he had left, MAP thought back to her session with him. Initially, she had fought the idea of doing it, but Randi had told her she had to, and that was that. Now it was all over she was surprised. The Duke and she had really hit it off, something she had not expected. In fact, she was sorry to see him go, and hoped he would be back again very soon. Sadly, fickle female that she was, she was now forgetting all about her cetacean friend Dirk, and was completely ignoring the good times she had had with her Guru.

At first, the Duke had had a little problem. She had gone to work on it with the professionalism the problem deserved, and slowly but surely it had become bigger ... thus (do you get the drift?) making the actual problem diminish in size, until it was a problem no more. He had left a happier man, she was satisfied she had done her job, and there was no doubt that he too had left fulfilled. But why did she want him to come back so very much? That was not like her at all; it was just a job ...

Some days later, she was collecting flowers for the next Satsang from Carnal House's lush borders, when unexpectedly a loud commotion startled her, the gravel on the driveway crunched wildly and a team of horses charged up at full pelt. MAP swivelled round, snapped her secateurs shut, almost removing two fingers in the process. First, she saw an alarming equestrian sight of considerable stature, four horses rearing up almost out of control, then a coach with a highly important person in charge, if it could be called that: some said the nearest the driver would ever get to a rein of his own.

The Duke had returned.

A huge, happy smile beamed across MAP's face, and she screeched with delight. She ran up towards the coach, her robes billowing backwards as she ran. Though she was smiling and happy, her actions were starting to worry the four horses pulling the Duke and his carriage, for the flowing white robes, the cascade of white hair and the accompanying war cry were sufficient to frighten even an experienced London Police horse. The blinkered horses not surprisingly looked straight ahead at MAP. She virtually flew down the gravel, which protested noisily at her every step. Her arms were wide open in greeting. The Duke looked down at her in wonderment, second thoughts about the day's jaunt entering his port- and brandy-scrambled brain.

The horses continued up the drive, first one, then another pulling, jerking at the reins. He held on for dear life, pulled back to slow them down, pulled back harder. MAP charged on. The Duke jerked the reins back, the horses responded by doing the same. He tried harder and harder to stop the coach from crashing onwards into MAP, for he knew not what damage she could cause it. He pulled back once again with all his aged might and in doing so forced the front of the horses up on their hind legs as if in a circus, front legs and hoofs flaying at the air. The coach stopped. MAP too stopped running. She looked up at the horses, who continued boxing the air. They sensed her presence, for as she reached up to grab them near their bits, they quickly calmed down, gently returning to earth on either side of the large white tent, totally under the control of the great female.

The Duke, though he knew it was she who had frightened the horses in the first place, was thankful that she had managed to calm them. But he could not help thinking that she was the only person he was ever likely to meet who could not only work in a circus, but could wear one.

"Now, that's quite enough of THAT!" she said, slapping each of the horses fiercely across the mouth with the back of her hand. The horses cowered. She looked up at the slumped figure of the Duke. "You alright?" she asked gruffly. "Don't you know how to drive these things? Good Lord, you nearly ran me over. Come on." She held her hands up. "Let me lift you down; looks like you need another session." The Duke's limp body touched the ground. He saw the woman who had somehow managed to frighten his imperturbable team of horses, thought of explaining what had happened, looked again, and then refrained.

MAP straightway carried him bodily from the coach to her own private room and once more set about relaxing and soothing the aching brow, and other assorted bits, of the old royal. On completion of her pleasurable task, she let out a stupendous gasp of pleasure and rolled back onto her side of the vast expanse of mattress she called a bed. After a moment's rest, she spoke.

"Well, we've certainly cured your little problem, haven't we?" she said, as she tickled him playfully. He twitched nobly, reacting to her touch. She *would* be gentle. "I feel like a new woman," she whispered lovingly. The Duke realized he had once again had one. "You can stay the night at Carnal House ...," she sighed, "will you?"

"One can't ...," he hesitated, bashfully.

"Why? Why not?" MAP looked crestfallen.

"... One can't think of anything nicer."

23. Three Ministers Of State

In an interview suite at Heathrow airport in London, another pair of lovers was talking, this time to a Detective Inspector of the Metropolitan Police. A policewoman was also in attendance, to record and witness the interview. Swami Tikka Masala, with his Nurse next to him, was trying to explain how he had come to be in possession of a very pornographic video tape, found in his luggage as they went through security. They were booked on a flight out that evening to Zurich, having sold the Rolls Royce the day before for a tidy sum, and had hoped to get away from it all to spend some of the money, and some time, together. But it looked like their plans might be scuppered and they might miss their plane.

"So, you 'forgot' you had this tape, did you, son?" said the Detective. "And you were going to hand it in, were you? Well, well ... I think you may be in big trouble, both of you ... possession of pornographic material intended to deprave, conspiracy to transport such material across state borders ... I could go on ..."

A sweating Tikka tried to explain what had happened. "... And I just threw it in my bag and left," he said. "We had to get away, both of us; the Guru is obviously evil and we had had enough ..."

"Now," said the Detective, "I'll make a deal with you. No promises, mind, but I will do my best to get you on your flight. Tell me all you know about this Guru – who is already on our radar – so no lies – and I'll see what I can do. Now, what do you know ...?"

Tikka started talking, and, with Nurse's help, after half an hour had given the Detective just what he wanted to hear.

"So," he said, " 'Shooby, Dooby, Wah', eh? That's quite some story. And you never suspected anything? Anyway, that's not important right now. What you have said stacks up with what we in Operation Figleaf already know, so I believe you. I shall keep this tape, which is useful evidence, and shall ignore your possible misdemeanours, though they will be kept on file. I'll give you a receipt for the tape, which I am sure you don't want, and you are both free to go. Be more careful next time, son. Here are your passports back. You've had a lucky escape. Interview over, recording stopping now ... Oh, and don't you think it's time to wipe off the bird dropping and wear some normal clothes? Eh, son? And change your name back ... you sound like something you get on a curry night in a pub!"

* * * * * * * * *

Two files marked 'Top Secret – For Your Eyes Only' stared up at the Right Honourable Winstanley Rutherford, KGB, Secretary for Home Affairs in her Britannic Majesty's Government. They contained reports about two subjects, apparently unrelated, but which had a geographical factor in common. The first report concerned something about which the Rt. Hon. 'Stodge' Rutherford was indeed very concerned.

It was the dreaded SLIM.

For the past two years the government Chief Medical Officer had been warning about the explosive exponential power of the disease, and now the first nationwide survey had been undertaken, the results of which were sitting on the Home Secretary's desk.

Picking up the report, he started reading its summary. The statistics were truly alarming, and it even implied that SLIM would reach the proportions of the

Black Death within five years, unless a huge advertising and educational programme was instigated nationwide. With the cutbacks ordered by his austerity minded Prime Minister, Stodge Rutherford did not see from where the money would come. By the end of the summary, though, he knew that he would have to find it – he was sure of that – even if it meant taking funds from the new national enterprise scheme which paid allowances to a million of the unemployed supposedly setting up new businesses and who came off the register of the out of work, something which considerably lowered the unemployment figures. The Employment Secretary wouldn't like that; he wouldn't like it at all.

He turned to the statistics section. The diagrams, graphs and maps were beautifully turned out, as usual, the final page telling the whole story in one fell swoop.

It was a map of the Kingdom, for once United under a deadly threat, with areas coloured in to represent percentages of people found to have antibodies to the virus. This apparently was the only way one could tell who would eventually contract 'full-blown' SLIM, as they called it.

Two areas stood out – the bright red over the whole of London was expected, but for some reason there was another blob in Devon. The centre of this random concentration was over the town of Totnes. Stodge wondered why. The only other places remotely coming up to the London percentages were the other big cities. Why Totnes, such a backwater?

He picked up the other report. It too concerned Totnes. Stodge assumed it must be something about the Monster that had been in all the papers. But no, it was about the local town council. Apparently, it had been taken over by some religious group, who all wore white, and whose leader was a Guru from the subcontinent.

What was going on? Two weeks before, Stodge had not even heard of Totnes. Now one thing after another! The intercom on his desk sprang to life.

"The Foreign Secretary is on the line, sir," said his PA. "Sounds a bit tipsy to me, sir. Apparently, it's very important he talks with you." Why on earth was old Tendon-Smythe ringing, thought Stodge; their departments were totally separate, and he hadn't heard from him for years.

"Put the old codger on, Jean," he said, and picked up the telephone. "Hullo ... Archie? To what do I owe the pleasure? How the hell are you, eh?"

"The aches and pains of old age are sometimes a burden, Stodge, but the Lord moves in mysterious ways, his wonders to ..." Onwards Tendon-Smythe slurred. Another two men who had been together at school, the Home Secretary having been the slightly older man's personal fag, and the loyalty built up then had evidently survived the decades. Stodge could almost smell whisky coming down the line.

"Archie," said Rutherford, "we must be quick. I have a report to write, recommendations to make. To what do I owe the pleasure?"

"Well, Stodge, Operation Figleaf ... you know, the Met's pet gripe of the moment ... older men usually, often foreign johnnies, sullying our young maidens ... that sort of thing ..."

"Please get to the point, Archie," said Stodge Rutherford.

"Yes, yes, just getting there ... you know when we met at the last Old Wallopian do – you remember you said to ring you if I ever needed anything – well, I don't really need anything, but it's about this man ..."

"What man is that?" interrupted a long-suffering Stodge.

"I'm coming to it; this man, that, er – has just come to my notice ... well, a video tape has come into my possession, kindly donated by the Met, of a foreign national, performing an unnatural act ..."

"Please come to the point, Archie ..."

"Precisely, Stodge – an unnatural act committed on the body of a young, innocent girl by this evil man. A man so evil, insidiously so, that I feel you ought to do something about banning him from the country."

"But you know," said the patient Home Secretary, "we can't just ban or expel a British National, now can we, Archie?"

"That's just it, Stodge, old boy." Tendon-Smythe was warming to the challenge. "As I said, he's not one of us. Operation Figleaf! That's why I have the tape. A colonial chappie, don't you know. Not British, so you can chuck him out; if, of course, you feel like it."

"Got to have bloody good grounds, excuse the French ..."

"Naw ... the fellow in it isn't from France either, he's ... Nepalese!"

Stodge Rutherford's ears pricked up. "You mean this fellow in the video is from Nepal?" he said.

"Exactly," continued the Foreign Secretary, "and with the evidence I have here, which amounts to pornographic, and when I say graphic I mean Graphic, evidence that the man is deranged, totally, and yet is in a very responsible position in charge of thousands of young people in this country, let alone abroad, you could get rid of him in no time at all. It's a long story, but it's true."

"Can't be having that, Archie," said the now interested Minister. "So what's his name?"

"Odd fellow, odd name – typical of him ... hope I can get it right. Something like Rancid, er ... that's it,

194

thinks he's God as well, and, believe it or not, the Master of the Vagina, whatever that is ..."

"Yes, but what's his name?" A certain tenseness had entered the Home Secretary's voice; could it be ...

"His name ... oh ... Guru Shami Randi – got it. Ever heard of him ..?"

Stodge Rutherford took a deep and meaningful breath. "Matter of fact, old boy," he said, "I've just been reading up on him. Where can we meet? We need to talk."

"Oh, come to the bar now, Stodge," said the Foreign Secretary. "I'm just having one or two with Na-Na from Defence. Why don't you join us? Eh!?"

And so three men who usually had surprisingly little in common, save the urge to become Prime Minister, would that day meet in the members' bar of the Commons. It was the place where stories were often swopped, embellished, made up, and often leaked. As Stodge Rutherford walked with speed towards it, three words went round and round inside his head: *Totnes ... SLIM ... Guru ...?*

A few minutes later, Her Majesty's Home Secretary was in deep conversation with the Rt. Hon. Archibald 'Achilles' Tendon-Smythe and the equally Honourable, but rarely right, Jason 'Na-Na' St. John Ambrigade, respectively the same Monarch's Foreign and Defence Secretaries, men not usually open to idle interdepartmental chit-chat.

"So, Archie," said the Home to the Foreign Secretary, "how long have you been after this Nepalese blighter?"

Tendon-Smythe knocked back his fifth large whisky of the day. "About three years, actually. Nasty piece of work. One of his top men fell out with him and gave us the tape. Foreign Office'll get him."

The Defence Secretary interrupted. "Sorry, Archie, but we're after him too. Got the Navy searching for his hush-hush submarine right now. Fleet up the Dart. Not bad, eh? Defence will get him ... no fear."

Stodge Rutherford, being a slightly more astute and honourable man than the other two, possibly more sober at that moment, then suggested something that sounded to his two listeners almost heretical. "If we all got together on this one," he said to a couple of gaping mouths, "united front, etc., don't you think we'd have more chance of actually getting rid of the man?" The other two looked at each other, then at Rutherford, in disbelief.

"Work together!?" they said, for once in unison.

"Yes," said the Home Secretary, "work together. I know this goes agin normal practice, but who knows. In the war we had a government of national unity, opposing parties in a coalition, so maybe with someone like this, someone so totally un-British, someone whom we all want to 'liquidate', we ought to have some interdepartmental unity. The electorate would expect it of us. Why no-one's thought of it before, I just don't know."

"Neither do I," said Archie.

"Nor I," said Na-Na. "Goes against the grain somewhat, don't you know. Have to think about this. You mean actually working together on something?"

"Liaising?"

"Exchanging information?"

"Wouldn't work," announced Archie. "Too dodgy. Defence might know more than Foreign or Home, or vice versa; might have to give too much away, departmental secrets, etc. I don't like it. Same again, gents?" They moved to lean on the bar. Rutherford spoke.

196

"May I suggest," he persisted, "that we give it a try? We really have nothing to lose, and everything to gain. We must, from everything we've said today, at least make this person an undesirable alien, and you know how hard it is to do that these days. Appeals could go on for years. We need a united front. If we work separately, we might end up embroiled in some long-winded legal process, department fighting department. Be as bad as getting a motorway through. Can't afford that. What do you think?"

"Well ... possibly. Just this once. As you say, Stodge, we do all agree on the result we want. What say you, Archie?" Defence had sprung to Foreign's defence.

"Very well, but only on this," agreed the Foreign Secretary. "After it's over, we revert to the status quo. Yes?" He was very wary of the scheme, having seen alliances like that before, and he was sure that they never worked. Too many cooks ... but his word was his bond.

And so it was that Her Majesty's departments of Home, Foreign and Defence affairs for once fought together for a common aim, an aim decided over many whiskies and sodas, an aim that concerned but one man, a man about whom at that moment the Good Lord above was also beginning to learn, and about whom even He was none too pleased.

* * * * * * * * *

The following day dawned once more and Stodge Rutherford sat at his desk, inspecting the display that the man from the Totnes Weights and Measures Office had so neatly laid out on it. Row after row of rubber appliances looked back at him. He reached out and gingerly touched one, then another.

197

"That one," said the W & M Inspector, "is known as the ... er, Chambermaid's Comforter; and that one – the Duchess' Delight. Note the small bumps and ridges all down the side of the shaft, and indeed on the tip. It retails at 85p, or £8.50 for a pack of twelve. Totnes now has more of these appliance vending machines than cigarette and chocolate ones put together. Of course, they are also freely available in newsagents, tobacconists and sweet shops, in an attempt to sell to the younger market, besides the traditional barber shop outlets ..."

Rutherford looked at the man talking, who seemed to know plenty about this subject. He was not too tall, not too short. He had brownish hair, receding at the temples and generally thinning. He wore a cheap brown suit, stained in various places, and smelt of a mixture of cigarettes, sweat, cheap aftershave lotion, and hair restorer.

"And you say," said the Home Secretary, with handkerchief hovering over nose, "that all these ... things ... have a common fault?"

"Yes, indeed they do," replied the inspector. "Each and every one has a minute pin hole in the teat at the end."

"Good Lord!" said Stodge. "Holy condoms!"

The Inspector held one up limply to Stodge's face for his edification. As it accidentally flapped against the Home Secretary's nose, the Inspector spoke. "There," he said, "right at the end. Now, usually with this type of appliance we receive many complaints of splitting and rupturing; often this occurs at just the wrong moment, if you get my drift." The man sniggered slightly, a small drop of fluid appearing at the tip of his nose, which he wiped away with the back of his hand. "We were surprised," he continued, "that we received no complaints like that at all with this make, so we randomly took samples from various outlets, and all the results were 100% consistent. Every single one has had a tiny hole in the tip."

"Why on Earth would they, the makers presumably, do this? I mean to say, someone's put a prick in all of them, but at the wrong end, so to speak," said Stodge in amazement.

"We are now sure," replied the humourless Inspector authoritatively, "beyond all reasonable doubt, that this was to make the appliances *appear* 100% effective. So often men just do not know how to wear these things; they forget to squeeze the air out of the teat and then the damn thing ruptures. Now these won't, of course not, because the pressure created as a result of the climax of the ... er ... sexual act is dissipated. Steam, so to speak, is let off. Consequently, these particular appliances are very popular, because they are known not to rupture. Further, they are very nearly the only ones available in Totnes – some contract the town council entered into with the makers to purchase them in bulk at an advantageous price."

"Yes," said Stodge, "I wrote to the council to tell them they had to do something about Totnes' particular, and peculiar, problem. Glad to see they tried."

"But, sir," said the Inspector, "as you well know, this pin hole makes every single one worse than dangerous, for the participating couple think they are safe, when they are not at all. They must be taken off the market immediately before Totnes has a huge population explosion."

"It's not the population explosion I'm worried about," said Stodge. "You see, the reason they are so widely on sale in Totnes is because of the SLIM epidemic there. You probably don't know about it;

we've tried to keep it hush hush so as not to scare the hoi poloi. Please keep it under your hat. Oh and thank you for coming up to London so quickly. This is bad – if what you say is true, the size of the epidemic could make it totally unmanageable."

"From a Weights and Measures point of view," continued the Inspector, not fully comprehending the import of the Home Secretary's statement, "I think we have a good case for prosecution. You see, the maker's whole advertising campaign, apparently funded by the council, concerns the reliability of the appliances – that they do not split. Here's one of the advertisements." The Inspector handed Rutherford a poster.

Stodge read the copy. What had the country come to when posters like this were freely to be seen on the highways and byways of the land? He was about to hand back the poster when he noticed the maker's name in small print at the foot of the page. One word ominously stuck in his head ... Randi. "This Randi Rubber Co. – what do you know about them?" he asked of the Inspector.

"Registered," the man replied, swiftly looking at his notes, "at a, er ... Carnal House, Totnes. One main shareholder, a Guru Shami Randi – an Indian gent, I believe. Keeps very much to himself. Directors – the above, a Ma Anna Poona, a Swami Tika Mas... er, no, he's just been voted off, looks like a bit of a shake-up's been going on, and a Premi Lax Sativa. If we can prove that the pin holes are manufactured after the rubber is moulded, which I am sure we can, and that they are put there deliberately to ensure that they never split, then we're home and dry."

"Did you say Lax Sativa?" The Home Secretary was certainly not happy. "Yes, Lax ... that's funny, the new chairman of the council is called that," replied the

Inspector.

"I know," said Stodge, "not funny at all ..."

He immediately ordered warrants to be issued for the arrest of the directors of the Randi Rubber Co. He then arranged to meet with St. John Ambrigade from Defence over lunch, the intention being to discuss overall strategy relating to the Totnes problem, or 'Monster', as Ambrigade kept calling it. But so good was the menu of line-caught smoked salmon, followed by Angus fillet steak (rare), washed down by a bottle of Chablis '83 and Margaux '68 respectively, that no relevant discussion took place. Straight after their lunch, at around four o'clock in the afternoon, the two Ministers finally got round to the purpose of their meeting.

"Got totally out of hand now, hasn't it, Stodge," said Ambrigade. "Place is run by a religious nut, it's riddled with the deadliest disease since the Black Death, the Navy's looking for a submarine with stolen top secret NATO property on board that has somehow managed to evade capture, there is allegedly a monster on the loose in the river, and the common factor of the whole affair, this Guru chappie, is missing presumed hiding. Maybe you should bring back hanging. Wouldn't have been good enough for the likes of him. Totnes," he continued, somewhat stating the obvious, "is certainly taking up plenty of time at the moment."

"As far as I'm concerned," continued Ambrigade, "the only thing to do is put the bloody place under a quarantine order and get rid of the town council – that's your side of it. My side would be to provide enough men to surround the town, cutting all the roads, and increase the naval presence up the Dart to finally nab the rogue sub. That should get this monster under control, or at least start to. What say you, old boy?"

"Sounds to me," said Rutherford, "that you're talking about an International Arrest Warrant for the Guru chappie, and declaring a State of Emergency or designating Totnes a Disaster Area."

"Something like that. What d'you think?"

"I think," said Stodge after a moment's thought, "I'll declare it a Disaster Area, then we can get the EU grant. A simple State of Emergency is considered more of a political problem and we'd get nothing. So ... Disaster Area it is. Agreed, Na-Na?"

"Agreed, Stodge."

The two men knocked back the last dregs of the 1948 Otard still left in their massive brandy glasses, stood up, at the second try actually remaining standing, and said their adieus. They then unsteadily wended their way back to their respective offices for a short, but absolutely vital, nap.

Stodge Rutherford awoke slightly earlier than his counterpart in Defence, at around seven o'clock, and tried to start enacting the various instruments needed to turn Totnes into an official Disaster Area, at the same time drawing up the quarantine regulations. Realizing his mental processes had been somewhat impaired by an over-generous luncheon, he left the job to his long-suffering civil servants, and went home.

Jason St. John Ambrigade had slightly more luck, in that he simply had to pick up the 'phone twice and issue two coded orders, one to the Chief of General Staff and one to the First Sea Lord, though these two high officers of Her Majesty did have some difficulty deciphering the codes, due to a number of eminently discountable and totally irrelevant hics and hups not mentioned anywhere in the cypher books.

By morning, as a result of this one lunch in the House of Commons dining room, Totnes was about to be governed directly from London, for officially Totnes and District Council would be no more.

The area would be under the strictest possible quarantine regulations, and the good citizens of Totnes were surprised to wake up the next day to the sound of tanks and armoured personnel carriers rumbling through their narrow streets, and to the sound of armed soldiers in full combat gear walking back to back, or lurking in shady doorways.

The Senior Service, too, was of course involved in the same containment exercise. By now, virtually a third of the British Royal Navy was steaming – as were its officers – at the very idea that the *Obtuse* was continuing to evade their blockade.

And that same evening, naval reinforcements were ordered to head for the mouth of the Dart in the hope of finally flushing it out and apprehending the submarine.

24. The Lord Above

The next morning in his vicarage, John Priestley woke early, a sweet dream about Mrs Jenkins and her broom being interrupted by the noise of the arrival of the daily newspaper coming through the vicarage letterbox. He was still exhausted; had been for days, weeks. Something was wrong – the exorcism *should* have released the evil spirit, and he felt sure it had not. He painfully extracted himself from his bed and went downstairs to pick up the paper. So – a whale had been seen near the river bank. Of course ... that must have been his monster! So it had *not* been his Omen. Oh, Dear Lord – the Exorcism! He read further ... there was yet another article about the Guru and his Devotees. How tiresome!

Suddenly, the tired Vicar realized the enormity of what he had done. He had exorcised something – a whale – that was not an evil spirit at all! It was the Guru on whom he should have been working his spells. He *must* make it up with the Good Lord Above. Quickly, he picked up the telephone, and once more dialled the Bishop's number. This time the call was answered by an answering device, a thing which invariably flummoxed the elderly, old-fashioned cleric.

"Good day," said the professionally recorded voice, a Gregorian chant mixed dolefully into the background. "You are connected with His Grace the Bishop's Palace telephone answering service. His Grace is otherwise engaged at this time, and would be pleased to reply to your call personally on his return, if you would be so good as to leave a telephone number where he may contact you. Please do so after the following tone. God bless you. Beeeeeee."

Though Priestley hated answering machines, a devils creation, he said, even he admitted that anything was better than talking to the deaf Verger, a man whose mental processes often made his own processes equally so.

"Hullo," said the Vicar into his mouthpiece, "Priestley here, Crumbleigh parish, Totnes. Re ... er ... previous exorcism. Evil spirit was not present, adjurations misplaced. Object of exorcism not monster as first thought, but ... um ... a large whale. Evil spirit in fact incarnate in man now resident here. Imperative exorcised forthwith. If no reply from Your Grace by early evening, will assume acceptance, and will proceed with the aforementioned exorcism." As the day was fine, he carelessly added, assuming the Bishop to be once again striding golf links somewhere, "and I hope the result of the match went Your Grace's way. Good day." The match, for Priestley was correct concerning the Bishop's whereabouts, had not in fact gone his way, and he had lost a three-figure sum in the process.

On his return to his Palace and his new answering device, the Bishop was in no mood to receive the sort of message Priestley had just left. So now, he thought, the senile idiot was asking for another exorcism. No-one else had requested even one in thirty years. As he listened to Priestley's message, he grabbed the telephone to talk to him and dissuade the man from these ancient holy rites – rites which, in the Bishop's opinion, had more holes in them than Gruyère cheese, and which he would much have liked to consign to his new shredding machine. But, unlike the Bishop, who appeared to spend more time with electronic business aides than with religion, the Vicar did not have an answering machine, nor a shredder, and was not in the vicarage. The telephone call went unanswered.

John Priestley had not bothered to wait, assuming that the Bishop would be out all day, and was in his disintegrating church, bathed in a ghastly, ghostly green light, alone, arms outstretched, head thrown back, wildly adjuring to the Lord. The Vicar was exhausted. It seemed as though he had been praying, chanting, adjuring and genuflecting for hours. His ancient frame was wearing out, he knew it. If he could just get through this exorcism, he would be a happy man. The Lord was listening, he could tell. He could feel it in those ancient bones.

And he was right: the Lord Above was hearing him, and might even hear him out, if HE didn't get too bored. HE was good like that, was the Lord Above; but HE knew when something was wrong. HE hadn't created the world, the solar system, the galaxy *and* the rest of the bloody universe just for this little twerp to be allowed to bother HIM each and every time it thought something was wrong.

Priestley had nearly got it right this time; he was much nearer than last, but he was still off the mark. The man he was trying to exorcise was not worth the time he was spending on him, though the Lord magnanimously understood the human logic involved. After all, HE had invented it.

Of course, it wasn't the Whale that he should have exorcised, but it certainly wasn't the Guru (who was in the great scheme of things as insignificant as the idiot Vicar himself) that was the evil spirit that needed annihilating. Once again, he was exorcising the wrong thing. The Lord was getting just a bit bored with the wailing and adjuring coming from the Vicar. Enough was indeed enough. So Priestley was bothered about the collapsing roof on the church that the Guru wanted to get his hands on. Rubbish! HE would show him

206

collapsing!

Priestley sensed something was wrong. He felt it go cold and heard a wind get up outside the church. Rain started suddenly smashing against the old stained-glass windows. There was thunder, he saw flashes of lightning. A storm had started from nowhere. It was coming nearer, he could tell. Priestley started to feel ill, and sank to his knees, his arms held out to the heavens, begging for the forgiveness of the Lord, who he knew was listening. What had gone wrong? Everything had seemed perfect until moments before. Had he said something? The thunder and lightning were almost simultaneous now: he had been counting the gap between them. Now there was none. Then he saw the Light. Priestley couldn't have missed it, for a bolt of lightning sent from on high had hit what was still left of the church roof.

The missing lightning conductor could have saved the church, but it had fallen off a month before with the piece of masonry that had nearly killed one of the lay preachers. There had not been the funds to replace it, nor the lay preacher. As the lightning hit the roof, the ancient timbers instantly caught fire. Water, huge chunks of stone, gargoyles and miscellaneous saints in kit form rained down into the nave. Most of the big pieces of stone narrowly missed the Vicar, for the Lord had intended only to teach him a lesson, and as he lay soaking wet in the ambulance en route to the hospital, Priestley realized that once again he had got it wrong. He had been trying to save his church, and now it was nought but a pile of rubble. He knew something needed exorcising, but what? Next time he'd be more careful.

(*The Lord knew he would.*)

25. SLIM

Down the road from the Vicarage, Totnes Council was in uproar – the very last meeting, it had been declared. There was even a small amount of wailing and gnashing of teeth, something not normal in polite Totnes society. However, the councillors who were not wearing white, now approximately only one quarter of the council, did not understand the monumental import of the developing situation, were confused by central government's quarantine regulations, by the soldiers in the streets, and as usual stayed silent, their voice having been heard less and less as the weeks had gone by. All, however, were aware of the import of the meeting that morning and had braved the sudden local storm to attend.

"Ladies and gentlemen, please may I have your attention?!" Councillor Lax Sativa addressed the Council members. "Thank you. I shall leave the most important item till last ... First item on the agenda today is the so-called Totnes Monster," he announced, as the hubbub died down. "This has unfortunately been proved to be a whale, a large sperm whale, apparently, that has for some reason strayed, and stayed, up the Dart. Our animal rights officer has confirmed this in writing to me, and advises that there is no danger to life from this ... er ... fish. Second item is oil ... There have been further reports, and sad to relate for the future of the town's finances, all have been negative. Our hopes had been raised, as one of the original exploratory drillings did find oil in fairly large quantities; but, as you discovered at our last meeting, it appears the drill hit the under-river pipeline from Plymouth. This has now been mended; there were no big spillages, as timely action was

209

taken and any environmental damage was minimal. I am pleased to say that oil is once more safely flowing to the petrol distribution facility in Torquay. Therefore, I feel the meeting ought to vote on reopening the beaches and the river to normal traffic. Maybe we can use the whale as a tourist attraction: 'The Totnes Monster'; indeed, I have taken the liberty to instruct Mr. ... er ... Premi ... our animal rights officer appointed at our last meeting ... to look into this possibility. Those in favour of reopening the river? ... Those against? ... Abstentions? ... Motion carried!" He looked at the papers in his hands.

"Today, with great trepidation in my heart," he announced dramatically, "I have to talk to you about the dreaded disease SLIM. We are told by central government that we here in Totnes have a problem, a big problem, a very big problem! I have here a letter from the Home Office, may I say the same department that has just authorized the detention of our ... the Guru, his assistant Ma Anna Poona and myself ... dated yesterday – matters which we will have to deal with urgently. Apparently, I will have to surrender to the Totnes police or face immediate arrest! I therefore intend to surrender myself as soon as this meeting is over. Anyway, that is personal and here we must keep to Council matters ... The Home Office communication explains that, as of tomorrow, Totnes will be governed directly from London, as this disease SLIM is reaching endemic proportions in Totnes, and if something drastic is not done, there will be an epidemic."

The sound of murmurs, much anguish and even some rending of clothes greeted this news.

"If we cannot contain the problem," continued Lax, "and it appears our problem is even worse than London's – in fact, worse than almost anywhere in the world – we, as a town, will be put in quarantine by the government. This would mean road blocks in and out of town, gunboats on the river, and the whole town encircled by the army. So, even though we have just reopened the river, the government in their wisdom may be about to shut it forthwith, and the roads too. This, ladies and gentlemen, we cannot afford to let happen. We are coming up to the peak holiday season, and 'Totnes Ltd.' could not stand the loss this would mean. The town would die. Even when the roads and river were once again open, no-one would come here for years, for fear of any residual problem. So I have thought about this and come up with one solution. This will be the ultimate enactment of the present Totnes Parish Council. We must start a huge educational programme to contain the disease, to stop it spreading. I fear people will have to change their sexual habits, and so I propose that every household in Totnes receives a free packet of condoms, also known as French letters, Johnnies, Ticklers, etc. Finally, that we pass a byelaw making unprotected sex an offence. What is the feeling of the meeting?"

There were murmurs of approval from almost all, save a lone Catholic, who pointed out that the use of anything such as a condom was deemed a sin. Lax pointed out that killing people actually already alive was also probably a sin, and the objector quietened.

"Very well," he said, "I propose that we action the purchase of enough condoms to cover at least six times the number of male, er ... members in Totnes, and that we pass a byelaw with the following wording:

That it be an offence for any resident of Totnes and district to engage in sexual intercourse until further notice, unless the male member ... strike member ... insert penis ... er, is completely covered with a council-

211

approved sheath. And further, that anyone engaging in unprotected sexual intercourse shall be liable to custody for a period not exceeding one year.'

"Those in favour? Those against? Any abstentions? Motion carried! Any questions?"

"How can we enforce this law?" asked Councillor Boti. "It's obviously a good idea, but if we can't enforce it, the law will look an ass."

"Boti," said Lax, "you and I know the law is indeed an ass, but what can we do; and I am personally about to be subject to its rigours! We have to satisfy central government to keep our roads open and we have to keep the burghers of Totnes ... er ... satisfied."

"But what about the voters?" asked a confused Boti.

"The voters are all burghers!" cried an exasperated Lax.

"Take that back, Councillor!" shouted Mrs Simpson. "I am a voter, and I have never been so insulted!"

The meeting droned on ...

The main shareholder of the Randi Rubber Co. would also have been very satisfied if he had been able to hear the outcome of the meeting – a huge boost for Randco sales: fifty thousand Randiconds being delivered to the Council stores within the week; but, having been tipped off that the Police were on their way to Carnal House to arrest him and Ma Anna Poona, the Guru had made himself very scarce whilst they were apprehending her, and he was now hidden away aboard the *Obtuse* in his very own aquatic grotto.

It had taken five big men, and a very large Black Maria, to get MAP under lock and key.

26. Abduction

The cells at Totnes police station were not exactly spacious. Councillor Lax Sativa had given himself in and now sat fairly well in his, but MAP had difficulty even with the simplest tasks. It would have been bad enough trying to swing a cat in hers, though this was far from her mind as she placed her huge rear end on the tiny pot supplied to her for fairly obvious purposes. As she was finishing her task, she heard the eyehole cover being pulled back, and she let out a stream of abuse.

A man with facial hair possibly purloined from the estate of W. G. Grace, wearing dark glasses, a fedora and trench coat, entered. The door was locked again behind him, leaving MAP and the bearded apparition alone. MAP swiftly kicked the pot under the bunk as she rose to her feet, while adjusting her clothing – another difficult task. The man spoke.

"You don't recognize me, do you, Anna?" he said through his beard, which he then pulled down on its elastic, at the same time raising his spectacles. Then, for the first time in a day, she smiled. She opened her arms wide and gave the man a huge hug, smothering him, whilst kissing all over his face.

"OH! Dukey," she cried, "what a surprise, what a disguise! But why are you here? To see me?" The Duke, for indeed it was he, cleared his throat as if to make a speech, and speech it was, written by his personal speech writer and memorized the previous evening with the aid of a bottle of Mme Bollinger's best. It was one of the few things he ever said to her, their relationship being frankly of a somewhat physical nature.

"Anna," he said, "I have come to see you and I have come to get you out of this hell hole. Arrangements are being made presently to bail you out, but I am afraid that your friend Mr Sativa will have to stay. That is the deal I have been able to arrange. I have come to see you here because I know we will not be overheard; and please excuse the silly disguise – an old royal tradition when visiting incognito. I have, for you and me, some bad news."

The Duke bravely cleared his throat. "My wife," he announced, "a powerful woman in this land of ...," he looked up at MAP, "powerful women, has found out ... about us. She knows I have visited you on more than one occasion and she does not approve. She perceives you as a threat. I don't know what sort of threat, because she and I have very little life together as it is, we even have separate bedrooms, but that is that. I have to do as she says, for she is rich and powerful, as you know. I am totally dependent on her for support. Without her I would have no horses, no carriages, no polo ponies, no yachts, no trips to Cannes, no ... nothing! And she has said ... NO! So that, I am afraid, dear Anna, has to be that."

"But Dukey," said Anna, "she doesn't have to know. We could still see each other in private somewhere. We could fly away together to an island in the sun. We don't need money, we have each other. Love conquers all."

"I'm afraid it does not, darling Anna, it does not pay bills, and of those I have plenty. Do not make this too hard for me, Anna," he said, as her hand slipped down his front towards the belt buckle on his coat. "Anna, no, not here. ANNA – Oh! Please don't make it har..." But it was too late. Ma Anna Poona then managed to do something in that tiny cell that few would

214

have dreamt was possible, for in its restricted confines she played a special kind of poker, and certainly made the royal flush.

Twenty minutes later, the Duke managed to escape from her clutches long enough to hammer on the door for help, and MAP knew that, at least for that day, the dice were no longer loaded in her favour, so she ceased her administrations. Presently, the door opened to reveal a smiling constable, who had plainly heard the goings-on coming from cell 3. As the Duke said a fond farewell, he handed her a bracelet made of pure gold, one with no 'best before' date, as a memento of their love. He turned and was gone. The door shut.

As she heard it lock, and then the sound of horses' hooves disappearing in the distance, MAP vowed that it would not be the last time she would see him. She lay in the cell awaiting her discharge and a cunning plan formed in her mind.

Two hours later, she was released into the siege atmosphere of Totnes, an atmosphere redolent of the last days of the war, with soldiers fraternizing with the locals, mainly the local girls, when they were under the strictest instructions not to. For security reasons, none of the men were told the reason for the blockade of Totnes – it certainly would have improved the health of their country if they had been. They were just following orders.

Now men will be boys, and, on the basis that rules are always made to be broken, many swift liaisons were made between soldier and country girl, liaisons which in the months to come, as soldiers on leave went home to their wives and girlfriends, increased the spread of the SLIM epidemic to uncontrollable proportions throughout the length and breadth of the whole Kingdom.

MAP returned straightway to Carnal House, having been warned under the terms of her bail that she had to keep the peace, and promptly started making arrangements to keep it not. She commandeered two strong Devos, had some uniforms run up in the clothes workshop, and ordered the repainting of the Devo ambulance. Then she confirmed where the Duke's itinerary would take him over the next few days.

The following afternoon, while the Duke was preparing to inspect a guard of honour of cadets at the Britannia Naval College, Dartmouth, MAP was putting the finishing touches to her single-minded plan. At two o'clock, she received the last item needed, a false pass forged in the Devo print shop, which would allow her in and out of the restricted zone around Totnes. He would not escape her! She was ready!

The Duke, though, was not. He was in the hospitality suite at Dartmouth, having a short rest before undertaking the arduous task of walking in front of line after line of smart young men who all looked identical. How he hated these inspections – all too often his sword would get tangled up with his legs and cause a frightful palaver. There was always something that went wrong.

After one hour's rest, the Duke rose from the chaise-longue. He shat, showered and shaved, and then started dressing. First, he donned a pair of white tennis socks. He eyed himself in the full-length mirror – he was definitely looking better, and now that he had made his decision about that woman, he felt good. His stomach was firm, for a man of his age, though why he'd had that small problem recently when he had often hoped for more than just his stomach to be firm was beyond him. He had to thank her for solving the problem. Well, that was that, he wouldn't be seeing her again.

Pulling on white boxer shorts and a cotton vest,

he looked again. He was feeling good, very good. He buttoned his officer's shirt and climbed into his dress uniform – a suitably grand affair with a nation's supply of gold braid festooned over the extra-large epaulettes, plus a supply of *ex gratia* medals completely covering the area of his heart. It was a uniform signifying the rank of Admiral.

Finally, he strapped on the scabbard and, after a few minutes' delay when much uncontrolled sword waving occurred, he inserted his sword. He vowed that, with the TV news cameras present, he would not permit his sword to attack him today. He was ready. Taking a deep breath, he stepped outside the room, looked right and left, trying to remember which way to go. He paused to think.

At that moment, Ma Anna Poona slapped a cotton wad soaked with chloroform over his mouth, bundled him under a blanket and bodily hurled him onto the stretcher her two male Devo assistants were carrying. She was neatly dressed in the starched white uniform of Captain Matron, and the two Devos were in the similar garb of navy male nurses. Anyone looking at the trio would not have thought twice at their authenticity, and neither indeed had the guards at the various security checks through which she had had to pass to enable her small party to enter the Royal Naval College at Dartmouth on 'Passing Out Day'; a day so called due to the number of young cadets who did the same, whose bodies just did not understand the import of remaining upright for hours on end on hot summer's days to be looked at for a moment by some ageing celebrity, who himself at that moment had also passed out.

They swiftly conveyed their unconscious charge through the corridors until they found the appropriate exit, where they had positioned their 'Navy' ambulance. On the way, MAP was often saluted, maybe a touch too noticeable in her high-ranking uniform, but the trick was working.

Having thrown the Duke's limp body into the back of the ambulance, one of the Devos tended to the unconscious man. MAP and the other ran quickly to the front and jumped in. The suspension groaned. On went the siren and, lights flashing, the party attempted an exit from the base. Three barriers lifted with no problem, but at the fourth and last a Petty Officer, who in MAP's opinion was certainly being just that, and a Lieutenant who later thought twice about obeying orders, asked to see papers. Summarily, MAP dispatched both to a period of temporary sleep.

The ambulance left at a pace, soon to be pursued by a fleet of cars, vans, trucks, personnel carriers, armoured personnel carriers and one helicopter. Many of the road vehicles were driving much too fast, and as the ambulance they were chasing had soon reached its destination, were running around in ever decreasing circles still searching for it. Even the helicopter's wise endeavours at directing from the air failed to stop a catastrophic and unexpected meeting of all and sundry at one five-way crossroads.

As the anaesthetized Duke started to come round, he was forced to swallow a small sugar lump, onto which some hallucinogenic acid had been dripped. MAP felt that if she and many others had been converted to Randism by this means, and mean it was, then so could the Duke be programmed to love her, and only her. She and the two men changed back into their white sheets as the journey progressed, discarding their mock naval attire. She then ordered one of the men to roll a reefer of stupendous proportions, a cocktail made up of the best the Lebanon, Afghanistan, Thailand and Mexico had to offer. Soon the happy crew could hardly see as far as the windscreen, let alone the road, and, as happens in situations such as this, the ambulance itself seemed to take over, and the journey continued in an apparently orderly manner – certainly if viewed from the vehicle's exterior.

MAP climbed into the back to minister to their now groaning charge. As the acid had not yet fully taken hold of his brain, she decided to speed up his conversion. She reversed the loaded reefer in her mouth and blew the smoke she had taken into her lungs back into his slack jaw. The poor man nearly choked, sat up coughing and spluttering, opened his eyes and then saw her. His mouth once more opened wide, this time in surprise, and he received another dose of drug-laden smoke. The combination of the hashish, the chloroform and the acid, which was now starting to take effect, took precedence over the off-the-cuff words the Duke was about to say; he sank back onto the stretcher, dazed and a touch the worse for wear.

On arrival at Carnal House one half hour later, to which den of iniquity MAP was certainly aiming, the by now happier and hallucinating Duke was propelled by his two Devo minders into a brightly lit room, filled with various adult toys and trinkets.

This was what the grand old Duke had been wanting; it seemed to him that he had been waiting for it all his life, and he was now happy beyond belief. The swimming and pulsating mandalas on the walls, the faces on the posters changing from Randi or the top Devo pictured to various world leaders, to his father, to himself; the right wall coming, the facing wall going away from him – was he in heaven, or was this hell?

Someone told him gently he had been given

LSD, and he remembered somewhere in his brain that the US Army had tried it once on its own soldiers to test its effectiveness as a weapon. No wonder they couldn't win wars, this was something else. Then, settling down to his trip, he discovered the secret of life, and spent the rest of it trying to remember it so he could tell all his new friends just what it was.

A Devo removed the Duke's dress uniform, and his other clothes, placing over his head a white robe similar to the one Randi himself wore, for the Duke was an honoured guest. They garlanded him with flowers and placed on his head the ultimate accolade – a rainbow turban.

The Duke was so happy. Damn the royals, he thought, this is the life. These men and women had something he had never known. A sense of peace and purpose – that's what it was. He tried crossing his legs, humming ommmmm, burying his head under a blanket, touching the back of his throat with his tongue, seeing the Light, and yes – there it was, changing, pulsating, going this way, then that. What he had been missing!

A young Devo girl of seventeen came in, long black hair cascading down her back, hand-picked by MAP because of her beautiful face and body, a present to the Duke for his personal edification and appreciation. She lifted his robe up to the top of his chest, then covered him with oil. Slowly, she massaged his muscles until they were completely relaxed, all his muscles save for one, which appeared not to wish to follow the others, possibly due to yet more blue pills to which the Duke had recently taken a shine. She removed her robe and, after liberally anointing him once more with oil, sat across him, and slowly lowered herself onto him.

The Duke thought he had never, never been

treated like this. The girl was fantastic. She rode him slowly with strokes that Henry Cotton would never have played, until the Duke could stand it no more, and once again discovered the secret of life. Maybe this time he would remember it.

The girl withdrew off his body and out of the room, pulling his robe down to his ankles once again, leaving him lying on the cushions. Once again, the walls started moving and once again the posters changed. The floor undulated, he floated, settled, floated. And then he slept.

While the Duke was flat on his back discovering the secret of life over and over, in another corner of the grounds of Carnal House a small Nepalese gentleman was emerging extremely carefully from a well-hidden submarine. It had all been too much for Guru Shami Randi. He had hated being cooped up in a submarine for over a day with a crew of Greek seamen, all of whom seemed to have some ailment or other. It was not, to put it mildly, his idea of fun ... but it was probably preferable than being taken into custody by the British border police.

As he emerged from the sub's hatch, a small group of Devos, who had been lazing around on the grass outside, cheered, and ran forwards towards him. Forgetting his need to remain discreet, he pulled himself up to his full magnificence to greet them, as a conquering hero would, and stepped out of the hatch, arms outstretched. The hatch cover duly fell down with a loud crash, fortuitously only trapping his steel foot, and one of the welcoming Devos was then obliged to help him lift up the hatch and reattach the appendage so that he could continue into Carnal House, on foot, or feet, so to speak.

Back inside the *Obtuse*, the men were becoming very restless indeed. Many were going down with peculiar ailments, lying in their bunks with swollen glands, uncomfortable colons, open sores, uncomfortable sores, even open colons. Some were throwing up into shaky hand-held bowls, throwing up a product very similar to the spaghetti or moussaka they had forced down their gullets only hours before, and this worried Captain Halitosis deeply. Not only was his submarine stuck up a one-way street with warships after it, but day by day his crew appeared to be more and more incapable of functioning at all.

Only he and Spiro, his number one, seemed well enough at all times to carry on their normal functions. Kamakis was no fool, and he could tell when something was up. And something definitely was. There was no doctor on board who could diagnose what the problem might be, but this normally wild bunch of zealots was not well at all.

He felt in his bones that it was time to move. If Guru couldn't give some indication as to when they were going to start the oil exploration for which they had come all the way from Greece, then he was going to up anchor and leave. His men couldn't languish in this mockery of a boathouse much longer, of that he was sure, and before Guru had left the sub, he had told him so in no uncertain terms. Randi's reaction had worried him somewhat, for the Guru obviously had something a lot more than the exploration of oil on his mind. He had not seemed bothered when Hal had threatened to leave, as though it was something fairly insignificant. So, thought Hal to himself, if we are that unimportant, that's the end of the matter. He had given Randi an ultimatum – get something moving within twenty-four hours or they would be, moving back to Greece that is, to their homes and, yes, to their loved ones, for even these men were privileged to have such attachments, and most of them now needed them badly.

Randi had momentarily worried about Kamakis' attitude, thinking it somewhat suppressive. It was obvious he had, in the language of Randism, some sort of admin or tech withhold, or just possibly it was simply a financial overt. Well, Halitosis wouldn't be getting on the Bridge to Total Freedom and Knowledge like that. By the time Randi had reached the side door to Carnal House, he had dismissed the problems of the submarine, knowing full well that his personal legal status was for him much more problematic. Ethics and justice tech were certainly being abused!

At the side door, the Guru found MAP. She had already heard from Hal Kamakis on the scrambled ship-to-shore that he had jumped ship and was nervously pacing to and fro, wondering how to tell him of the 'siege' of Totnes, that she had been in jail, that their council takeover had been scuppered, that there was no oil, that the whale was the monster, and more – much more. And knowing how jealous he was of the Duke, how on earth could she tell him that the same royal personage was tripping out of his brains in the play room downstairs? MAP had been so single-mindedly blinkered that, when abducting the Duke, she had totally ignored the Guru's presence nearby, thinking he would remain sensibly submerged.

Ma Anna Poona now had the weight of the world on her shoulders. Thank Guru they were broad.

27. Too Many Cooks

Whilst a worried MAP was greeting and meeting an anxious Randi at Carnal House, two other nervous souls were steaming towards each other, a stream of semaphore messages criss-crossing the mouth of the Dart as they converged at a combined speed of approximately sixty knots. Henry Potts-Johnstone and Hugo Horneyolde-Foxe individually knew they might never have a chance like this again, naval engagements being at a premium, and each wanted any glory that would be available all for himself. Each, like MAP, were totally blinkered and were ignoring the messages from the other's ship telling them to keep away, and each was still awaiting final instructions from their respective HQs: Henry from the British Royal Navy's command centre at Northwood, and Hugo from NATO in Brussels. Both men were being very focussed in their endeavours, as they had been trained to be, and neither stopped for a moment to think whether too many cooks, two to be precise, might be spoiling the proverbial broth. Indeed, neither listened to the bleatings of their first officers, who had realized that rude ambition and hubris was getting in the way of good Navy discipline and procedures. Both were trying to tell their Admirals that they had lost the sonar trace of the submarine they were following due to the close proximity of the other's warships.

Under the terms of the North Atlantic Treaty, Brussels had no need to inform Northwood of its intentions for the *Valiant* and the *Victor*, and as the *Superfluous* and its flotilla were operating in British territorial waters, there was certainly no need for Northwood to inform anyone at all. As a result, and also, of course, because of their usual sibling rivalry, both men felt very strongly this was their own command, and that the other was distinctly getting in the way, little realizing just what effect their ambitious actions were now having on their sonar crews' peace of mind.

Stodge Rutherford, Her Majesty's Home and Commonwealth Secretary, was at the same time in his office in London signing a destruction order for the contents of a council warehouse in Totnes, where fifty thousand unusable condoms were now stored, and was conversing on the telephone with his friend the General Secretary of NATO. From the conversation he gleaned that satellite locators had confirmed the position of the *Obtuse* right up to the mouth of the Dart, but that NATO ships had lost track of the submarine since, due to sonar reflections from too many other ships nearby. Stodge knew what two and two added up to. In this case it was Totnes – and Carnal House. He immediately telephoned Aldershot, spoke to the Army General in command of the Totnes detachment and ordered that Carnal House be surrounded forthwith – with force. Then the Guru should be 'flushed out' and held.

One could not tolerate international arrest warrants being ignored. An example had to be made.

After his telephone call with Stodge, the General Secretary of NATO had made a telephone call of his own. Though he knew that under the terms of the North Atlantic Treaty there was no need for the call, he felt that, as in order to capture the *Obtuse*, NATO might actually need to use force within the borders of one of its own member states, he ought to at least make his intentions clear to that country's Foreign Secretary, with whom under the Treaty he had to liaise. The self-same

Archie Tendon-Smythe, who had recently finished yet another rather good lunch, could see no reason for objecting to NATO's presence in Sovereign waters; after all, the submarine had stolen from NATO, it was owned by the horrible little Guru that Stodge Rutherford was trying to apprehend, and what it might get it would definitely deserve. He was only too happy to let the NATO ships retrieve, with force if necessary, what was rightfully theirs, and happily gave his slightly slurred blessing. The NATO General Secretary immediately ordered the transmission of Plan 6A to Horneyolde-Foxe on the *Valiant*, authorizing him to enter the Dart, to use force to retrieve the various bits of hardware taken from the NATO base at Paleocastritsa, and to board and arrest the *Obtuse* and its crew.

One could not tolerate such flaunting of the honourable aims of the North Atlantic Treaty Organization. An example had to be made.

At the moment these important decisions were being made, a message was received at the Royal Navy's command headquarters at Northwood from HMS *Superfluous*, flagship of the British flotilla searching for the *Obtuse*. It confirmed that the submarine in question was definitely in the waters of the River Dart, but that sonar had lost its fix due to certain other craft in the vicinity. The Flag Officer asked permission to go in with depth charges in the hope of making the rogue sub come to the surface. Northwood thought it was a capital idea, and contacted the Defence Secretary, J. St. John Ambrigade, for final clearance. He could see no reason to hold back, also thought the idea somewhat capital, and gave his assent immediately. Northwood then transmitted Plan R to the *Superfluous*, authorizing the use of depth charges, and other force if and as

226

necessary, to bring the submarine to the surface.

One could not tolerate such flaunting of British Sovereignty. An example had to be made.

So two flotillas steamed up the Dart from its mouth, until they reached a point offshore from Carnal House, where the draught of the river became too shallow for them to continue, and there they anchored. Both Rear Admirals were still ignoring the other, chins were set firm and proud, backs straight, tummies held tightly in and buttocks clenched. Nothing would deter them now. Both were happy at the prospect of flexing their powerful maritime muscles, not for a moment believing that their opposite number, with their own flotilla but a stone's throw across the water, would also have permission to do just the same.

And Old Carthusian General Sir Edward Cluete De Sworder, MC, hero of the Burma campaign – though some said he had never actually been present with the Forgotten Army, but then no-one could really remember – and commanding officer of the British land forces surrounding Totnes, was equally happy at the thought of some action at last. He liked his orders. He liked action.

He was a man with a moustache and really not much else, but now he had a mission. He'd jolly well flush out those little brown chapatti wallahs.

Yes indeed he would, SAH!

28. General De Sworder

"This," shouted General De Sworder into the megaphone he held aloft in one hand, "is the British Army. Now come ite with your hends in the heir, and all will be well. If you do not, my min will farstly shoot in the heir and then, if you still do not upyour, will be farced to take your mans – wait for it ... SHUN! – by farce. Is that understood?"

The General stood proudly at the gates of Carnal House, which had, as ordered, been completely surrounded by his men from the Queen's Own Fusiliers, with the megaphone in one hand and a pistol, attached to his wrist by a lanyard, in the other. He invariably had trouble with his vowels, and due in part to this slight case of verbal dyslexia, he always ate a diet high in fibre. He was a very regular chap, in the regular army ... regular. After some minutes shouting, which made the great warrior feel somewhat equestrian for a man who had spent his life in the footsloggers, he ordered the colonel next to him to go and knock on the front door, as it was even obvious to him that his ministrations were probably going unheard. The colonel told the major, the major the captain, the captain the lieutenant, and so on until, five minutes later, a private did arrive at the door, and when it had been opened, explained to the startled Devo who answered that his General wished to shout at him from the roadway. The private then withdrew back till he was, as the General put it, 'behind our lines'. The General recommenced his shouting.

MAP, who had been summoned to the front door, listened carefully, but had great difficulty understanding more than a few words. She put her hands to her lips and verbally pointed this salient fact out to the man with the megaphone. She did, however, notice that Carnal House was surrounded, and that the soldiers wanted something. "WHAT-DO-YOU-WANT?" she yelled at the top of her powerful voice.

"Would you be so good as to arsk the little Indian gentleman to step forad?" shouted back the General. "We know he's in thar. Now come orn, be a good chap." MAP did not like being mistaken for a 'chap'.

"Which 'little Indian gentleman'?" she screamed back at one hundred paces. The duel was on.

"Your leader, the man Randi; we have an international warrant for his arrest. If he does not come ite, we shall go orn in. We hev orders to take him by farce if deemed so, don't y'know. So come alorng now. Let's be hevving you."

"Hang on a minute," said MAP, playing for time. "I must go in to consult; won't be two ticks." And she slammed the huge front door shut.

Whilst the army were clicking their heels and twiddling their thumbs, the navy, or rather two incommunicado sections of it, were upping anchors in preparation for the submarine operation. It quickly dawned on the first officers of both flagships that the other ships were undertaking similar actions – guns were being manned, depth charges readied, and men could be seen on all the ships scurrying around in flash hoods; but, as the two commanding Rear Admirals were refusing to talk to each other, and their orders originated from differing sources, little could be done to unite their forces. And being too busy for such trivia, neither had heard the big news of the day.

The disappearance of the Duke from Dartmouth was an embarrassment that the Royal Navy could have done without. Only as a favour had he been there in the first place, and now, for a reason unknown to anyone at the base, he had been spirited away by a team posing as a Captain Matron and two Orderlies. The Navy ambulance could not be found, and, at the five-way crossroads where all the chasing vehicles had suddenly met, was now positioned a pile of twisted and smouldering metal. Eight Navy vehicles had been written off in one moment, with twenty-eight dead or dying. A catastrophe was not the word. But where was the Duke? He had disappeared into thin air, lost somewhere in the south of England. And where do you start looking for a Duke? England had never misplaced one before.

Inside Carnal House, Ma Anna Poona had quickly consulted with Randi, and they had decided to arm all the Peace Corps present with M16s from the basement armoury and to use the Duke as a bargaining ploy. Randi had been shocked to hear of his presence in Carnal House, but when he realized that the Duke could be used to safeguard his own freedom, he was a touch happier. MAP, toting one of the rifles, then walked boldly to the front door and explained, through her own loud hailer, the position they were adopting to the waiting forces.

"I say," shouted back the General, assuming MAP's suggested possession of a right royal person to be a bluff, "that's a bit steep, y'know." He then turned to the men next to him and asked if anyone had heard anything about any recent royal abductions. No-one had. So De Sworder ignored the bluff.

At the same moment, a loud explosion occurred, and all in a line the General, the Colonel, the Major, etc., saw, through their regulation for the use of field glasses, a rather large splash of water three hundred

231

yards away across the beautifully tended lawns. The water then rained down on this well-kept grass, obviating the need for the following week's watering, any discussion of which, due to subsequent events, anyway becoming something totally academic.

Rear Admiral Potts-Johnstone saw the splash. He had, however, also seen the flash, which in his opinion had emanated from a deck gun on Horneyolde-Foxe's *Valiant*. So Hugo was flexing his muscles! That was something he too could do. He immediately ordered the dropping of a brace of depth charges in the vicinity of the *Valiant*'s initial splash.

The men in the *Obtuse* started to throw up in unison. The rocking and rolling they were receiving from the armouries of the two ships was beginning to affect their inner souls. What were they doing here!? In between bouts of chunder, the Greeks voiced their opinions, simple opinions, opinions such as 'come on, Hal, we must leave now': opinions that carried a lot of weight when only Hal and Spiro were still functioning properly. Kamakis didn't want to run, but maybe he'd have to. His Neanderthal brow furrowed deeper, and it wasn't the only brow ready for planting.

General Sir Edward De Sworder's Cro-Magnon version of the human forehead – high, imposing, with not much in it – also formed distinctly parallel lines at the same time. He had now heard two or was it three explosions, and yet had no idea that there were a couple of naval flotillas sitting so close to him on the Dart. He assumed the firing must have come from the mansion, and that his men were now under attack. Luckily, the amateurs hadn't got their range yet. He immediately radioed for reinforcements, urgently requested air support, and ordered his men in.

When MAP saw the charging, yelling, minstrel-blacked-up men firing their guns at random, and at her, she ducked down and slammed shut the massive front door to Carnal House.

She barked out orders to the already armed Peace Corps like the Sergeant Major she should have been, and the Devos scattered to every corner of the mansion, taking up defensive positions wherever they could. As they did so, they returned the army's fire. Not expecting such a powerful fusillade to be returned, the General ordered his men to retreat and regroup.

The two Rear Admirals heard the firing; each assumed it was they who had located the submarine and were under attack. They both immediately ordered their deck gunners to fire volleys in the direction of the gunfire. Obviously, the submarine crew had taken up defensive positions and were holed up in the large mansion they could see on shore.

And so it was, some time later, that five amphibious landing craft loaded to the gunnels with still-incommunicado NATO and Royal Marine Commandos, with the air support of three Sea King helicopters, approached the Totnes Randicentre by way of the River Dart; and at the same time, a battalion of men from the Queen's Own Fusiliers, with their own air support in the shape of two VTOL Harrier 'jump' jets, approached from land.

Thus, three sections of Her Majesty's forces, each still receiving their orders from a different source, arrived at Carnal House at precisely the same time. The chaos and mayhem that followed is now legendary, the loss of life and machinery astonishing, and a winner has yet to be found.

After the first hour of fighting, when it was finally noticed that Englishman was killing Englishman, soldier was killing sailor, sailor – soldier, airman – etc., etc., and that most of the gunfire was missing Carnal House, a co-ordinating officer, one Hugo Horneyolde-Foxe, was appointed under NATO auspices on board his flagship the *Valiant.* A fuse was nearly blown in Henry Potts-Johnstone's ambitiously jealous head when he heard the news. The brief was simple: to capture the *Obtuse* and Guru Shami Randi.

A short summary of the two hours' fighting is as follows. Royal Marines stormed off the landing crafts, which, prior to depositing their loads, had narrowly missed a small uncharted boathouse in which were secreted one Oberon class submarine (the *Obtuse*) and approximately thirty-five tired, ill, hungry and above all angry seamen (the Crew).

The marines charged forward, soldiers dropped down ladders from helicopters, the two Harriers flew just above the Randicentre, showing off their amazing powers for going slowly forwards, backwards and sideways, creating an horrendous jet-stream downwards, but doing little else save using up an average family's year's fuel needs, and the marines and soldiers fell right over, unable to stand up under the blast from the Harriers' engines.

From Carnal House, MAP and Randi had seen the attack intensify considerably, and she had broken out more hand grenades and ammunition, distributing it amongst all the Devos. She barked out orders into a compact personal radio she carried, and thus was able to control her outside forces from the relative safety of the mansion. The Duke was still downstairs, unaware of almost anything but the still-pulsating room.

Onto the huge lawn, which swept right down to the river, charged the Devos and their Peace Corps, firing their M16s and hurling grenades. As most of the poor marines and soldiers were just getting to their feet again, having been knocked over by the Harriers' downdraft, many were mown down like skittles in a bowling alley.

On the *Superfluous*, from which the view to shore was better than from the *Valiant*, Henry Potts-Johnstone saw his chance. He was horrified watching the soldiers fall, and realized that no-one would be becoming First Sea Lord if a bunch of religious nuts could beat Her Majesty's combined forces, as was happening at that moment. But if someone came up with a plan that virtually guaranteed success, that used the chaos on the lawn as a diversion, that used stealth and intelligence, then maybe ... It looked as though the submarine had, so to speak, gone to ground. But if that Guru was in the building ...? He'd know where the sub was ... That was it! Henry had found his Plan.

He ordered a small detachment of men to skirt Carnal House, avoiding the main attack, to make their way into the building and, locating Randi, take him prisoner. Then, using the one Sea King helicopter under his control, bring him back to the *Superfluous*. And when this feat had been accomplished, and only then, he would raze the building to the ground. If nothing else, the successful instigator of a plan like that deserved a few medals.

The group of marines duly sought a side entrance, and, under the cover of various rare arboreal specimens, now blazing merrily, they made their way into the house. Room by room they searched, until, in a downstairs room, they found their quarry. It had to be him – he fitted the description perfectly. Alone in a large meditation room they found their man, lying back, with a serene smile on his face. Not taking any chances, they quickly dispatched him to sleep, so that the poor man in question now had an extra bump on his head. They hustled him into the waiting helicopter, where he was unceremoniously winched up and flown over to the *Superfluous*.

On arrival, the white-robed and turbaned human was locked up in a lower cabin with an armed guard at the door, who was instructed to contact Henry the moment the man stirred. Then Henry would drag out of him the whereabouts of the missing sub.

The Harriers went into action, sending their powerful and lethal rockets flying, though none too accurately. One collaterally missed Carnal House and hit the family house next door, the explosion of which rocket virtually collapsed the house, and four floors concertina-ed into one on the ground. Luckily, hearing and seeing the mayhem, the family had escaped moments earlier and were sheltering up the road behind a hastily constructed Police cordon.

Not so the au-pair. She had been in *flagrante delecto* in her room on the top floor with her legs high in the air, her spotty biker boyfriend deep within her, chewing ravenously at her neck. Maybe he had not eaten for weeks. Neither had noticed the commotion outside, neither had heard the whoosh of the rocket, and, as the house collapsed and they fell four floors, neither noticed their fast accelerating downward movement. They continued banging into each other, the boy still eating, now almost through to her oesophagus, until they landed with a huge thud and clouds of dust on the ground floor. At that moment they climaxed in unison, and again, and again, then the bed bounced twice and all was still. She was later taken to hospital to have her neck stitched and, though hard to believe, was the only civilian casualty of the affair.

At least two of the rockets did hit their mark, and large portions of the beautifully restored

Randicentre fell away. Up till that moment it had seemed as though the Devos were gaining ground, Her Majesty's forces being slowly but surely pushed back towards the river and the waiting landing craft.

Both Rear Admirals were worried. At least, thought Henry, the horrid man was in his brig. He'd wheedle out of him the truth about the whereabouts of the sub, and the stolen torpedoes, and the gun. But their forces were certainly under pressure and their socks would soon be getting wet. He was loathe to use the *Superfluous'* big guns, never yet fired in anger. Who knows where the shells might land? Knowing his luck so far, they'd probably land in the General Hospital where, at that moment, a surgeon was putting neat little stitches into a young girl's neck, and a Vicar was in bed recovering.

The Harriers' rockets had, however, done their job, and the startled Devos were running back towards their mansion, thinking that their beloved leader was inside, seeing huge chunks of it crashing down. Quickly, the marines, who up till that moment were almost back in the boats, charged forward towards Carnal House, into the remains of which the Devos were fast disappearing.

Whilst all the mayhem and slaughter had been underway, certain very ill Greek seamen had given their leader a final ultimatum. Either they were to leave Totnes now by any means at all, even by submarine, or they would all abandon ship and give themselves up. Halitosis Kamakis had no choice. Even in the partly submerged sub, they could hear something happening outside. Dull thuds and various miscellaneous noises could be felt and heard through the hull, and most, being navy men, recognized the sounds as those of war. They'd better leave, and fast. Luckily, they were in one

237

of the world's quietest submarines, and running on the batteries they could with luck escape up the river without detection.

And so the ancient Oberon class submarine the *Obtuse* edged its way out of the small boathouse into the channel. Nothing but a little ripple showed, for the Greeks, as usual, were stealthy in their endeavours. Very slowly, Kamakis upped the low-power periscope for a look around and was astonished at what he saw. So as not to alarm any of the crew, he kept his face poker straight, but nevertheless shuddered slightly.

To the right of the sub were beached landing craft, and on the gently sloping incline towards what used to be the Randicentre were charging detachments of marines and soldiers in front of fleeing Devos. To the left, in open channel, were two groups of warships. They would have to be exceedingly careful yet quick. He knew the *Obtuse*'s batteries needed recharging after the lay-up, and that meant reaching the sea before they could come up for air.

Their greatest problem would be navigating the channel without getting stuck. There could be no deep diving here to escape detection; in fact, they would have to do it all on the periscope. "Absolute quiet," came Kamakis' order. "Stay at periscope depth, ahead slow, dead slow."

Gently, the *Obtuse* moved away from its mooring place and into the channel. Kamakis assumed that if they went around the other side of the nearest destroyer, unless there was a sharp-eyed watch, they would probably be missed, as everyone would be watching the now-burning Randicentre. And that's what the man did. How he ever reached the open sea without detection was a naval feat that will be written about at length, but not at this moment, though some of his success can be put down to an unhealthy rivalry between his two opponents. Only one turbaned person in a cabin low down in the bowels of a destroyer, almost on the waterline, noticed first the wake then the periscope, but he thought he was hallucinating once more and fell back to sleep.

Half a mile up the river there appeared another wake, but no periscope. Noticing the departure of that submarine which had been ignoring him, the massive owner of the wake headed straight to the boathouse, which resting place he had been eyeing jealously for a couple of days, and then all was quiet.

In Carnal House, MAP was urging Randi to escape. The tired Guru, though, wanted to stay with his Peace Corps. This was in no way due to the concept of the captain not deserting the sinking ship, for this man would have deserted his own mother, but because he thought the Peace Corps were the only people in the world who could now defend him. MAP bellowed at him until if he had not agreed to go he would very soon have become deaf. Anything was better than being bellowed at by a mountain.

She dressed him quickly in the naval uniform taken from the Duke, which almost fitted, though there was much room to spare. She thought it unlikely any of the opposing forces would take a pot shot at an Admiral, and, after removing Randi's turban to his cries of anguish, stuffed the cap on his bald head, being careful to tuck his long side hair under. She gave him her walkie talkie, thrusting it in his hands, and told him to get down to the *Obtuse* and escape in it, for at least their attackers had not yet found the submarine.

Randi did not like running, he found it difficult, but he sensed that if he did not he, even he, might be forced to meet his maker sooner than intended.

So he ran, and ran, and ran. He ran down the sloping lawn under the cover of some now very dead arboreal specimens, down towards the river and the little boathouse where his submarine awaited him. Thank god he still had Kamakis, the *Obtuse* and freedom. But Guru Shami Randi was running away. It was something he thought he had never done before. Money, property, towns had been his, and now he had to run. It was downright jealous persecution, racial too. The British obviously did not like successful colonials like himself. Panting, he rounded the corner and was swiftly in the boathouse. There in the gloom he could see the hulk lying next to the landing stage. Thank God it was there. Quickly he ran down the steps, along the dock and down the ladder. Damn, the tide was going out, he thought, less depth, more chance of detection. He carefully hopped onto the black slippery looking deck. To his surprise it gave slightly. He was worrying too much.

"Open the sub door, Hal," he spoke quietly into his radio. Nothing.

"OPEN THE SUB DOOR, HAL," he said louder. Again nothing happened. The huge hulk under him moved slightly. Odd, he was having difficulty balancing with only one good leg and did not like the rippling he now felt. They weren't going to leave him on deck! He couldn't swim.

"OPEN THE SUB DOOR, HAL!" he screamed, not caring that he should be heard, and at that moment he saw the front of the submarine astonishingly rear up. He was face to face, literally, with something he had hoped he would never have to face again.

Guru Shami Randi, God the Enlightener, Giver of Knowledge and Master of the Vagina, was once again

240

in the company of his Nemesis, his very own personal Totnes Monster.

Big Dirk, for it was indubitably he, smiled the widest smile Randi had ever seen, covered him from head to foot with a jet of water, winked wickedly and was off.

Randi held on for dear life. Was this a nightmare? Quick, wake me up! But there was no waking up, and no turning back. Straight out into the channel and past the now quieter ships charged Dirk. He'd have some fun with this little man. Though the man on his back was disguised as a naval officer, Dirk knew it was his old friend Randi, sensed it, recognized the slimy voice, could feel the difference between the one real and one false foot.

It was fun to see him again after so many years.

Randi was absolutely petrified and in the now gathering dusk was almost glowing white with fear. He was just about keeping his balance: he mustn't fall into the water. Past the nearest destroyer they went, their passing coinciding with the reawakening of the Duke, who stretched, looked out of the porthole once more, saw himself shoot past on the back of, what was it, a whale? But he was here, not there. Something went snap in his brain, and at that moment royalty lost their oddest Duke, who became even odder and who never spoke any sense ever again, though to be fair few noticed the change.

One or possibly two sailors on the ships, leaning over the rail, watching the sun go down and having a quiet smoke after all the mayhem and fighting, noticed the swim past of Randi and Dirk, but kept quiet about it in case they might be thought to be suffering from battle fatigue.

And two men who were now counting the cost of

their ambition and jealousy were also somewhat tired. Neither Henry Potts-Johnstone nor Hugo Horneyolde-Foxe did ever make it to First Sea Lord. The former, unfortunately, even lost his commission due to the discovery of the babbling Duke in his brig, whilst the latter only missed demotion as a result of the inordinate loss of life, and yet no submarine, by the skin of his teeth.

Ma Anna Poona and the few Devos eventually found still alive in the smouldering ruin of Carnal House were rounded up, incarcerated for a short time, and then released, as there was no proof that Randi had ever been there, MAP eventually becoming both halves of a successful celebrity chef.

General de Sworder became a security consultant to the Republic of South Africa.

Fred Lukes, to the relief of the town, was given back his Council, Lax Sativa became Frank Lee once more, and they started having lunch together again, surprisingly ending up in a civil partnership.

The Swami and the Nurse never returned, made many babies; in fact, the hills were alive with them.

And Big Dirk, with his little friend on his back who was now white as a sheet with fear and who was madly reckoning where it had all gone wrong, reckoning ... reckoning ..., swam off into the sunset.

At long last, Dirk was just having a whale of a time ...

EPILOGUE

John Priestley, suffering Vicar of Crumbleigh, lay in his bed in the casualty ward of Totnes General Hospital, having an armful of blood extracted for a routine blood test. The radio was on, and he was surprised to hear of the news that Carnal House had been razed to the ground and that the Guru was missing, presumed dead. So the Lord Above had got rid of the Guru – and maybe he had listened to his own adjurations about him. Priestley thought the Lord had been ignoring him – the fact that he now no longer had a church was enough proof for him, so why the change of heart? Maybe, thought he, the Lord was a bit human after all, and had second thoughts about the disaster he had wrought on the parish church. It was just possible, and if so, he knew he was one of the few clerics still around who had a direct hotline upstairs. He said a silent prayer of thank you, a prayer that was received loud and clear by the Lord above.

All of a sudden, Priestley felt he needed the toilet. He thought this somewhat unusual, normally being fairly continent, and rang the bell for the nurse.

"Well, Vicar, what can I do for you?" asked the nurse.

"I need relief," he stammered, not used to having to ask to go.

"Vicar, this is a hospital. I've heard of men like you. Really!"

"No, you see, I need you to help me go ... to the toilet," he whispered.

"Well, why on earth didn't you say so? Come on then." She lifted him forward, and helped him steady his feet.

They walked slowly, the Vicar still in some pain from his injuries, towards the toilets. "What's that ward?" he asked, seeing a ward of very thin young men. "Looks unusual to me, they all look the same. Like, er ... clones, that's the word. What's the matter with them?"

The nurse lowered her voice almost conspiratorially. "That's the SLIM ward, poor lads. None of them will last the course. They come and go every few weeks, but none actually get better. Eventually, we put them in the hospice over the road, where they die. Can't even use their bodies for research, too risky." They had reached the toilets. "Here we are," she said. "Now, you don't want me to hold it for you, do you?"

"Er ... no, of course not. I'll only be a minute. But what's SLIM?"

"I'll tell you on the way back," said the nurse. Fancy the Vicar not knowing about SLIM. "Now come on, hurry up."

When John Priestley was safely back in bed, he thought on what the nurse had then told him. The prospect for the young men was horrifying. They had no life at all. But worse was what she had said about the spread of the disease nationwide, and in particular about its hold on Totnes of all places. Priestley lay back in his bed. He could not stop thinking about SLIM. Of course! – It must be SLIM that was the actual Totnes Monster! If anything, that was what he should have exorcised.

The Lord above smiled. How convenient, he thought, the toilets being next to the SLIM ward; for the Lord really did move in mysterious ways his wonders to perform, and John Priestley's sudden need of the toilet had in reality been naught but celestially inspired incontinency. The Vicar had finally got the message loud and clear.

Two days later, in a wheelchair, John Priestley was discharged from the General Hospital. Driven back to the vicarage in an ambulance, he was unceremoniously wheeled into his dusty sitting room. To Priestley it looked as if Mrs Jenkins had once again not touched the place; he'd get her working – no fear. The ambulance men said their goodbyes and left the Vicar alone.

Peace at last. Then the telephone rang.

"Good day," said a fruity voice that he thought he should recognize, "have you recovered, Priestley?"

"This is Priestley, and as far as I know I've never been missing ..."

"That, Priestley, is a matter of opinion. Now I want to talk to you about your parish." Dear Lord, thought the Vicar, it's the Bishop. Putting on his most erudite accent, he cleared his throat to speak.

"My Lord Bishop, how wonderful to talk to you. I have been trying to contact you for days. Is the golf going well? It is such a shame about the church, is it not, but I suppose you are ringing to tell me when the rebuilding will start. Am I right?"

"Once again, Priestley," said the Lord Bishop, "you are not. Far from it. I am 'ringing', as you say, to tell you man to, er ... man that ... well, your days in Totnes are numbered. The church is damaged beyond repair, your attendances have fallen similarly and I understand from the last stocktake that most of the church's priceless relics are even missing, absent, gone ... perhaps stolen? The final balls-up, if I may call it that, is that apparently the mediaeval testicles of Saint Ethelred the Ready and Willing are now misplaced, something that would have been very painful both to the saint and to your congregation – if, of course, you still had one. All that the commissioners' agents could find were the two spherical containers used since the Dark Ages to hold the Saint's manhood! Empty! Not a ball in sight!

"Further, I understand that you too have sustained some sort of permanent damage. I feel that perhaps you too have become something of a relic ... so, under the circumstances, we should call it a day. Retirement for you, demolition for the church and a new place of worship for your mean – and may I say your collection plates have never been emptier (you must tell me one day how you managed a negative figure on the last service you took) – congregation of, I believe these are the latest figures," the Bishop looked at the printout from his computer, "three."

Priestley gulped. One thing was indubitably leading to another. He knew in what bones he had left that the whale that had started off the whole ghastly episode was somehow linked to the Guru, and to the crumbling church – but how? And now he was being made redundant; he couldn't get another job, not at his age. It was fine for the Bishop in his palace to waffle down the 'phone about attendances, demolishing churches, lost balls and taking away people's livelihoods; he was all right – he had a good income, nice though pretentious clothes, an easy life. Priestley had nothing to look forward to but incontinence and early senility.

"So that's it, is it?" he said. "No job, no parish, no – nothing! Thanks very much. Well, at least I have my health, of sorts. I suppose the church commissioners will be in touch with me, am I correct, my Lord Bishop?"

"You are, for once, Priestley, you are. And may I, on behalf of Christians everywhere, thank you sincerely for the work you have done over the years in

God's name."

"You may ..." said Priestley.

"Pardon?"

""... thank me. You may thank me."

"But I just have!" The Bishop was confused.

"My Lord, forgive me, but you only asked if you might thank me. I do not think you have yet actually thanked me."

"Priestley, you are tiresome. Goodbye and ... thank you." It was always wise to cut out the dead wood, thought the Bishop, as he put down his telephone. The day was going well. Now to buy back the river at a very advantageous price – there was no oil ... the price would be rock bottom. The Bishop poured himself a large whisky, before making what would be a very profitable call.

In the vicarage, Priestley wheeled himself over to the drinks cabinet and poured himself a stiff sherry, knocking it back in one. Once again the telephone rang.

"Hullo," replied Priestley, "Crumbleigh Vicarage, Totnes ..."

"Good morning – is that the Vicar? Aah ... good! This is your doctor's surgery here. We have just received the results of the blood test that was taken when you were in hospital. Would you like to come to the surgery to discuss them? Doctor needs to talk to you about them. When would be convenient?"

"Now would be," said Priestley. "What's wrong, and what bloody test?"

"Blood test," corrected the doctor's receptionist. "As I said, the routine one you had in the hospital. New government regulations are now in force, and every hospital admission now automatically has their blood tested for the SLIM virus."

"Good God," said Priestley. Right now God

248

didn't seem to be too good. "And what's this guff about my blood, eh?"

"Can you come to the surgery to talk to Doctor? He wants you to have a session of counselling. It's your legal right under the new situation and it's free. When can you come?"

"I can't. I'm in a wheelchair." Priestley was not happy.

"We could send an ambulance, or I suppose ... I could explain over the telephone as you are the Vicar."

"I've been messed about enough today," said Priestley. "What is going on? Tell me now. I'm getting tired of all this."

"Very well," said the receptionist. "Are you sitting down? I'll give you the results."

"Sitting down? I can't get up. Come on, what's the damn news?"

"Well, Reverend, the results of the blood test taken last week in the Totnes General Hospital under the regulations now in force ..."

"Yes?"

"... show that you, I'm sorry to have to tell you this, Vicar, are – are you sure you want this news over the 'phone?"

"YES!"

"Vicar, you are antibody positive. Do you understand what this means?"

"I certainly do not. I trained to save people's souls, not their bodies. What does it mean?" replied a still unworried Priestley.

"It means," said the patient girl to the impatient patient, "you have antibodies in your blood, little organisms if you like, that are there to fight a specific disease, and these particular antibodies are there to fight the disease SLIM."

"Brilliant," chortled Priestley. "So I am immune! Praise be to the Lord!"

"I am afraid it rather means the opposite," said the girl. "The Doctor could explain it better ... shall I ask him to talk to you?"

"NO," the Vicar said positively.

"Very well, I shall try," continued the girl. "You see, you only have these antibodies if the virus has entered your body. We can't test for the actual virus, as yet, only the antibodies. What I am trying to tell you, Vicar, is that you are very likely in the next few years to develop what we call 'full-blown' SLIM – the disease itself, plus possibly other complications, and at the moment there is no known cure for it. Now, do you understand? Vicar ...?"

John Priestley did understand. He was going to die.

"Thank you," he said down the line. "I shall have to think about this. Goodbye." He slowly put the telephone down and quickly knocked back another sherry, his mind in turmoil. How long did he have? Where did he catch the disease? Were they positive he was antibody ... whatever it was?

He suddenly felt extremely mortal. What could he, John Priestley, still just Vicar of Crumbleigh, do to improve the situation?

And then it hit him. As quick as he could, he rushed, wheelchair wheels almost spinning, to the space that was now the shell of his once-beautiful church.

Once again he commenced adjuring and praying to the Lord. This time he had not contacted the Bishop for permission, for he knew in his bones that ultimately he had got it right, and in any case he had no Bishop any more. The very thing he was praying for was in his bones – the doctors had told him so. He was trying to

250

exorcise his own personal Totnes Monster.
THE Totnes Monster ... *SLIM!*

In the nave of the condemned church in his wheelchair he sat, with the faithful Mrs Jenkins now in attendance, right in the centre of the aisle where so often, cricket lover that he was, he had walked up its length and wondered if it could take spin.

John Priestley would not be genuflecting, genuflecting, genuflecting this time. And he would certainly not be bowling any maidens over. After the lightning had struck him, his knees had locked solid, and he was now unable to walk.

He looked up to the open sky, and as he did so the sun broke through a gap in the clouds over the top of the ancient roofless edifice, sending a shaft of Light shimmering down through the rising dust of the dying church.

And the Lord saw that it was good. And John Priestley, arms outstretched, had cried up, "Lord, Lord, why hast thou forsaken me?" Which being translated means, "Ελοι, Ελοι, Λαμα Σηαβακτηαν?"

And the Lord saw he was not really doing any exorcizing, was being somewhat anally precious, and decided it was time for his long recall.

John Priestley again felt the searing pain in his chest, and this time the Lord's very own clot halted the flow of blood into his heart for good, and, as he looked up to the Light streaming down onto his radiantly calm face, he remembered, as his life flashed before him, when it must have happened. It *must* have been that Kenyan Deacon who had stolen all his leather appliances, his chains, his straps, his ropes and his whips. It had been one evening after drinks, four years before, at the Brighton Synod.

251

At last, in his dying breath, he had at long last found his Monster!

Just one night's sin. That was all it took. Yeah!

And then he gave up the Ghost, and Mrs Jenkins screamed. And the Lord saw that he was dead.

And the Evening and Morning were at opposite ends of the Day ...

𝕬𝕸𝕰𝕹